FOR YOU

Always

BOOK 4 OF THE PEACE FALLS SERIES

HANNAH JORDAN

About This Book

Peace Falls Series **Reading Order:** *For You Always* is a stand-alone novel; however, Cammie and Wyatt are featured throughout the original trilogy of the *Peace Falls Series*. *For You Always* occurs chronologically after the first three books and contains spoilers for each.

Content Warning: This book contains potentially upsetting subject matter, including references to domestic abuse, drug use, and incarceration. It also contains multiple blush-inducing sex scenes, so if you're looking for a sweet, small-town romance, best put this one down.

Published by Hannah Jordan Books 2025

Cover Design: Kaytalin McCarry, Duskbound Books

ebook ISBN:979-8-9905868-7-1

Paperback ISBN: 979-8-9905868-6-4

www.hannahjordanauthor.com

To the families we find

CHAPTER ONE

Cammie

I KNEW THE TEN o'clock patient might be trouble when he scheduled his appointment. First, he sounded young and flirty on the phone. Second, he'd injured his back in a parkour accident. Any person willing to jump between rooftops and do flips out of trees was bound to take the simple risk of asking out anyone he wanted.

I did my best to look unapproachable, yet even with my resting bitch face, no makeup, and my hair in a messy bun, the guy's eyes lit up the moment he entered the physical therapy office.

"Well, hello there," he said, walking straight to my desk, which, granted, was what most patients did.

"Good morning," I said. "Dr. Cardoso will be right with you. Please take a seat in the waiting area." Clipped, but polite. Maybe he'd get the hint.

Brad/Chad, I could have looked at the schedule, but honestly, I didn't want to know his name, glanced at the vinyl-covered chairs pushed against the wall, then back at me.

"I don't think we've met," he said, holding out his hand. "I'm Thad."

"Cammie," I said, but kept my hands on my keyboard, typing gibberish into a word doc at a rate that implied I was extremely busy. My pulse pounded and my palms started to sweat while I waited for him to walk away.

He didn't move.

I was not in the mood for this. I hadn't had my second cup of coffee yet and working two jobs was tiring me out.

"Nice to meet you," he said after dropping his hand. My obvious rebuff did nothing to squelch the spark of interest in his striking blue eyes.

I should have worn the pale gray scrubs that made me look ill. Instead, I'd chosen my brightest pink pair this morning to perk myself up. Sure, the color sometimes attracted attention, but I loved cheerful clothes. Bold pinks, yellows, even neons. Unfortunately, there's only so much a color can do for your mood when you're rolling on five hours of sleep.

Thad didn't seem to notice my general exhaustion and lack of interest. He was extremely good looking and knew it. No doubt he assumed his attention wouldn't come off as creepy because most women wanted what he had to offer.

Too bad for Thad, I wasn't most women.

He glanced at my left hand, flashed me a huge smile, and pressed against the desk, showing off his toned forearms. I should buy myself a wedding band and be done with it. But the sliver of my heart that still believed in love and happily ever after balked at the idea. I stared over Thad's shoulder, hoping to get my boss's attention. Unfortunately, Cal was focused on his 9:15 patient.

I almost didn't take this job when I met Dr. Cardoso. With a face to rival any male model, he'd looked like trouble. I'd been terrified of working together, but Cal's professionalism quickly put me at ease. He was just an associate at the practice then, and we bonded over our mutual dislike of the owner. Before long, Cal picked up that men, especially young, fit ones, made me nervous, and carved a place in my life as a brother figure. An extremely protective one. Now that Cal owned the practice, I could tell Thad to screw off without fear of losing my main job, but as usual, I froze.

"Are you new in town?" Thad asked. "I'd remember meeting someone as gorgeous as you."

He was correct that our paths hadn't crossed. I'd have remembered a guy with a man bun and the body of a gymnast. Apart from the PT office and Karma, the coffee shop/bookstore where I worked evenings and weekends, I didn't get out much. Thad looked like the type of guy who drank mushroom tea instead of caffeine, so until he tweaked his back, we wouldn't have had much chance of meeting.

As the silence stretched, my tongue started to feel too heavy, and my breathing hitched.

Thad noticed and misread the change as excitement instead of fear. "Let me take you out," he said, leaning so close I could smell the patchouli oil rolling off his body. "When are you off?"

I hated that my mouth stopped working every time something like this happened. How hard was it to say "No thanks" and point to the chairs in the waiting area? After everything I've been through, turning down parkour Thad shouldn't be a problem. But it was. It'd been over two years since I ran from Bishop, and my stomach still bunched with nerves any time a guy got too friendly.

Bishop hated when I spoke to other men. No matter if all I did was tell someone to back off, the second we were alone, he'd make me pay. Even with years and the state of North Carolina between us, he might as well have been standing right behind me.

Thad flashed another smile. "I see. You want me to work for it, don't you?"

No, I want you to leave *it* alone. I looked past Thad again to the center of the room, willing Cal to look up. He didn't, but his dog, Skye, did.

Before I knew what was happening, the Weimaraner shot across the exercise mats like a silver bullet and started growling at Thad. Cal's attention snapped to his dog, and he narrowed his eyes when he took in his next patient leaning across my desk.

"Sit," Cal said with authority as he crossed the room to us.

Skye plopped on the floor by Thad's feet and glared up at him, which was a very un-Skye-like expression.

"Dr. Cardoso," Cal said, holding out his hand to Thad, his voice unusually cold. "Sorry about Skye. Something must have spooked her."

As they shook hands, they eyed each other like a pair of boxers about to go twelve rounds. Thad's forehead bunched with confusion when he saw Cal's wedding ring. Guys often assumed Cal and I were together and backed down when he acted protective. Since Cal married my friend Rowan a few months ago, his big-brother act had led to more than one perplexed stare. No one would confuse us for siblings with his classic tall, dark, and handsome looks and my blue eyes and pale blonde hair. I guess we're both tall, but that wasn't enough to suggest we shared DNA.

"Have a seat there," Cal said, pointing to the table farthest from my desk. "I'll be right with you."

As soon as Thad started across the room, I let out a relieved breath.

Cal frowned. "Do you want me to dismiss him?"

"No," I said quickly. It warmed my heart that he wouldn't hesitate to put my feelings before his business, but I couldn't let my past hurt Cal's present. "He didn't do anything wrong. It's just me being me."

Cal nodded, though he still looked pissed.

"I'm fine, really. Get back to your patients."

"Stay with Cam," he said to Skye before returning to the older lady he'd left in the middle of a set of lunges.

Skye walked around my desk and plopped by my feet. I blew out a long breath, trying to get my heartbeat under control.

"You're such a good girl," I said, bending to kiss the soft fur on the top of her head. She flopped on her back, and I gave her belly a good scratch before returning to my computer. I deleted the gibberish from the patient letter I'd been typing when Thad arrived and quickly finished it before moving on to July's billing.

My little interaction with Thad had made the August heat even more noticeable. By afternoon, our fourth-floor office would be stifling, even with the AC and overhead fans going full speed. Skye panted beside me, and I decided it was time for her to have some water and for me to have some coffee.

Not that hot coffee was going to cool me down. As much as I wanted to head to Karma for something iced or frozen, I'd cut down on my coffee runs since I started working there part time. The owner, Lauren, refused to charge me, even when I wasn't on the clock, which didn't sit right with me. Instead, I limited myself to one Karma coffee before work and made frequent use of the single-serve machine in our building's waiting area.

Before I walked down the four flights of stairs to the lobby, I filled a pitcher from the water cooler and refilled Skye's bowl. She quickly lapped all the water and gave her food bowl a hopeful nudge with her paw.

"Don't tell the boss," I said, slipping her a doggie treat. "Thanks for having my back earlier." She was still chewing as she made her way across the room to Cal, who was focused on Thad now that his other patient had moved to the treadmill for the cardio portion of her session. If I didn't work so much, I'd consider getting a dog of my own. A big, scary one who loved me fiercely and greeted me at the door with tail wags and kisses. Sadly, I was only home to sleep and shower, and Skye was bound to get into mischief if I brought another dog to the office.

As I huffed down the stairs, I berated my yesterday self for not making a batch of cold brew. At least we'd be closing early. Starting last month, Cal and I decided to skip our usual mid-day break and book patients from seven to three. He insisted I still take my lunch break. I insisted on eating at my desk, so I could still answer the phone. I hated getting up an hour early, but it was that or sweat through the worst of the heat. The new schedule meant Cal and I could put in a full day's work before it got too uncomfortable and gave me a couple extra hours at Karma. Unfortunately, the temperature was already brutal today.

When I reached the lobby, I dropped my favorite hazelnut pod into the machine and waited for it to brew. The air conditioning blasting through the lobby quickly cooled my heated skin. Just looking at the steam rolling from the paper cup made me question my logic. If I drank the coffee back in the office, I'd be sweating for sure.

I took my cell from my pocket and checked the time. Cal's 9:15 patient wouldn't be leaving for at least ten minutes. I could probably chug my coffee in the comfort of the lobby before I needed to be back upstairs to schedule her follow-up appointment. After the machine sputtered the last drops into the paper cup, I added more creamers than usual, hoping to cool the coffee as much as possible, and took a seat in one of the comfy chairs facing Main Street.

The building housed several healthcare professionals, making it a centralized location for most of the town's medical needs. Technically, the gilded sign out front said *Everson Tower*, which was a grandiose label for a four-story structure with an elevator the size of a coffin. The locals seemed to agree and called it "The Doctors on Main" instead. It'd taken me a while to learn all the quirky nicknames of places in town, but the temporary confusion eventually gave way to a feeling of belonging once I could converse like any born-and-raised resident.

I'd really lucked out landing in Peace Falls. When I left Charleston, I'd planned to disappear into New York City. On the drive north, I'd chosen the scenic route through the Appalachian Mountains instead of the main interstate to make the long drive somewhat interesting. After the chaos of my relationship with Bishop, the name of the town had called to me like a siren, and I'd decided to break up the trip with an overnight stay. By the next morning, I knew I'd found home.

The arbitrary nature of my decision felt right, safe. Why would Bishop look for me in a place where I had zero ties and never planned to visit, let alone live? I often wondered how different my life would be if I'd taken the other route to New York.

I slurped my coffee as fast as the temperature allowed and pulled out my phone again to keep an eye on the time. I almost dropped it when it buzzed with a call from the Broad River Correctional Institute. I answered on the first ring, my heart in my throat. When the typical prompt for an inmate calling played, I let out the breath I'd been holding. A call directly from the prison staff would only be bad news. Still, it wasn't like Daddy to make an unscheduled call, especially when he knew I'd be working. With how much calls cost per minute and the limited opportunities he had to make them, we typically planned our conversations days in advance.

"Hey, Millie," he said as soon as we were connected.

Hearing my childhood name in his deep voice made my heart ache. We emailed, called, and video chatted as much as the system allowed, but it felt like a lifetime since I'd hugged my dad, and in many ways, it was. I wasn't the same person who'd left South Carolina. I'd have legally changed my name if I'd had the money. Instead, I'd settled for the nickname my mom had used for our shared first name. I never wanted to be Millie again, but I made an exception for my dad.

"Daddy, what's wrong?" I asked, squeezing the paper cup in my hand.

"Nothing, sweetie," he said. "Nothing at all. Just wanted to hear your voice."

Best way to lie: Say something true. Of course he wanted to hear my voice, just like I always looked forward to hearing his. But my dad didn't make spontaneous calls. Ever. He should know better than to lie to me.

After all, he's the one who taught me how. It wasn't a skill I'd needed before my mother died, but after everything fell apart, it'd become a necessary evil.

"And," I said.

The line went quiet a moment before he blew out a breath. "And I wanted to make sure you're doing all right."

The hand holding my coffee started shaking, so I placed it on the floor while I waited for him to elaborate.

"Are you?" he asked without further explanation.

"Is there a reason I wouldn't be?"

"You know I always worry about you, Millie."

True, but something had made him worry more than usual. "Come on, Daddy," I said, irritation slowly taking the place of my anxiety. "You and I both know you wouldn't be calling like this if that was the only reason."

I'd taken care of myself far longer than most people my age. I may be his little girl, but I was long past the time for sheltering. Intentional or not, he'd made sure of that when he started using again.

"I don't want to worry you if it's nothing," he said, dropping his voice to a near whisper. I pictured him pulling the phone closer to his mouth and curling his body inward to hide his words from anyone listening. Because there was always someone listening. Always.

"Go on, Daddy. I'd rather know. Whatever it is."

"Folks on the block say Bishop's been looking for you again."

I almost laughed with relief. "Did he ever stop?"

I knew Bishop better than I knew myself. No matter how much time passed, he'd never forgive me. Maybe he could get past me leaving, but he'd never forgive me for stealing from him.

"It's different this time, Millie," he said, his tone serious.

"How?"

"His brother's been moved to my block."

We stayed silent, letting the cost of the call tick up until he cleared his throat. "You know I'll never tell him where you are, but I have friends here. I've been racking my brain trying to remember if I ever told them anything that could lead Bishop to you. I don't think I have. Still, I want you to be careful. More than you already are. Maybe even think about moving."

I sucked in a pained breath. "I love it here," I said, staring out the window at the postcard-perfect Main Street. "This could be a good thing. I've almost saved up what I need to pay Bishop back. Maybe you could help me coordinate with Todd—"

"No." My dad hadn't spoken so sternly to me since I was a little kid about to burn my hand on the stove. "No matter what you give that man, he'll never consider your debt paid. You bruised that boy's ego."

"Yeah, well, he bruised me." The words slipped out before I could stop them, and I instantly regretted bringing up the past.

"I know, sweetie," he said, his voice full of pain. "I'm not making excuses for Bishop. There aren't words harsh enough for what he is, which is why you need to be careful."

"You too, Daddy," I said, worrying my bottom lip. My dad was only fifty-three and in great shape, but prison was dangerous, especially when you mixed in old grudges between families. Todd and Bishop were close, or at least they had been when Bishop and I were together. And Daddy would never stop fighting to protect me. Putting the two of them in the same block could be a recipe for disaster.

"I'll video call you Sunday like we planned. I love you, Millie."

"Love you too."

I stared at the phone long after the call disconnected. What my dad said made sense. Moving would ensure Bishop's brother couldn't piece together tidbits of information Daddy had shared over the years. But I'd built a life for myself in Peace Falls.

I had friends. More than that, I had people like Cal and Lauren who treated me like family. I hadn't had that since my dad fell back into addiction. When he'd gotten clean in prison, it'd felt like a double-edged sword to the heart. Daddy returned to the man he'd been before my mom died, but I was still on my own in the foster system. Even now, we could only share so much of our lives while I hid in the mountains of Virginia, and he served a life sentence in South Carolina.

I'd grown so much here. I still froze when guys asked me out, but I'd relaxed around Cal's best friends, once I realized they had zero interest in me. I'd even started working my Karma shifts with Wyatt, who should terrify me as much as Bishop. Not because Wyatt was violent, but because he woke butterflies in my stomach that I'd rather stayed dormant. I treasured each and every person who had welcomed me to this small town. I didn't want to leave them.

I jumped when Cal's 9:15 patient walked by, reminding me I should have been upstairs a while ago. I tossed my half-full cup in the trash and sprinted upstairs, the heat and parkour Thad no match for the ice-cold fear coursing through my body with the knowledge I could lose everything again.

CHAPTER TWO

Wyatt

I LIFTED MY T-SHIRT and wiped the sweat from my face. The heat was brutal, especially on the roof. Since I started working for Aiden's construction company full time, I'd hopped from crew to crew, learning new skills and helping where I was needed most. So far, I'd been able to avoid roofing, which suited my fear of heights just fine. But this Victorian remodel had ornate trim work in the gables that needed repairing, and unfortunately, I knew exactly how to fix it.

Who would have thought all those woodworking lessons with my *abuelito* would have led to me balancing on a roof in the stifling heat? Certainly not me.

"Make sure you drink water, *Novato*," my foreman Sam said, pushing a bottle of water into my hand.

The nickname grated a little. I wasn't exactly a newbie. I started working with the company part-time almost a year ago while I was still a full-time barista at Karma, but Sam wasn't wrong. I hadn't adjusted yet to working long hours in construction day after day. I dutifully chugged the entire bottle and tossed it over the edge onto the debris pile.

Sam leaned closer to check my work and let out a long whistle. "Damn, Wyatt. You're going to make the rest of us look bad."

"Aiden didn't hire us to whittle," Mateo said in Spanish.

Sam laughed. "Guess I can't talk shit about you in English now?"

"Your funeral," Mateo said in heavily accented English. Everyone on the roof laughed.

Sam glared at me, but I could tell he wasn't really pissed. I'd been teaching some of the guys slang to help them improve their English. Sam and I were Aiden's only fully bilingual employees, and while the boss spoke decent Spanish and the rest of the guys spoke English and Spanish with varying proficiency, the two of us bridged everyone together.

"When you finish that trim work, I could use you in the primary," Sam said. "The homeowner wants to expand the closet, but I think we could get the storage space she wants with built-ins and keep the floor plan intact. Thought maybe you could take a look and sketch something."

"Sure," I said, trying not to sound too excited. I'd rip out a sewer line if it meant getting off this roof, but the rest of the guys would be here all day. "I should be done in a half hour or so."

"Drink more water," he said, tossing another bottle at me. "You look like shit. *Toma agua*," he shouted to everyone else.

My phone vibrated in my pocket as I caught the bottle. Damn it. I needed food, not water. I unscrewed the cap and drank slowly, waiting for Sam to climb down from the roof and the rest of the guys to turn back to their work before I pulled my cell from my cargo pants.

I swiped open the notification from my blood sugar monitoring app and blew out a breath. 68. I could finish up the trim work and grab something to eat from my car before I checked out the primary. I got to work and ignored my phone when it vibrated again. I'd already eaten all the candy in my pockets, so the best I could do was finish up quick. By the time I started fitting the last piece of trim, sweat poured down my face and my hands felt shaky.

"Wyatt," Aiden called from below.

I looked over the side of the roof and found him standing next to the trash pile with his hands on his hips. All the chatter on the roof stopped at once. Aiden was supposed to be overseeing the crews at the housing development site, not here.

"Now," he said, sounding pissed.

The guys stayed silent while I climbed down the ladder to our boss, who looked ready to throw a punch.

"Everything OK?" I asked, stepping onto the grass. The world spun, and I sucked in a breath.

Aiden gripped my shoulder and pushed me toward his truck. "Get in."

He'd left the air conditioning running, and despite the nerves twisting my stomach, I practically melted into the passenger seat.

"Here," he said, handing me a can of soda. "Drink some of that before I chew your ass out."

"I was going to—"

"Drink it, Wyatt, before you upset Lauren more than you already have."

His phone rang, and he answered it immediately, putting the call on speaker. "He's here. Give him time to drink it."

My hands shook as I popped open the can. The anger drained from Aiden's face, and he looked at me with genuine concern.

"I'm fine," I said after swallowing a gulp of soda.

"Your blood sugar is 62, Wyatt," Lauren yelled through Aiden's phone.

Fuck. That was low. I quickly drank half the can. I'd rather chug juice than soda, but I didn't want to risk walking to my car for one of the boxes I kept there.

"Why did you ignore the alerts?" Lauren asked. The worry in her voice shot a hefty dose of guilt to my chest.

"I was—"

"In the basement," Aiden said, shooting me a glare. "Reception is shit down there."

"OK," she said, letting out a breath. "It's going up. How do you feel?"

"I'm good."

Aiden studied me like I was a wet spot on a ceiling he'd just installed. "We'll hang out in my truck until he's back to normal."

"You should take tonight off," Lauren said.

"Absolutely not," I said, trying not to sound half dead. Now that I wasn't focused on trim work or falling off a roof, all the crappy side effects of low blood sugar slammed into my awareness at once. I could barely keep my eyes opened, and my lips felt numb, making it difficult to speak. "You're not working late, and neither of us wants Cammie working alone."

Aiden raised his eyebrows at my tone, yet far from looking pissed at me for talking back to his girlfriend, he seemed strangely impressed. The dynamics of their relationship confused the hell out of me, but it was clear they loved and respected each other.

"I don't know, Wyatt," Lauren said.

"You can't treat me like glass every time my numbers dip."

And I didn't want to miss the best hours of my day. I'd been hung up on Cammie Gibson since the first time I saw her at Karma a year ago. Before that moment, I'd have laughed at anyone who said they believed in love at first sight. Lust maybe. But the feeling that slammed into me the second we locked eyes was unlike anything I'd ever experienced before. I knew, with absolute certainty, she was it for me. Unfortunately, she avoided me like a cockroach.

For months, I'd watched her charm customers with her warm smile and bright personality, but the moment we were alone, she clammed up. I kept my distance until she started looking at me when she thought I wouldn't notice. I finally worked up the nerve to ask her out, only to receive a head shake in reply. Not even a no. My stupid heart didn't care, though I knew better than to push someone after they turned me down. I figured things would stay awkward between us forever, but once we started sharing shifts, she began to relax around me. And yes, I knew how pathetic it was to be completely in love with a woman who only tolerated my company. It didn't change the fact that I looked forward to every moment I spent with her.

"I'm just worried about you," Lauren said, pulling me from my thoughts.

"We've got this, Princess," Aiden said, softening his voice. "I promise."

The idea of the two of them being together and expecting a baby would never have crossed my mind a few months ago. Yet, they were, which was exactly why I was sitting in my new boss's truck, drinking a soda, because my old boss was the big sister I never had who insisted I share alerts from my monitoring app to her phone while I struggled to figure out how the fuck to get through the day with a newly defunct pancreas.

"How are you really?" Aiden asked as soon as he ended the call.

I pulled my cell from my pocket and saw that my blood sugar had crept back to 67. "Getting there."

Aiden rubbed his forehead and blew out a breath before he turned to face me. "I'm impressed with your work, Wyatt, but if I ever find out you've ignored your blood sugar on one of my sites again, I'll fire your ass. And not just because you scared my pregnant girlfriend. You were on a fucking roof. I know you're smarter than that."

I nodded because of course he was right. If I'd gotten much lower, I might have passed out and fallen.

"I know this violates HIPPA and probably a half dozen employment laws," he continued, "but you could send the alerts to me. Or Sam. Any of the guys, really. Hell, you could keep us all in the loop if you wanted."

I shook my head. "I don't want everyone fussing every time I dip below 70. And so far, you're the only person here who knows I have diabetes. I'd rather keep it that way."

Aiden let out a huff. "Fine, but handle your shit, Wyatt. And if you ever tell Lauren I had you on a roof while your blood sugar crashed, boss or not, I will kick your ass."

"I'm not that stupid," I said. "I was going to tell her I was inside a closet with horsehair plaster walls."

Aiden laughed, and the knot in my stomach loosened.

"Speaking of which," I said, hoping to move on from any conversation about firing me. "I better get back. Sam wanted me to sketch out custom shelving for the closet in the primary." I held out my phone and showed him that my blood sugar had gone up to 69. "I'm sorry for ignoring the alert and making Lauren worry. It won't happen again. I mean, my blood sugar will probably drop again at some point, but I'll handle it before she gets concerned."

Aiden shook his head. "When it comes to you, she's always concerned. If you weren't so good at woodworking, I'd send you back to Karma full time, just to put her mind at ease. Still might."

Which was exactly what he'd done when Lauren was suffering through terrible morning sickness and hadn't found my replacement. I'd been glad to jump back to my old job to help her, but now that I'd trained and hired two new full-timers for Karma, I wanted to keep learning my way around construction sites.

Not only did it give me health insurance and allow me to send more money to my family, it made me feel like I hadn't completely given up my dream of becoming an architect. Reading how homes were built was one thing. Actually using my hands to construct them was something I could carry with me back to college. Because despite the curve ball life threw me, I would go back.

"I could stop sending alerts to her phone," I said, taking another sip of soda.

Aiden laughed, and I joined him. No way in hell Lauren would let that happen.

"I'm good," I said, showing him that my blood sugar had jumped to 71. It'd probably spike even higher before falling again, but I'd shove a few snacks and some candy in my pockets before I returned to the roof.

"All right," Aiden said, knocking my shoulder. "Get back to work."

I climbed out of his truck, taking the can of soda with me. Hammers thudded on the roof, though I knew they'd fall silent the moment I rejoined the crew.

The only issue with having a great boss was coming up with an excuse for why he'd looked ready to murder me before chewing me out in his truck for fifteen minutes. Aiden liked people to think he was a hard ass, but apart from Lauren, I'd never worked for anyone who cared more about their employees. I'd have had to do something truly stupid to bring him from another job site to yell at me. *Like letting myself go hypoglycemic on a roof.*

I stopped at my car and shoved a few packets of mixed nuts, a juice box, and some gummy worms in my pockets before climbing up the ladder. The heat rolling off the roof had jumped several degrees since I'd left, and everyone was dripping sweat.

"What'd you do, *Novato?*" Mateo asked when he saw me. The entire crew stopped working and waited for me to answer.

"Pissed off his baby mama," I said, which was 100% true. No doubt, Lauren would hang around Karma until I got there to give me an earful.

"What'd you do?" Mateo asked again because, like everyone else in Peace Falls, he knew Lauren was one of the kindest, most giving people in the world.

"Forgot to feed the cats last night," I answered in Spanish. "Poor things were howling mad when she got in this morning. She called Aiden, crying. Pregnancy hormones, you know."

I felt terrible lying about Lauren, but I couldn't think of any other reason Aiden would tear into me that wouldn't make the crew look bad since I was the newbie in training.

"*Estúpido*," Mateo said, giving my back a good-natured slap. "Her cats her babies. Don't mess with *Mamá*." His Spanglish was definitely improving.

I nodded and everyone went back to work, satisfied that I hadn't fucked up something on any of the sites.

I picked up the piece of trim I'd abandoned and fit it in place. The last piece I'd attached was off kilter, further confirming how bad my blood sugar had gotten. I gently removed the piece and reset it correctly. I really was stupid.

I glanced at the guys working around me. They teased each other mercilessly, yet every one of them would give the shirt off his back to anyone who needed it. No doubt they'd help keep my sugar levels steady, but I hated the idea of anyone else worrying about me like Lauren did. Most of the guys had wives and kids or older parents who needed their help when they got home. They didn't need to babysit a twenty-two-year-old on the job. Hell, I hadn't even told my family. The only people who knew were Lauren, Aiden, my endocrinologist, and the doctor at the college clinic who diagnosed me last year, which meant I had to do a better job of responding to my monitoring app.

I pulled my cell from my pocket, turned up the volume, so I wouldn't miss any alerts, and swiped away the notification of a missed call from Lauren before texting her.

Sorry. Won't happen again

Proof of life

I smiled and snapped a selfie in front of the trim work.

"Quit showing off to whatever girl you're trying to impress and get back to work," Mateo said in Spanish.

I quickly sent the picture to Lauren and pocketed my phone. If only I could text the girl I wanted to impress. Cammie probably wouldn't talk to me again if I sent her a random photo of myself, no matter how good my trim work looked in the background.

CHAPTER THREE

Cammie

I WENT TO MY apartment just long enough to change out of my scrubs and eat a protein bar before heading to Karma for my second shift of the day. Cal paid me well. Too well, if I'm being honest. But the extra income I got from Karma had helped me save up nearly enough to pay back Bishop, hopefully without seeing him, and ensured Daddy always had a healthy amount in his commissary account and enough credits to call, video chat, and email whenever he could.

Lauren greeted me with a hug when I pushed through the swinging door from the back room to the coffee bar. Her adorable baby bump pressed against my stomach, and despite the unsettling phone call from my dad, I smiled.

"How are you today?" I asked, stepping back. After she'd lost so much weight early in her pregnancy, it was a relief to see the healthy glow on her face.

"Oh," she said, grabbing my hand and holding it to her swollen stomach. A tiny flutter brushed against my fingertips. "Did you feel that?"

"Oh my stars," I breathed, laying my other hand on her abdomen as well. I'd been trying to feel the baby move for weeks, but this was the first time I'd been able. Tears filled my eyes and slipped down my cheeks. My beautiful friend had really found the happily ever after she deserved.

"Hey," Lauren said, wiping the tears from my face with a napkin because I refused to take my hands from her stomach while I could feel the baby move. "What's wrong?"

"Nothing," I said a little too quickly. "I'm just so happy for you." Which was 100% the truth. "And finally getting to feel Logan move—it's amazing."

"I can't wait to meet him," Lauren said, smiling.

She'd come a long way in a short time. When she first found out she was pregnant, she'd considered giving the baby up for adoption or relinquishing all her parental rights to Aiden because she didn't think she could be a mother. Her own mom had set a terrible example, and Lauren had done things to make it through foster care that weighed on her conscience. Having spent a few years in the system myself, I could empathize with her fears, but I never questioned her ability to be an amazing mother. The woman mothered everyone around her. Case in point, she was studying me again with a furrowed brow.

I reluctantly pulled my hands from her stomach and walked to the display case. "What time is Rowan stopping by with the bakery delivery?"

"Just before closing," Lauren answered, eyeing me skeptically. "Like always."

Rowan and her sister, Poppy, opened a bakery just down the street from Karma that specialized in custom cakes, but supplied several of the local businesses with desserts and pastries. Karma's display case looked just sparse enough to shift Lauren's focus off me. "I'll text her if we run too low before then," I said.

Lauren glanced at the pastry case and frowned. "I'll text her now," she said, pulling out her phone just as it let out a horrific, and irritatingly common, wail.

"Can't you change that?" I asked, tensing at the noise. "It sounds awful."

"It's meant to get your attention," she said, frowning at her phone.

"What's it for anyway?" I asked, stepping closer. She blushed and shoved the phone in her apron pocket.

"Lauren?"

Several emotions played across her face as if she was having a raging debate in her head before she let out a huff. "It's a cat tracker, and if you laugh at me, I swear I'll never let you feel my stomach again."

"What's a cat tracker? I can't laugh if I don't know what you're talking about."

"Follow me," she said, sounding resigned. We wove through the café tables, which were only partially filled with customers this time of day, to the front window where Karma's two cats, Desdemona and Medusa, were curled together asleep. "I got them collars with air tags, so I can check on them at night."

I slapped my hand over my mouth to cover the laugh bubbling from my chest. Both cats sported new collars with shiny tags.

"I know," she said, rolling her eyes. "But ever since I moved in with Aiden, I've been worried one of them would get stuck in my office or somewhere after everyone left. Sometimes Desdemona gets herself into places she needs help getting out of. Medusa manages pretty well on her own, considering, but I couldn't stop imagining how terrified she'd be if she was separated from Desdemona, which got me thinking about what could happen if one of them accidentally wandered outside, and the next thing I knew, I was buying cat trackers."

"Makes sense," I said, forcing all the humor from my voice. Moving in with Aiden had been a gigantic step for Lauren, and I could see her fixating on something like the cats to work through her feelings about leaving her safe space. Neither cat would have been happy moving with her. Medusa, who was completely blind, had Karma and Lauren's apartment upstairs completely memorized. Desdemona would have fared better, despite missing a leg, but she and Medusa were bonded. "Though I don't think your app is working right," I said, frowning at the sleeping cats. "When is the alarm supposed to sound?"

"Oh," Lauren said, blushing again. "If they go through one of the external doors. The front window sticks out past the entrance, so that must be it. We better get back to the coffee bar. I see Dr. Evers and Maddie headed this way for their afternoon lattes."

We'd just stepped behind the counter when Dr. Evers and Maddie Hendricks pushed through the front door.

"Hot or iced?" Lauren asked Dr. Evers, heading for the espresso machine.

"Iced," he said, giving her a smile. "You look well today, Lauren. But you'd look even better going home and resting."

"She would," I said, filling a to-go cup with ice and coconut milk. Dr. Evers and I had this routine down. He rented office space in the same building as Cal. Sometimes I wondered if he kept an eye out for when I left just so he could wander into Karma a half hour later and help me convince Lauren to leave. The woman arrived before five in the morning and worked without breaks most days. It made my feet hurt to think about it, and I wasn't growing a baby. In the last week or so, he'd recruited Maddie Hendricks to Operation Send Lauren Home.

"What about you, Maddie?" Lauren asked, choosing to ignore us both.

"Same as Dr. Evers," she said, tying her long brown hair up into a messy bun.

She'd picked up a serious afternoon mocha habit that probably had more to do with helping Dr. Evers and me convince Lauren to leave early than getting extra caffeine.

"How's the studying going?" I asked as I filled another cup with ice.

She blew out a breath. "It's going. Dr. Evers has been a lifesaver. I don't know what I'd do without our afternoon pep talks." She'd been studying for some test called Step 1 since she finished her second year of med school. As the weeks passed, the circles under her eyes had darkened, and I suspected part of Dr. Evers's reason for recruiting her for our daily guilt trip was to check on her as well.

"I don't know about that," Dr. Evers said. "But I'm happy to help." He gave Maddie a pointed look and she leaned over the counter.

"Does Aiden know you're still here?" she asked Lauren.

Lauren ignored us all and smacked the side of the espresso machine. It let out a short sigh before shutting off completely. "Ugh, not again," she said, giving it another slap. "I'm so sorry, y'all. Wyatt planned to give this diva a tune up during his shift, but I guess it couldn't wait."

"Don't give it another thought," Dr. Evers said. "I'm fine with iced coffee as long as it's got mocha syrup."

"Admit it, you just want the chocolate," I said, smiling at him. He winked at me as I squirted enough chocolate sauce into the cup to wire an entire kindergarten class. For whatever reason, older men like Dr. Evers didn't make me nervous. Often they reminded me of my dad, and I suppose Bishop never considered them enough of a threat to punish me for talking to them. I stirred in some cold brew while Lauren tried to convince Dr. Evers and Maddie they didn't need to pay the price of a latte. My thoughts drifted to the phone call with my dad this morning. I kept stirring both drinks as I replayed the conversation, trying to decide if Daddy was being overprotective or if the threat of Bishop finding me had grown.

"Just put it in the tip jar then," Lauren said, taking the drinks from me and adding whipped cream and chocolate shavings on top before handing them to the doctor and Maddie. They each paid for an ice coffee before Dr. Evers dropped a five in the tip jar.

"Go home and rest," he said. "Doctor's orders."

"You know I'll text Aiden if you don't," Maddie added, dropping her bag onto one of the empty bistro tables where she'd probably study until closing.

"Listen to her," Dr. Evers said. "She's a brilliant young lady."

Both women smiled at him as he pushed out the front door sipping his mocha.

"He's such a peach," I said, giving the espresso machine a hopeful shove. "And you should absolutely take his advice. I've got everything handled here, minus this beast."

"Don't bother trying to fix it yourself," Lauren said. "Wyatt should be here soon. Aiden shut down the sites early because of the heat."

"All the more reason for you to go home," I said, putting away the coconut milk and whipped cream. "You'll have a lot more fun with Aiden than standing here with me. We aren't even that busy."

Lauren bit her bottom lip and pulled out her cell.

"I can see the cats from here," I said. "They're fine."

She let out a long breath and nodded.

"Everything OK?" I asked.

She narrowed her eyes at me. "I was just about to ask you the same thing. You stirred those mochas so long I'm worried about your wrists."

I crossed my arms and glared at her. "You looked worried before I did that."

"How's it been working with Wyatt?" she asked. If I didn't know her better, I'd say she was trying to change the subject, but she bit her lip after she said his name, a clear tell that she was nervous asking the question.

"Fine," I said, keeping my voice steady. Better than fine. Just like him. Would I choose to work with a guy I found not only attractive but endearing? Absolutely not. Unfortunately, evenings and weekends were the only times either of us could work at Karma, so we worked together.

I didn't want to quit my second job. After I had enough to pay back Bishop, I planned to save up for Daddy's next appeal. I also didn't want Wyatt to lose hours because he occasionally popped into my head when I reached for my vibrator. If Lauren knew how uncomfortable I felt working with him, she'd limit our shifts together.

"You sure?" she asked, worrying her lip.

"Why? Did he say something?"

"Of course not," she said. "Just be careful with him."

"Careful?" It was an odd choice of words, especially after the conversation I'd had with my dad. Until now, I'd never considered Wyatt a threat to anything but my resolve to keep my orgasms self-induced. Some of the panic I'd been feeling all day must have bled into my face because Lauren quickly put a hand on my arm.

"Careful you don't upset him," she said. "He comes across as easygoing, but he's more sensitive than he lets on."

Don't make him angry. Don't argue. Keep your eyes down. Let him have his way. If you upset him, whatever happens after is your fault.

I bristled. I knew Wyatt had liked me enough at one point to ask me out, but he'd taken my rejection in stride and had gone out of his way since to make me feel comfortable around him. I figured he realized I turned down everyone and didn't take it personally. Even if he didn't, that was his problem, not mine. Plus, Wyatt didn't seem at all fragile to me. He always came across as confident without being an alpha-hole.

When I didn't say anything, Lauren added, "He's sweet, and you can be a little—"

"Guarded?"

"Cold," she said, narrowing her eyes at me.

Somewhere in the past year, we'd stopped being overly polite with each other and became the type of friends who spoke the hard truth when necessary. That still didn't mean we told each other everything.

We stood there, eyes locked, waiting for someone to break under the weight of the silence and speak the whole truth. Whatever that was. My past with Bishop? Her reasons for protecting Wyatt so fiercely? The silence stretched. Both of us had survived too much to crumble easily.

"Go home," I said, eventually. "I promise to make sure the cats are good for the night. And as for Wyatt, he's a fully capable adult. You know I'd never intentionally hurt anyone's feelings. Yes, he's sweeter than most guys, but even if I accidentally did or said something to upset him, he's responsible for his own emotions."

It took a lot of pain, self-help books, and distance to believe that, and I did.

She nodded, looking flustered. She opened her mouth, then pressed her lips together. Instead of speaking, she pulled me into a strong hug that I returned, each of us pressing all the words we wouldn't say into the embrace.

CHAPTER FOUR

Wyatt

I PULLED INTO THE parking lot behind Karma, glanced at the clock on my dashboard, and decided I couldn't wait a minute longer to hear how Wade's evaluation went. He accepted my video call with a huge smile on his face.

"Well?" I asked. Given my twin's expression, I knew the answer, but I figured he'd been dying to tell me all afternoon.

"I've been cleared."

I let out a whoop, and his smile widened. Our images on the phone screen looked nearly identical. He wore his hair a little longer than mine, but the color and texture were the same. If not for the slight droop on the left side of his face, we would be indistinguishable with matching haircuts and clothes.

"Congrats, man," I said. "I know you worked really hard in OT. What was the driving eval like?"

"Hard," Wade said, gripping the back of his neck. "For a minute, I didn't think the rehab specialist would clear me. I'll need a vehicle with a shit-ton of modifications, but I can get my learner's permit. Finally."

"What kind of modifications?" I asked.

"Well, other than the usual for wheelchair access, I'll need hand controls, safety bars and straps, and a bunch of other things. The specialist wrote it all in my clearance."

"Do you have to have a vehicle before you can get your permit?" I asked, my stomach sinking.

"I guess not. But these are the only wheels I'll be driving until I do," he said, panning the camera down to show a flash of his wheelchair before lifting the phone back to his face, which looked much less excited than when I called.

"We'll make it happen," I said with more confidence than I felt.

"Aiden give you a raise already?"

No. He almost fired me. "Nah, but I've been getting a ton of hours at Karma, since none of the new hires want to work evenings and weekends in the summer."

"You shouldn't want to either," Wade said, frowning. "You've got to be busting your ass at your day job. Abuelito always worked more hours in the summer. Seeing what he did day after day was downright inspiring, but even he didn't have a second job after working overtime. Aren't you tired?"

Yes. Fucking exhausted. "I'm fine."

"I don't need your money, you know. I work too."

But I wanted to help him. Because I knew he couldn't work the hours I did, and the only jobs for people our age without college degrees paid minimum wage or required manual labor, like construction.

"I need a DD," I said.

"Uber is cheaper, moron."

"And Cammie is warming up to me."

His eyes brightened, and the smile returned to his face. "You going to ask her out again?"

I shook my head and looked at the back of the Karma building. "She turned me down. I'll assume her answer hasn't changed unless she tells me otherwise."

"So take someone else out."

"Like that worked before."

"You haven't tried that hard. When was the last time you went on a date?"

Too long. I shrugged. "I can't break the pull she has on me. Speaking of which, I better get inside and start my shift. I'll call you after we close."

Wade smirked. "Don't bother. I'll be out celebrating with Megan. Her best friend is single, by the way, if you want me to set you up the next time you're home. She's cute."

"Word of advice, don't tell Megan you think her best friend is cute."

Wade glared at me and I laughed. His rizz was better than mine, and we both knew it.

"Have fun," I said. "And congrats again."

After we hung up, I blew out a breath, opened the group text I had with my parents, and started typing in Spanish.

> *How much is a van like he needs?*

Papá

> *Don't worry about it, kid.*

Mamá

> *Up to $15K for modifications plus the cost of the van.*

Shit. That was a lot of money.

Papá

> *We might be able to modify our van for $3K.*

Still a shit-ton of money, but if we all pitched in, we could save up enough in a couple months.

Mamá

If you joined your grandfather's old crew in Alexandria, you wouldn't have to pay for an apartment. It wouldn't take any time at all to save the money.

Papá

He can't live up here. He's going back to school.

Mamá

You're taking classes fall semester?

No. Hopefully spring semester.

Mamá

So come home and save your rent money for tuition, if not for your brother. You can work construction here as well as you can there.

It was the same argument I had with my mother every time we spoke. I could save money moving back home, but I loved living in Peace Falls, and part of me knew if I moved back to Northern Virginia, I'd never return to college here. Maybe anywhere.

Papá

Nina let it rest.

Given the time of day, it was possible they were both home, texting back and forth on the couch with my brother in the next room or even watching TV beside them. They wouldn't want him to be a part of this conversation any more than I did, which sucked. Truth was, I'd always felt conflicted about these side bar conversations with my parents. We never wanted Wade to feel like a burden. He knew I transferred money to our parents to help out, just like he did, but he didn't know exactly how much I'd given over the years to get him what he needed.

Mamá

> *It was different when you were in school. If you don't want to take classes, come home. Your family is here. Your friends.*

I wanted to take classes. I hated that I'd had to drop to part-time and then completely out after I was diagnosed. My insulin and all the other medical crap I needed, plus my living expenses and tuition, were too much. I didn't want my family to know my body had crapped out on me, at least not until I got a handle on my blood sugar, so they just thought I needed a break from classes. Lauren was nothing compared to my mother in the worry department.

> *Love you both. I've got to go to work.*

My phone dinged again. Instead of answering, I slipped it into my pocket and rested my head on the steering wheel. Between the heat and my fickle blood sugar, I felt like I was recovering from the flu. As much as my body begged me to curl up and take a nap, I didn't want to miss another minute of my time with Cammie.

I climbed out of my car, relieved to see Lauren's beater wasn't in the parking lot. No doubt she'd be calling after my shift to make sure I was OK before ripping into me.

"Hey, Cam," I called out as I stepped into the back room and closed the heavy exterior door. Since Aiden fixed the squeaky hinge, I'd given Cammie more than one unintentional jump scare when I joined her in the narrow space behind the coffee bar.

She pushed open the swinging door to the front and smiled at me. My heart did the usual skip beat at the sight of her, and my steps quickened.

"Hey, Wyatt," she said. I loved how she said my name, the second syllable always a little raised like she was excited. I'd gotten off more times than I could count, imagining what she'd sound like screaming it mid-orgasm. Fuck, I was pathetic.

In my defense, she was absolutely stunning without trying. Her blonde hair was in a messy bun that showed off her long neck. A few strands had fallen free, framing her gorgeous face. She didn't wear makeup; however, the bright colors she often wore made her cheeks look rosy and her eyes sparkle. I'd always preferred brown eyes to blue, but hers were a shade that somehow managed to be both warm and piercing. Seeing her wide smile aimed in my direction had me almost tripping over my feet to get to her.

"Not too busy tonight," she said, holding open the door for me.

As I walked by, her scent made my pulse race like it did every time I got close to her. Warm, alluring, like stepping into a patch of sunshine on a cold day.

Fuck, I needed to get a grip. Wade would say I needed to get laid, which was definitely true, but I'd rather take care of my own needs than explain the sensor shoved in my bicep to a complete stranger, who given the size of this town, would likely be linked to someone else I knew.

"What time did Lauren leave?" I asked, grabbing a fresh apron from the hook on the back wall and tying it around my waist.

"Around three-thirty," Cammie said as she wiped down the counter. Her body was long and lean, her movements graceful, almost like she was dancing while she worked. "Dr. Evers came in and gave her a hard time."

"Good for him," I said, smiling. Lauren was even more of a workaholic than me. Thankfully, she'd started taking better care of herself since becoming pregnant.

Cammie beamed back at me, and I had to turn away before I did something stupid like kiss her senseless. I moved to-go cups from the cabinet to the stack on the counter while I tried to regain my self-control.

"I can do that," she said, stepping closer. "I need you for something else."

Not helping, Cam. All the blood in my head rushed south.

My hands stilled. I stared at my shoes to keep from looking at her. If I were alone in the shower imagining this scenario, the next words from her mouth would be erotic. "What do you need?" I asked, my voice rough despite how hard I fought to sound normal.

"Um—"

My eyes moved to her face, and I glimpsed her reddening cheeks before I forced myself to step away. Fuck, I'd made her uncomfortable.

"The espresso machine is acting up again," she said in a rush. "It just conked out right after I got here. I haven't been able to use it at all. Lauren said you were going to work on it tonight and—"

"Let me see what I can do," I said, walking past her to the silent machine, cursing myself. It'd taken her months to thaw after I'd asked her out, and that one little slip might have set us back completely.

It wasn't until I watched her freeze up when a customer hit on her that I realized what a monumental mistake I'd made. Not only was she not interested in dating, she seemed genuinely terrified of most men. She only relaxed when it was clear the guy just wanted to be friends. She'd been a wreck around Aiden until he got together with Lauren. Now they chatted with ease, though I'd noticed he didn't tease her like he did his other female friends. I had a feeling it was because he didn't want her to think he was flirting, even in jest, since he was head-over-heels for Lauren.

Hence my problem: I wanted Cammie. Badly. But the only chance I had to get close to her was to pretend I didn't.

Which I obviously sucked at doing. My best bet was to focus on work and ignore the voice in my head that suggested the many ways I could coax the fear out of her and replace it with pleasure. Therapy by orgasm. Instead, I removed the portafilter, hoping the machine would run without it. Filters were easy enough to clean and replace if the issue was there. When the machine still didn't function, I figured I either had a blocked or failed pump. After taking it apart, I cleaned out a clump of grinds, put everything back together, and was able to start up the machine.

"Wow," Cammie said, creeping closer to me. "It's amazing how quickly you fixed that."

I shrugged. Pleased with both her compliment and her willingness to speak to me. "What else do we need to do before closing? Any new inventory for the bookstore?"

"No, we're all good there, but remind me to make sure the cats are OK before I leave."

I glanced at Desdemona and Medusa, who were stretched across the desk in the corner that Lauren called the career center, which was really just a computer with a printer/copier/fax and a corkboard for posting job listings. "Is something wrong with them?"

I might have used Lauren's cats as an excuse earlier with the guys, but honestly, I doted on them just as much as Lauren did.

Cammie surprised me by placing her slim hand on my shoulder and laughing. "Oh my word, Wyatt. You won't believe this. Lauren's phone made this ear-splitting sound, and it turns out she's got air tags on both cats. The software thought they'd left the building when they were sleeping in the front window."

Her hand slipped from my shoulder, but the smile stayed on her face.

"A cat monitoring alarm?" I asked, my stomach sinking. My blood sugar had been dipping and spiking all afternoon. Given how upset Lauren was earlier, it wouldn't surprise me if she'd turned up the sound on her phone instead of letting the alerts vibrate like I usually did. I hated that she'd had to lie to Cammie because of me.

"Come see," she said, walking around the counter. I followed her through the seating area to the career center. Medusa turned her sightless eyes toward the sound of our footsteps, and Desdemona let out a soft meow, either to greet us or to let her BFF know friendly people were approaching.

"Hey, girls," I said, rubbing them each behind the ears. They started purring in tandem and bumping their heads against my palms. Sure enough, they each had a new collar. I flipped over the shiny disk on Desdemona's and confirmed it was, in fact, an air tag.

I laughed so loud both cats jumped.

"She said she checks on them at night to make sure they aren't stuck somewhere," Cammie said, watching as I loved on the cats. "I told her I'd make sure they weren't anywhere that didn't have a cat door before we leave. Maybe you can move the sensor or something, so it doesn't go off every time they're in the front window."

"Sure," I said, though my gut told me the alarm had been for my blood sugar. Most air tags just gave a location. Setting up a perimeter with alerts would be a whole other level of sophistication, and as much as Lauren babied her cats, that seemed excessive, even for her.

"She's going to be a great mom," Cammie said, petting Desdemona. Our fingers were so close, they almost brushed. "Overprotective but great."

I couldn't agree more. Deep down, I knew Lauren was still terrified she wouldn't be good enough. We'd all do our best to reassure her, but until she held Logan in her arms, she'd doubt her ability to be a mom. She didn't need to worry about me as well.

It was the same reason I'd kept my diagnosis from my family. Type 1 diabetes was common, and if managed well, wouldn't limit me from doing anything I wanted. Cerebral palsy like Wade's came with a mountain of challenges that required money, time, and an intense amount of effort to manage. I was constantly amazed by his determination to gain more independence, but he had some physical limitations he'd never be able to overcome.

"I hope you can figure out a way to keep that alarm from going off," Cammie said.

"I'm positive I can."

Our hands met on Desdemona's back, our fingertips touching. Neither of us moved until the cat wiggled, breaking wherever the moment could have led.

Chapter Five

Cammie

WHILE MOST BARS WOULD be fairly empty on Sunday evenings, Church Street Brews was packed as usual. In a stroke of luck or marketing brilliance, "going to Church on Sunday" was a tradition with multiple meanings for the good people of Peace Falls.

"I'm so hungry," Lauren said as she read over the menu. "I think I might order fries *and* onion rings with my burger." Her brown hair looked sun kissed, her tan had deepened since I saw yesterday, and her eyes sparkled. She'd spent all afternoon outside with Aiden's large family, and I'd bet the glow surrounding her had more to do with them than her time in the sun.

"Go for it," I said, filling my glass from the pitcher of frozen mango margaritas I'd ordered when we sat down. "You're eating for two."

She eyed my drink with longing before shaking her head. "You didn't see the amount of barbequed chicken I had at the picnic."

"I'm sure you burned off all of it playing with Aiden's nieces and nephews."

Her face lit with joy, and the corners of my eyes stung. Lauren finally had the family she deserved. Not just the one she'd cobbled together with her friends, but a loud, multi-generational group who filled her life with unwavering love and support. I'd been so relieved when Aiden's family welcomed her warmly into theirs. I'd heard enough in-law horror stories to worry. Luckily, all my fears for Lauren evaporated the moment I met the O'Malleys. I admit, I might even be a tad bit jealous, if only because I'd never get over my fears enough to find love like she did, let alone with someone who came with a family I thought only existed on sappy TV shows.

"Will someone please tell my sister I don't have to wear a wedding dress," Poppy said, slamming her messenger bag on the table and sliding into the seat next to Lauren.

"What do you plan to wear, then?" Rowan asked, dropping a pillow on the hard booth bench before sitting down gently beside me. Despite making significant progress in her PT sessions with Cal, she was still recovering from back surgery.

"Something black," Poppy said, gesturing to her outfit. No one could ever accuse her of not being loyal to a color choice.

"You could always wear a black wedding dress," I said before taking a sip of my drink.

Poppy's eyes widened. She quickly grabbed her phone and started typing. "They exist," she said, sounding breathless as she held her phone out for us to see.

The second I heard Poppy and her tattoo artist boyfriend, Theo, had gotten engaged, I immediately pictured her in a black wedding dress. Poppy was a romantic like me. Not that either of us would admit it, but I figured it was 50/50 she'd go goth or a white princess ballgown, which was why I hadn't mentioned my idea until she turned down the more traditional option.

Poppy let out a squeal, and we all leaned closer to see the image on her phone: a puffy princess ballgown in black lace.

"It's perfect," Rowan said.

"It is," Poppy whispered. She put the phone down with a sigh.

"What's wrong?" Lauren asked, taking her hand.

A look so vulnerable crossed Poppy's face my breath caught. Beneath all the eye liner and badass attitude, she was incredibly sweet. Every time Poppy allowed me to see her soft side felt like a privilege and a step closer in our friendship.

"I hate being the center of attention," she said quietly. "The idea of standing in front of everyone I know, even to marry Theo, makes me want to throw up."

She looked so embarrassed by her admission I spoke before I considered the conversation I was inviting. "Been there. I puke every time I perform."

At least I had since Bishop broke my hand.

Lauren, Rowan, and Poppy stared at me with matching frowns.

"Bullshit," Poppy said. "I watched you sing at Rowan's wedding. You didn't sound nervous."

I wasn't. I loved singing, and watching others enjoy listening filled me with joy. I had many reasons to hate Bishop, but tainting my post-performance high topped the list. Just thinking about him soured my stomach. Daddy had missed our usual Sunday call, which sadly wasn't out of the ordinary, given the steps he had to go through to make it. Still, waiting another day to hear how he was doing with Bishop's brother in the unit had my nerves pulled taunt.

"Have you ever seen me right after I leave the stage?" I asked, pouring Poppy and Rowan glasses from the pitcher. I pushed the drinks to the sisters, hoping to distract them. The better I got to know these women, the harder it became to keep my past to myself, where it belonged, festering a hole in my stomach.

"Is that why you don't perform more often?" Rowan asked gently, ignoring the glass in front of her. "You've only done one open mic since I moved back to Peace Falls."

Instead of answering, I took a sip of my drink.

"That's the only one she's ever done," Lauren said, looking around for our usual server, Brandi. "Maybe I should just order my food at the bar."

I'd forced myself to sing at the open mic, hoping Bishop's hold on me had loosened after living in Peace Falls awhile. But the moment I finished the song, I'd had to run out the door to be sick in the alley behind the bar. The same thing happened when I sang at Cal and Rowan's wedding.

"Getting back to Poppy," I said, hoping to dodge any more questions about me. "Don't you want to celebrate your love with Theo?"

"We celebrate it every night just fine," she said, sniffing her glass before taking a delicate sip.

I bet they did. The heat between those two could start a wildfire. I'd never experienced that kind of sexual tension with anyone—until recently. My cheeks heated at the memory.

"What do you need?"

An ache formed deep in my core just remembering how Wyatt sounded when he asked the question. He definitely wasn't thinking about inventory or the espresso machine, and after hearing his husky words, neither was I. The longing in his voice was undeniable and spoke to my body in a way I'd never felt before.

I knew he was attracted to me when we met, and the realization he still was made me ache to feel his touch. The impulse scared me enough to yank me from his pheromone cloud. I started babbling about the espresso machine and the moment evaporated like so many chances I'd let pass over the years. Only I couldn't stop thinking about it and found myself inching closer to him any chance I could.

What did I need? Sex with Wyatt, apparently. I'm embarrassed by the number of times I'd gotten myself off imagining all the ways I could have answered him.

"But weddings are so—" Rowan started.

"Unnecessary," Poppy said, glaring at her.

"Romantic," I said, forcing my mind back to where it belonged.

"Says the woman who freezes every time anyone shows interest in her," Poppy said.

I waved my hand as if to brush off her words. "I love romance. Just not directed at me."

"Admit it, Poppy," Lauren said. "You want to put on that great big morbid ballgown and watch Theo's reaction as you walk down the aisle to him."

Before Poppy could answer, Brandi came over to the table, and Lauren shocked everyone by ordering two burgers with fries and onion rings.

"OK, fine," Poppy said, slamming her half-full glass on the table. "It might be nice to have a small ceremony. But if I give in to that, Mom will go overboard and invite half the town."

"Not if she doesn't know about it, until she's there," I said.

The Stevens sisters looked at me like I'd suddenly turned teal. Lauren smiled.

"You think I can plan an entire wedding without my mother—the local florist—finding out about it?" Poppy asked, eyeing me skeptically.

"You do hate cut flowers," Rowan reminded her. "You could make them out of paper."

"Or metal," Poppy said, her eyes glazing over. Poppy was an amazing sculptor, and I'm sure whatever she was picturing in her mind would be incredible.

"Then you could keep them forever," I said and smiled at her.

Her eyes brightened and a soft smile crossed her face. Yep, definitely a romantic.

"When do you suggest we have this flash wedding?" Poppy asked.

"Halloween?" Lauren suggested.

Poppy glared at her. "That's cliché. Though a fall wedding would be nice. It gives us enough time to pull it together without dragging out the prep work. Plus, Theo wants us married ASAP."

"October 12th," Rowan shouted.

"My birthday?" Lauren asked, her forehead scrunched in confusion.

"What better excuse to get Mom to a party without her suspecting it's Poppy's wedding?" Rowan said. "I mean, unless you don't want to share your birthday with her anniversary. Or do you and Aiden have something planned?"

We all leaned forward.

"One life event at a time," Lauren said, placing her hand on her stomach. "I can't imagine a better birthday gift than celebrating your wedding, Poppy."

"You're welcomed to marry Aiden on my birthday," Poppy said with a smirk.

"So, October 12th?" Rowan asked, deftly moving the conversation along.

"If Theo's OK with it, fine," Poppy said. "But you three are helping me."

"Of course," Rowan said, giving her sister's hand a squeeze.

My chest warmed. I'd never been part of a wedding until Rowan and Cal's. I looked at each woman at the table, grateful they had made space for me in their lives. Bishop narrowed my world until only he remained, yet each friendship I formed in Peace Falls seemed to bring me another. Lauren might understand how I felt, though I doubt Rowan and Poppy had a clue what it was like to be entirely alone in the world. I could never explain to them what their friendships meant to me, but I could show them. "I can sing, if you want."

Poppy shook her head, and I wanted to hide under the table. I shouldn't have assumed she'd want me to perform. I wasn't tone deaf, but I wasn't Adele either.

No one really wants to hear you sing. Your voice is nothing special. They're just staring at your body.

"As much as I'd love to hear you perform again," Poppy said, "I can't ask you to after what you just told us."

"You didn't ask. I offered," I said, telling the voice in my head, that sounded an awful lot like Bishop, to shut up. "How many people are we talking?"

Poppy's lips moved like she was listing names in her head. "No more than fifteen. Wait, maybe twenty. I should probably invite everyone from art class, since they worked so hard to get us together."

"That should be fine." I'd just throw up and not tell her. The size of the crowd didn't matter. I got sick because of the fear that dumped into my system after I performed. Yet another trigger response I hadn't been able to work through.

The sisters accepted what I said at face value and started chatting about venues. Lauren shook her head. I silently pleaded with her to let it go, which she did. But after Lauren had inhaled her dinner, and we'd said goodnight to the Stevens sisters, she walked with me to my car.

"It's time, Cam," she said without a hint of pity in her voice. "You've got to stop letting whatever happened keep you from doing what you love."

"I just get nervous. That's all."

Lauren shook her head. She could read people better than anyone I knew and had yet to believe any of the excuses I gave everyone else. "You offered to sing at the wedding to give Poppy something meaningful. But I want you to be able to sing for yourself whenever you want. You can start by singing for me, then we'll add Rowan and Poppy, and then the guys. You'll keep singing, and we'll keep listening. If you do it enough times, you'll break whatever it is holding you back."

I nodded. It might actually work.

"And by guys, I'm including Wyatt," she said with a smirk.

I shrugged like the idea of him watching me sing didn't fill me with equal parts fear and longing. I never wanted him to hear. I desperately wanted to know how he'd react if he did. Yet again, Wyatt created a battle in my head I was destined to lose. I'd either give in to my attraction to him, making myself vulnerable to a man yet again. Or I'd keep him at arm's length, always wondering what would have happened if only I'd been brave enough to let down my walls.

Chapter Six

Wyatt

WHEN I ARRIVED AT Karma on Monday, Lauren was working alone.

"Is Cammie all right?" I asked, joining her behind the coffee bar. "I thought the PT office had been closing early."

"She's fine," Lauren said, flashing me a bright smile. "She needed to finish up some things for Cal, but she'll be in soon. How's your family?"

"Good," I said, pulling out my phone and showing her the picture Wade had sent me this morning. "My brother got his learner's permit."

She smiled at the photo of my twin holding up a shiny plastic ID. "He must be so excited."

"We're all excited for him."

"Tell Wade congrats from me," she said and gave my arm a squeeze. "Won't be long until he's driving down here to visit you."

I nodded. I wasn't about to get into all the things that'd have to line up before that could happen. If I mentioned my twin needed money for an adaptive van, no telling what Lauren would do to help him, and she had enough on her plate running Karma and preparing for the baby. But, fuck, I missed my brother.

I hadn't made enough effort to see my college friends since I stopped taking classes. That's a lie. I'd basically avoided everyone. It hurt too much to see them, knowing I wasn't living the same life as them anymore, despite how much I wanted to be. I'd turned down so many invitations in the past year, they'd stopped coming. My social life was basically nonexistent at this point. Lauren had filled much of the void my friends left behind, but as grateful as I was to have her in my life, I missed Wade.

Lauren cleared her throat and shifted her weight from one foot to the other. "While it's just the two of us, there's something I'd like to discuss."

"Sure," I said, dread settling like a bowling ball in my stomach. Discussions never meant good news, especially when the other person looked as nervous as Lauren did. Growing up, it was how my parents started any conversation about adjustments they needed to make to the household budget. Wade's OT copays went up fifty dollars a session. Would I mind sitting out travel soccer? Wade needed a new wheelchair. Would I be able to get a job after school to help? The answer was always of course.

By some chance of fate, I was born healthy while my twin faced struggle after struggle from the moment he took his first breath. What was travel soccer compared with Wade building up strength and mobility in his arms? Or a few hours working a crummy retail job if it meant Wade could get a new chair that didn't glitch on the regular?

Some of the worry must have bled into my expressions because Lauren placed a gentle hand on my arm and said, "Nothing's wrong, Wy."

I started to relax when she hit me with the second part of her sentence.

"But things could be better."

I tried to recall any way I'd messed up during my shifts at Karma and came up blank. "How so?" I finally asked.

She chewed on her bottom lip a moment as she worked on what she wanted to say. "You should get an insulin pump," she blurted out.

I shook my head. "I've already looked into them. Even with insurance, pumps are outrageously expensive. It's just not something I can swing right now."

"I could," she said, her eyes pleading, like handing me thousands of dollars topped her life's wish list. She was generous to a fault, and I wasn't about to take advantage of her.

"I'm not taking your money, Lauren."

Her face softened. "I get how important it is for you to stand on your own feet, so I'd just loan you the money. You could take however long you need to pay me back."

I shook my head. "I finally got you to agree to hiring more help around here. If I take thousands out of your savings, you'll worry you're spending too much."

She let out a tiny huff because she knew I was right. "Fine, take Aiden's money then. He's actually the one who suggested the pump. He might not have shown it, but you really upset him last week."

Oh, he showed me all right. "I'm just figuring it out is all," I said, rubbing my forehead. "It's been hard to gauge how much I need to eat to offset the work I do. Things like electrical don't require many more calories than what I burn here, but days when I'm demoing or framing, I need a lot more."

"Which is why a pump would be ideal."

It would be. However, if I had $6K to spare, I'd be putting it toward a van for Wade. I remember how excited I was to get my learner's permit, then license. It had taken Wade six more years of hard PT and OT to build the strength and coordination to pass the evaluation he needed to even get a permit.

"I've worked with Aiden long enough to know he wouldn't let me pay him back, and I don't want or need a handout," I told her. "If I ever get a pump, I'm buying it myself."

"Yeah, I figured," she said with a smirk that made the dimples on her cheeks appear. "Which is why you should move into the apartment upstairs."

"Your apartment?" I asked. Until recently, Lauren had lived in the two-bedroom apartment on the second floor above Karma. Except for the occasional nap, she'd rarely used it for the past couple months.

"Things are going really well with Aiden. Great even," she said with a small smile. "There's no reason you should pay rent when there's an entire apartment sitting empty upstairs. Your lease is month-to-month, right?"

I nodded.

"And with the semester starting soon, I'm sure your landlord will easily find a new tenant."

Since the building was within walking distance of campus, I knew he would. Lauren's apartment was much nicer than mine, which had thin walls that let in every noise, heat wave, and icy draft. My place was also inconvenient, located on the opposite side of town from Karma and the new housing development where I worked most days.

Inconvenience was relative. Back home, I crept through DC suburban traffic at a snail's pace, stopping every few feet for a red light. Here, the biggest nuisance was being on the wrong side of the tracks from where I wanted to be when a freight train came through and having to wait five minutes to cross. Even if it only saved a few minutes a day, I'd wanted to move to Main Street for a while but couldn't justify the higher rent prices.

"It's not a terrible idea," I said.

She did a little happy hop and clapped her hands.

"But I'm paying you rent."

Lauren shook her head so hard her long braid flew over her shoulder to her back. "You'd be doing me a favor. I hate that the building sits empty overnight. Not only does it make it more vulnerable to break-ins, I worry about the cats being left alone for so long."

"Did you really put trackers on Desdemona and Medusa?" I asked.

Lauren straightened her spine and shot me a look that would have intimidated anyone who didn't know her as well as I did. "Yes. And I'll be keeping those collars on them whether or not you move in. They could wander outside and be lost forever."

Doubtful. Both cats knew they had a good thing. They'd probably lie down and wail the second their paws touched concrete. That wouldn't stop Lauren from worrying about them when she wasn't in the building.

I took a moment to consider her offer. I couldn't argue that having someone in the apartment overnight would deter anyone from breaking into Karma, not that Peace Falls was a hotbed of crime. But everyone in town knew Lauren no longer lived upstairs, and the business generated a significant amount of cash each day.

"You'd still use the apartment like you'd planned for the baby's naps when you're working, right?" I asked. "I'd just be staying in the second bedroom."

"You could have my old room, and I could put the baby in the smaller one," she said, her eyes brightening. "The shower is in the en suite."

She knew how close I was to agreeing, which was why she hadn't called it "her room." She didn't need to know that I'd be sending every dollar I saved back home for Wade's van.

"I'd consider it if I stayed in the smaller room, and you took the cat monitoring software off your phone. You can put it on mine if you want, but if you're monitoring my blood sugar, I'm monitoring the cats."

"Deal," she said, holding out her hand to shake mine.

After I dropped her hand, I cleared my throat and looked around to make sure a customer hadn't approached the counter. "The alarm Cammie heard last week was mine, not the cats, right?"

She nodded and a huge grin broke across my face. "Nice save. She asked me to fix the sensors, so the cats can nap in the front window without setting off the alarm."

Instead of laughing like I thought she would, Lauren frowned. "I hate lying to Cammie. To anyone, but especially to her. She doesn't trust easily. Honestly, I'm surprised she believed me."

The guilt was clear on her face and added to the weight I carried each day for keeping my health a secret from my family. "I'm sorry, Lauren."

She placed her hand on my shoulder. "I just wish you'd realize it's nothing to be embarrassed about."

"I'm not embarrassed," I said, even as I felt my cheeks warm.

She glared at me.

"It's not what you think," I said, trying to put into words something I didn't completely understand myself. "I'm not embarrassed that I have diabetes. It's not like I have a choice in the matter. I'm just uncomfortable with how people treat me when they know."

"I've made you uncomfortable?" Lauren asked, looking horrified. Her hand fell from my shoulder and immediately went to her midsection.

"No," I said quickly. She looked so hurt, I pulled her into a hug and kissed the top of her head. "You're the best."

"But?" she asked, stepping away. She wasn't letting me off the topic that easily, and we both knew it.

"I don't want people defining me by it. It's just not that big of a deal."

"What the hell, Wyatt," she said, surprising me with the anger in her voice. Pregnancy hormones had her swinging hot and cold more than usual, but this was different. I'd never seen her so pissed, at least with me. "Not a big deal? You could have fallen off a roof."

My mouth dropped open.

"Basement my ass." She shoved a finger in my chest. "Don't think for a second I bought that lie. I figured you were using a power tool or something marginally dangerous. When you sent that proof of life shot, I knew you'd been on a damn roof when you crashed. Let me guess, you knew it was happening but didn't want to tell your coworkers you needed a break to take care of yourself?"

Aiden hadn't mentioned my blood sugar crash since our talk in his truck, though judging by the wrath on Lauren's face, he might have received a chewing out on my behalf. "You didn't yell at Aiden, did you?"

"Of course, I yelled at him. He's operating under the delusion that pregnant women shouldn't get angry and raise their blood pressure, so I gave him a pass after he told me he'd fire you if it happened again."

"Everything OK?" a soft voice asked behind us.

We both froze.

Lauren shot me an apologetic look before she turned and faced Cammie. "I'm just giving Wyatt a piece of my mind he didn't ask for and might not deserve." She blew out a breath and shrugged. "Hormones."

My heart cracked. She was trying to cover for me. Again. Lauren was a huge believer in karma and, in her mind, lying to Cammie would offset some of the good she'd put into the universe.

"Nah, I deserved it," I said, turning to face Cammie as well. Her eyes looked impossibly large as they ping-ponged between Lauren and me. "I got dizzy while I was working on a roof last week and didn't tell anyone or take a break."

"Well, that's just stupid," Cammie said, putting her hands on her hips. "The heat was terrible. You're lucky you didn't pass out and fall."

I nodded, relieved she hadn't heard enough of the conversation to know the heat hadn't been the reason, and feeling like a piece of shit for not correcting her. Lauren didn't need to tell me about Cammie's trust issues. I'd been chipping away at them for a year. Lying to Cam, even by omission, felt like a huge step back. It also put in perspective how terrible Lauren must have felt covering for me.

Lauren looked between Cammie and me and smiled, which seemed an odd reaction. I certainly wasn't coming across well in this conversation. Maybe she was just pleased to have someone else tell me what an idiot I'd been. Sadly, Cammie's reaction felt a little too close to Lauren's big sister response for my liking.

"I'm sure it won't happen again," Lauren said, practically beaming.

"I'll make sure it doesn't," I said, reassuring them both as best I could. Conversations like this were exactly why I didn't go around telling everyone about my health problems.

"Guess what?" Lauren said, gripping Cammie's hands. "Wyatt's moving in upstairs to look after the building and the cats at night."

I figured Cammie didn't give a shit where I lived, but to my surprise she looked as excited as Lauren by the news. "That's wonderful," she said, flashing her brightest smile at Lauren. "Now you can actually relax when you're home."

"When can you move in?" Lauren asked me.

"Let me talk to my super. The original lease asked for a month's notice, though if there's a waiting list, I could probably move out right away."

"Let me know when, so Aiden and I can help you move," Lauren said. "Do you need to put anything in storage?"

I shook my head. "My place came furnished. I don't need storage space or help moving."

Lauren smiled so big her dimples sunk deep in her cheeks. "The cats will be so happy."

I doubt the cats cared, but I smiled at her anyway.

"Go home, woman," Cammie said, playfully pushing Lauren toward the swinging door leading to the back. "Wyatt and I have it from here."

I hated how my stomach dipped when she referred to us together. When did I become this pathetic? We were coworkers, for fuck's sake, and Cammie was just trying to get Lauren off her feet.

Soon after Lauren left, the evening rush began. Fewer people ordered coffee to go, but plenty met up with friends in the café or shopped for books. The last couple hours were always too busy for Cammie and me to be alone for long, and over the past month, we'd fallen into a comfortable rhythm working together.

It would only be awkward after we closed the front door and flipped the sign. When we first started sharing shifts, Cammie didn't speak a word to me as we cleaned up and readied the café for the morning rush. She'd slowly warmed up to being alone with me. A couple weeks ago, we talked about the weather like we were complete strangers making small talk. I'd been as thrilled by the conversation as a new parent hearing their child's first words. I figured it'd take another month before she worked up to anything meaningful, but to my surprise, Cammie looked eager as she ushered the last customer out the door.

"Oh my word, Wyatt. Do you know what you moving in means?"

I save a shit-ton on rent. "Lauren doesn't worry about the cats as much?"

She smacked my arm playfully, and I fought the urge to grab her hand and kiss each of her fingers.

"She's all in with Aiden," she said, smiling. "No way would she sell the building if it meant you wouldn't have a roof over your head. Plus, she didn't correct me when I called Aiden's place home, like she's done in the past."

Last month, Lauren had upset everyone when she put Karma on the market after deciding she couldn't stay in Peace Falls and watch Aiden raise their child. Thankfully, she'd changed her mind and seemed committed to Aiden and becoming a mom, and offering me the apartment upstairs was definitely proof she didn't plan to sell.

I smiled so wide my face hurt. "You're right."

Before I knew what was happening, Cammie had wrapped her arms around my waist and pressed the side of her face to my chest. I hugged her back almost as a reflex while my heart thudded so hard, she had to have heard it.

Lauren and Cammie were both huggers. It wasn't uncommon to see them hugging it out, and Lauren hugged me every time she said hello or goodbye. Cammie had never once embraced me. She seemed to realize this and stiffened in my arms. I waited for her to let go, but when she didn't, I ran my hand along her back. She melted closer, her fingers gripping my shirt. My excitement that the woman of my dreams was finally in my arms soon gave way to concern when her shoulder hitched. Shit, she was crying.

I was too dumbfounded to ask what was wrong. Instead, I kept rubbing her back while she cried into my shirt. After a while, she dropped her arms and stood back.

"Don't mind me," she said, wiping at the mascara cutting lines down her beautiful face.

I thought her eyes had looked different today, and seeing the black bleed down her cheeks confirmed she'd been wearing a little makeup. She was gorgeous with or without it, but nothing compared to how she looked now. Her eyes were bluer filled with tears, and her full bottom lip trembled as she fought to regain her composure. Sad shouldn't look so good. I was an asshole for being so attracted to her when she was clearly upset. In my defense, the fact she'd felt comfortable enough to break down in front of me amped up my usual longing. The urge to hold her again was so strong, I shoved my hands in my pockets to keep myself from reaching for her.

"I'm just relieved," she added.

She didn't look relieved: worried, upset, embarrassed, yes. I'd be crazy to call her out on it, yet I needed to say something to put her at ease. Wade would crack a joke. Too bad I didn't have his sense of humor.

"I get it," I said. "Lauren scared the shit out of me last month. I didn't catch a good night's sleep for days. I kept thinking I'd come in to open and find she'd left town in the middle of the night."

Cammie blew out a breath and wiped the last of her tears from her cheeks. "Thanks for understanding, Wyatt. Sorry I cried all over you."

"No need to apologize. Lauren does it all the time."

Cammie laughed, even though I was stating a fact.

"You're a really good friend," she said, smiling at me.

And even though I smiled back, my heart splintered as I crash landed in the friend zone.

Chapter Seven

Cammie

My breath hitched the moment the video call connected. Dark bruises marred my father's face, and his left eye was so swollen he could barely force it open. He'd gotten into a few fights since he'd been inside, but this was unlike anything I'd seen before.

"Hey, Millie," he said, like he wasn't battered and bruised. As if this were any other Sunday evening call, and we had a half hour to chat about the book he recently checked out from the prison library or the song I'd taught myself to play on my guitar.

"What happened?" I asked once I could breathe again.

"Looks worse than it is," he said. "How you been?"

"Daddy!" I yelled.

He let out a sigh. "It's nothing, honey."

"If you want to pretend I'd believe that, I might as well hang up now."

He pressed his lips into a grim line and nodded. "I didn't want to upset you, but I guess you should know. Todd and I got into a scuffle. It's all good now."

I figured it would happen eventually. Still, seeing the marks Bishop's brother left on my dad's face filled me with rage. Had Todd started it or had Daddy used Todd as a surrogate for Bishop, inflicting an ounce of what he'd threatened to do to my ex if he ever got the chance? "I need details."

"It's fine, Millie. He thought he could intimidate me, and I'd tell him where you were. Taught him real quick that wasn't going to happen. Only cost me a day in solitary."

I blew out a breath. All things considered, it wasn't the worst thing that could have happened.

"Almost got thrown back in though when I found out my cellmate let the asshole sit on my bed while I was gone. Fucking Phil can be bought for two soups and a coffee."

An overwhelming sense of dread tightened my stomach and chest. "Todd was in your cell?"

"Don't worry, I know Phil's a talker. He doesn't even know I have a daughter. We practically communicate in grunts."

"But Todd was in your cell!" I screeched. "With all your stuff."

"It's not like I have much to steal."

"Did you keep any of the letters I've sent you?"

His faced paled, and I knew I was screwed. Tears leaked down my cheeks, and it took every ounce of self-control to stop myself from sobbing. The life I'd built in Peace Falls was over.

"I checked my stuff when I got back to make sure Phil hadn't gotten into it. All the letters were there."

"He didn't have to take them to read the return address," I forced out. My breaths were coming in quick bursts. I needed a paper bag or something before I passed out.

"Millie, honey, you don't even know if he saw them. Plus, you use a PO Box," he said, but it sounded like he was trying to convince himself more than me.

"In Jericho," I shouted. "Fifteen minutes from where I live. How many days ago was this?"

"It hasn't even been a day. I got out of solitary this morning."

OK. Even if Todd found the letters and contacted Bishop right away, and I'd bet my right hand and both my legs he did, it would take a while for Bishop to trace the PO Box to my physical location. Thank heavens I didn't open a box at the Peace Falls post office. For once, my paranoia paid off. Still, if Bishop had my PO Box, he'd know the general area of where to find me. Rural Virginia wasn't like NYC. I couldn't hide in a town like Peace Falls, not once he knew to look around here.

"Millie, honey," Daddy said, pulling me back to our video call. "I promise I'll make Phil tell me about every second that shithead was in our cell."

I forced myself to stop crying so I could speak. "Before you do, get rid of anything with my PO Box on it," I said. "On the slim chance Todd didn't see it, we don't want to give him another chance if you get thrown back into solitary."

Daddy nodded, his eyes shining. "I'm so sorry, sweetie. I shouldn't have kept the letters. It was stupid. I just wanted something I could hold of yours, since I might never get to hold you again."

"It's OK, Daddy." It wasn't, but I straightened my spine and looked him in the eyes. "The only person who should feel guilty is Bishop."

"Please, be careful," he said in a strained voice. "If anything happens to you—" He shook his head, unwilling or unable to voice what his reality would become.

"I love you, Daddy."

"Love you too, Millie. I'll talk to Phil and get in touch as soon as I can."

After the call ended, I sat on the couch I'd thrifted from Goodwill and stared at my studio apartment. It wasn't much. Honestly, even with saving a huge chunk each month to pay back Bishop, I could afford a bigger place. But I knew I'd sleep easier if I could see every door and window in my space. I loved every inch of my tiny apartment because it was that: mine.

The mismatched dishes and used books I found at yard sales. The bright pink bedspread Lauren gifted me after I'd saved up to buy a mattress. The crocheted pillow shams that reminded me of the ones my mom used to make, her delicate fingers working the hook and yarn while she listened to me sing. And everywhere pictures of the people and places I loved in Peace Falls.

The sob I'd held back for my dad burst from my chest, and before I knew what I was doing, I'd dialed Lauren's cell. When she answered, I didn't say a word. After a moment of listening to me cry, she calmly said, "I'll be right there."

She must have been visiting the Stevens sisters or somewhere else in town because I barely had time to hunt down a box of tissues and blow my nose when a loud knock sounded on my door.

My heart rate sped up, even though there was a 99% chance it was Lauren. I looked through the peephole, relieved to see she'd come alone.

I unlocked the door, removed the chain, and cried on Lauren's shoulder for a good ten minutes with zero explanation.

"Why don't we sit down," she said when I'd finally cried myself out. I lifted my head and realized we were still in the doorway to my apartment. I motioned her inside and then locked the door behind her.

She sat down on the couch and patted the cushion beside her. I suddenly felt exhausted, like I could lie down on my shabby-chic rug and sleep for days while Lauren watched over me. I sank onto the couch beside her, and she took my hand. "Whenever you're ready."

I blew out a breath and spoke, my voice drained of all emotion. I could have been giving her an inventory update instead of the sad details of my past. She remained quiet, listening without pity because she understood one sympathetic look would break me.

When I fell silent, she squeezed my hand and said, "Pack a bag. You're coming home with me."

"Absolutely not," I said, sounding firm for the first time since she entered the apartment. "If Bishop tracked me down at your place, I'd be too far from town for the police to get there in time to help. Plus, I'm not putting you and the baby at risk."

Lines settled across her forehead, and I could see her running through every option she thought I had besides the only real one: Leave. "You could stay with Wyatt at Karma until you deal with your ex," she said, her eyes brightening. "Maybe if you pay Bishop back, he'll leave you alone. Until you do, stay with Wyatt."

"Are you insane? I won't date a man. Why on earth would I live with one?

"Not just any man. Wyatt."

"I know you see him as a brother, but trust me, he's a man and as dangerous as they come."

Lauren morphed from kind friend to full mama bear mode. Her eyes hardened, and she leaned forward, getting right in my face. This wasn't good.

"How many times has he asked you out?" she snapped.

"Once," I mumbled.

"And when you told him no, did he keep asking?"

I shook my head. "But he's still a man."

"Who's proven he respects you and does everything he can to make you feel comfortable around him."

I crossed my arms over my chest. "He's still dangerous."

"Because you like him," Lauren said.

I did, but I could barely admit that to myself. If Lauren knew how I felt, no telling what she'd do to push us together. Though I couldn't think of anything more *together* than living in the same 900 square foot apartment.

"I agree the farmhouse is too remote," Lauren said softly. "So, you have two choices: Either live with Wyatt or move in with Cal and Rowan. You know Cal will never let you live alone if he thinks you're in danger. And, I'm sorry, this is one secret I can't keep. Not when I could lose you."

I let out a huff. Darn her for being so rational. "There's a third option," I said.

"No, there isn't," she said firmly. "You've built a life here, and you're surrounded by people who will stand up to this asshat if he ever dares show his face in this town."

I wanted to stay so badly it hurt, but I couldn't see how. "I can't live with Cal and Rowan for the same reason I won't live with you. I'm not putting them at risk if Bishop finds me."

"Do you have a picture of this guy?"

"What?" I asked, genuinely confused. "Trust me, I don't need pictures. He's burned in my brain."

"Fair. Answer me this: does he own a gun?"

I squirmed on the sofa. The thought of Bishop armed made me want to climb in my car and leave without packing, but he'd only ever hurt me with his hands and words. I shook my head.

"Is he someone who'd fight anyone, or one of those pissant fuckheads who hurts people smaller than him to make himself feel big and bad?"

I raised my eyebrows at her, and she raised hers back at me. If she ever got the nerve to talk about her life before she came to Peace Falls, I'm sure we'd have more than one terrible memory in common. "He talked a big game, but I never saw him hit anyone other than me. He's about my height and average build."

"So, Cal could handle him."

"I'm not moving in with my boss, Lauren. Not only would it be weird, even for us, but they're newlyweds. I'd be a third wheel."

"Great. So you'll move in with Wyatt. He's taller than you, and Aiden says he's one of his strongest guys."

And didn't I know it. Wyatt's arms, which had always been frustratingly toned, had become down-right mouthwatering since he started working construction. And brilliant woman that I am, I'd gone and hugged him. The warmth of his touch, coupled with the realization that I'd almost lost Lauren and could lose the life I'd built in Peace Falls, had hit me hard. He'd held me as I fell apart, leaving me feeling safe, comforted, and incredibly turned on.

"Don't mistake his sweetness for weakness," Lauren said, misreading my lust-filled pondering for doubt. "He's incredibly protective. Aiden told me he got right in his face when he found out about the baby and only stepped down when Aiden said he wanted to step up. No question, Wyatt wouldn't let your ex try anything."

I didn't doubt it. What's worse, it made him even hotter. Still, if my options were to leave Peace Falls or live with Wyatt, I was willing to test my self-control. "I'm not giving up my apartment," I said. "This would only be temporary until I figure out how to deal with Bishop, or I'm confident he doesn't know where I am."

"That's reasonable," Lauren said with a nod. "Plus, you want Bishop to think you still live in this apartment, so he won't have a reason to look elsewhere in town."

"What on Earth are you going to tell Wyatt?" I asked.

"The truth? If he's in danger, don't you think he ought to know?"

"No, Lauren. I'm certain Bishop is only dangerous to me and any woman who gets between me and him. As long as I keep an eye out for him, no one needs to know. I don't want Cal or anyone else looking for him. And you know that's what would happen if you told anyone he'd abused me. I wouldn't put it past Poppy and Rowan to hunt him down with a baseball bat."

Lauren let out a sigh. "I don't agree with keeping everyone in the dark, but it's your choice. And it's my apartment, so I'll just tell him you're staying there temporarily to save money on rent, same as him."

"I thought he moved in to watch the building and the cats? Does Aiden pay him that bad?"

Lauren opened her mouth and then pressed her lips into a tight line. A million thoughts seemed to cross her face at once before she finally blurted out, "He sends money home to help his family. He's been doing it since he started at Karma." She narrowed her eyes and pointed at me. "Now forget I told you that. Saving money is a good reason to give him for why you'll be there."

I shook my head. "That's too convenient. He'll get the wrong idea and think I'm signaling I want him to make another move."

"Fine," she said, throwing her arms up in the air. "We'll say you have black mold in your apartment, and it's being cleaned or abated or whatever." She let out a groan and rubbed her forehead. "The number of lies I tell for the two of you is seriously negating my positive energy. My car is bound to crap out soon."

I didn't miss that she'd included Wyatt in her lying lament. It made me wonder what secrets she was helping him keep. I wanted to ask her, but I knew Lauren would never tell, minus her earlier slipup, unless he also had a crazy ex hunting him down and needed protecting. Sending money to his family didn't seem like something to hide, yet I wasn't surprised he hadn't told me. Our conversations tended toward superficial, which was completely my fault. "Your car is always a left turn signal away from crapping out," I said instead.

"True. Good thing you're following me back to the farmhouse tonight. Get packing. I doubt Bishop could find you so quickly, assuming he even has your PO Box, but I won't sleep if you stay here. I also need to at least give Wyatt some warning before you move in, if for no other reason than to manage his expectations. Unless you don't want them managed?" She smirked at me and waited.

"No, it's a solid plan. I'll get what I need tonight, and I'll pack the rest tomorrow after work."

Lauren shook her head. "Pack what you'll need for a while. I don't want you coming back here alone."

Lauren helped me put all my scrubs into the only suitcase I'd brought with me from South Carolina. We also packed up a decent chunk of my summer wardrobe, my toiletries, and my tablet. I grabbed the perishables from my fridge and dumped them in a tote bag before unplugging the window unit and checking that all the lights were off.

"I've got this," Lauren said, grabbing my guitar case.

"I don't need that," I said. She ignored me and walked into the hallway. I slung the tote bag on my shoulder and dragged my suitcase out of my apartment with no clue when I'd be back.

Chapter Eight

Wyatt

Sam was showing me the blueprints for the newest job site at the housing development when Lauren's old beater pulled to a stop beside the huge dirt pile Mateo had made digging the foundation.

Aiden stopped talking with the cement truck driver and headed straight for her with a huge smile on his face. "Wyatt," he called without stopping.

"What you do now, *Novato*?" Sam asked.

I shrugged. My blood sugar was fine. I hadn't lost a cat. "Guess I'll find out," I said, dropping the edge of the blueprint I was holding and crossing the site to my bosses.

"Hey Wyatt," Lauren said, pulling me into a hug. "Aiden, the coffee's in the backseat if you want to give it to the guys. I threw in a couple dozen of Rowan's apple tarts too."

"Thanks, Princess," he said, laying a kiss on her that was definitely NSFW. "Sam, get your ass over here and help me," he said when he came up for air.

When I started toward the car to help as well, Lauren laid her hand on my shoulder. "Can I talk with you a minute?"

I nodded and we stepped aside while Sam and the rest of the crew made a beeline for Lauren's car and the unexpected mid-morning break. They looked thrilled and entirely distracted. I sensed an ambush.

"Might as well just spit it out. Whatever it is," I said calmly.

"Cammie's going to stay in my old room for a bit. I wanted to give you a heads-up in case you had any medical supplies in the living area. She'll also need help carrying her suitcase upstairs tonight. Though knowing her, she'll try to do it herself."

For a second, I thought I was suffering another bout of low blood sugar and had hallucinated the conversation. Living with Cammie Gibson was a dream I hadn't even dared to entertain. It couldn't be real.

Lauren placed her hand on my arm and her tone became serious. "Don't read anything into it, Wyatt. Her apartment has black mold, and she just needs a place to crash for a while. She has no idea how long. You know black mold can get in everything."

Something in Lauren's expression looked off. Even if she wasn't telling me the entire truth, she was crystal clear on one thing: Cammie moving in had nothing to do with me. Lauren's warning not to get my hopes up was all the assurance I needed that my brain hadn't concocted the entire conversation.

"So," she said, "make sure you put away anything you don't want her to see before your shift."

Shit. How was I supposed to manage my blood sugar without Cammie knowing? I was pretty good at hiding my supplies and ducking into the bathroom for my injections when I was around people. But I stored my insulin in the fridge and turned up the alarm on my monitoring app when I slept. Not to mention the hunk of plastic in my upper arm. OK, that last one was wishful thinking. I wouldn't be parading around her shirtless even if my sensor wasn't a dead giveaway that something wasn't quite right with me.

"Yeah, sure," I said, sounding anything but.

Lauren's eyes softened. "You could just tell her. It's not a big deal."

Leave it to Lauren to use my own words against me. It also hadn't escaped my notice that she didn't ask if Cammie could move in. Not that she had to, but it was very un-Lauren like not to discuss something as big as cohabitating with the woman of my dreams before hard launching Cammie into my living space.

Which I'd been in less than a week. Lauren had also waited until my old apartment was taken, so I had nowhere else to live.

"How long have you been working on this plan?" I asked.

"What?" Lauren said, her eyes widening. "I just found out Cammie needed a place to stay last night. Ask Aiden. She spent the night at our house, but didn't want to intrude any longer."

I shot her a look. Their farmhouse was massive and could easily accommodate a woman who worked two jobs. No doubt Aiden's close-knit family dropped in to intrude several times a week.

"OK, I know she could stay with us. She'd rather stay in the apartment."

My eyebrows raised in surprise, and an ember of hope flickered to life in my chest.

"It's an easier commute," she added quickly. "And fine, I sort of encouraged her to stay with you, but not because I'm trying to get the two of you together."

"You just want me to tell her I'm diabetic and figured you'd make it logistically impossible not to."

Lauren scrunched her nose and frowned. "Well, when you put it that way, it sounds bad. It's more like I'd worry less if you had someone to help you if you needed it. Your building was full of people, and even if no one knew you had diabetes, anyone would call 911 if you knocked on their door in distress at two in the morning. You're completely alone in the Karma building overnight."

She'd clearly been imagining worst-case scenarios for a while.

"Everything good?" Aiden asked, stepping up to us with two iced coffees. He handed one to me and wrapped his arm around Lauren. "I shoved an apple tart in my pocket before the rest of the guys inhaled them. If you don't want it, Wyatt, I'll eat it later."

Lauren shot him a horrified look.

"I wrapped it in a napkin first," he said with a smirk.

"That's both incredibly sweet and gross," she said with a sigh.

Aiden pulled his gaze from Lauren to me. "So you're good with Cammie moving in with you?"

Lauren's cheeks pinked, either because she realized she hadn't asked me or because she'd led Aiden to believe she would.

"Of course," I said, hoping to put her at ease.

"Thank God," Aiden said, giving Lauren a squeeze. "Hopefully, this one will stop worrying about both of you now."

Lauren glared at him. "It's your fault I'm hormonal. Deal with it."

"Oh, I will," he said, giving her a wink.

Lauren cleared her throat, looking flushed. "Well, I better get back. Enjoy your coffee." She waved at the rest of the crew, and they shouted their thanks as she climbed into her car.

Aiden and I watched her drive away before he burst out laughing. "You know that mold excuse was bullshit, right? Creative, but total bullshit."

"Really?"

Aiden nodded.

"You think Lauren is trying to get the two of us together?"

Aiden rubbed his beard a minute before shaking his head. "I know she'd love to see you two together, but she'd never force it. There must be another reason. Though on the off chance this is some elaborate setup by Lauren, I suggest you don't hit on Cammie. Let her make a move, if she's interested. Otherwise, you'll make her really uncomfortable."

"Pretty sure just being in the same room with me makes her uncomfortable."

Aiden shrugged. "Must not or else she wouldn't have agreed to move in with you for whatever reason. That's something."

And I realized it was. Aiden slapped my back and headed over to Sam and the rest of the guys.

It's true, the more time I spent with Cammie, the more comfortable she became with me. *Because you're her friend.*

It wasn't the first time I'd seen Cammie relax around guys who once made her freeze. She'd been terrified of Aiden for a long time. Surprisingly, she came around much faster with Theo Makris, despite the guy looking scary as hell *to me*. He's actually one of the nicest people in town, which I guess goes a long way to explaining why she warmed up to him. It didn't hurt that, at least to my knowledge, Aiden and Theo had never asked her out.

I wanted her to feel comfortable enough around me to be herself. But fuck, I hated being in the friend zone, even if it was a step in the right direction. I couldn't show her how great we could be together if she was too afraid to interact with me.

I blew out a breath and started across the site to the guys, making a mental list of all the things I had to hide before Cammie moved in.

CHAPTER NINE

Cammie

I'D NEVER FELT SO awkward in my life, and that's saying something for a woman with uncontrolled selective mutism. Wyatt was doing his best to put me at ease, never letting the stretches of silence get too long, even if I'd barely been able to mutter a few words all evening.

"I can grab your suitcase when I take out the trash," he offered casually. Like it was no big deal we'd be living together for the foreseeable future. "Is your car locked?" he asked when I didn't answer.

Since his question only required a yes or no, I bobbed my head and fumbled in my pockets for my car keys before putting them on the counter by the register. Two questions answered with a single nod. I should have handed him the keys, but the thought of accidentally brushing his fingers made my heart beat faster.

"Great," Wyatt said with a smile, pocketing my keys as if my behavior was perfectly normal. He was by far the most patient man—make that person—I'd ever known.

"Have you eaten dinner yet?"

When I didn't answer, he started talking again. "I try to meal prep on Sunday, so the options are pretty good tonight. There's a whole rotisserie chicken upstairs and some veggies I roasted yesterday. There's also leftover chicken parm I made myself for dinner last night." He stopped and scratched his cheek. "That's a lot of chicken now that I think about it. I should have made barbacoa."

"Beef wasn't on sale this week," I said, surprising myself.

"Chicken breasts were," he said, smiling at me. "And I can never leave the grocery store without one of their rotisserie chickens. So I guess it's a double poultry week."

My lips quirked up, missing the memo from my brain to stay in full body lock down. The thought of Wyatt pushing a shopping cart through the local grocery store with a meal prep plan designed around the sales made me smile. Bishop never cooked. He also never liked anything I cooked, or at least he always used it as an excuse to berate me.

Wyatt smiled back at me, then quickly turned and started wiping the counter for what would hopefully be the last time tonight. It was adorable how hard he was trying to calm me down.

I blew out a breath and told my panic response to simmer. For once, it listened. "I'm going to do the walk through and let the stragglers know we're closing in five."

Wyatt nodded without turning to face me, but his shoulders visibly relaxed. Thankfully, everyone respected the posted hours, and we completed all the closing tasks by eight-thirty.

"I'll get your suitcase," Wyatt said, hefting a jumbo trash bag through the swinging door to the back. By the time I double checked the lock on the front door and walked around flipping off lights in the stockroom, I heard Wyatt reenter the building. I paused a moment in the dark to avoid being cramped on the stairs together, because I'm that awkward. Once I heard his footsteps overhead, I made my way up to the apartment.

When I entered the living room, Wyatt was carrying my suitcase toward Lauren's room. "You don't have to give me the big room," I called after him.

"I'm already unpacked down the hall," he said without stopping.

I sure as heck wasn't going into a bedroom with Wyatt, so I headed for the fridge and the promised chicken.

"Parm or rotisserie?" I shouted.

"Whichever you want," he said, far closer than I was expecting. I jumped like he was a deranged clown with a chainsaw popping out of a closet.

"Sorry—" he started.

"Don't apologize," I said, letting go of my death grip on the fridge door and turning to face him. "I'm jumpy. It's just going to take me a bit to get used to living with someone else."

"Maybe I should wear a bell like the cats before Lauren went hi-tech."

I held back a laugh. "I actually miss the bells, but no. How about chicken parm?"

He popped the container in the microwave while I set the table. I'd been in Lauren's kitchen enough times to know exactly where she kept everything. The familiarity eased some of my tension. Desdemona and Medusa pushed through the cat door into the apartment as the room filled with a delicious smell. Before I knew it, I was sharing a meal at a two-person table with Wyatt Romero. It felt too close to a date. All we needed was a couple of votive candles and wine.

"Do you want a glass of wine?" Wyatt asked, cutting into his chicken. "Lauren has a couple bottles of red in the cabinet."

Yes. I wanted an entire bottle. But no way was I lowering my inhibitions around Wyatt. "I'm fine with water, but you can open a bottle, if you want."

Wyatt shook his head. "I don't drink much. It makes it harder to—get up early."

"This looks great," I said before shoving my first bite of chicken into my mouth, which was better than anything I'd ever made. It was also unlike any chicken parm I'd had before. "Does this have nuts in it?"

Wyatt's eyes widened. "It's breaded in almond flour. Are you allergic?"

"No, I'm not allergic to anything that I know of. I just noticed it tasted different. I like it." Wyatt looked slightly flustered, and I regretted saying anything. He'd probably panicked, thinking he'd poisoned me. "What time do you usually leave in the morning?" I asked, hoping to change the subject.

"We get to the site around six, so I'm usually up by five and out the door by a quarter to six. It feels like sleeping in after working the opening shift at Karma."

Which meant I wouldn't see him in the morning. The disappointment I felt surprised me, and I quickly pushed it down.

"I've only worked the opening shift a few times and hated it," I said. "Mornings aren't my favorite. I need at least one cup of coffee and a shower before I'm human."

He nodded. "I guess we should work on a shower schedule," he said, staring at his plate instead of me.

How the heck did I forget Lauren only had one shower? Attached to her room. The room where I'd be staying.

"I take one as soon as I'm off the job site since I'm usually a mess," Wyatt said. "Typically around four, but later if we're trying to finish up something."

This I knew. Wyatt's schedule at Karma didn't have set start times, since it was hard to predict when he'd finish working with Aiden. It was a nifty perk of working for a couple, though it meant Lauren sometimes stayed later than she should or worked alone when Cal and I kept our normal hours. "Use the shower whenever," I said, sounding more cavalier than I felt. "Just knock if I've got the bedroom door closed."

"So you're OK with me waking you up every morning at five for a shower?" he asked, his dark eyes dancing with mischief.

I must have made a face because he burst out laughing.

"Don't worry, Cam. I only shower once a day, and I'll try my best not to make too much noise in the kitchen when I make breakfast."

He could try all he wanted, but I knew my eyes would fly open the second he stepped foot outside his room. At least until I got familiar with the sounds of someone in my living space. I doubt I'd be getting much sleep for at least a week.

"Well," he said, standing with his empty plate. "Five comes early."

"Your schedule is crazier than mine," I said, joining him at the sink with my plate. And no doubt more tiring. All I did was sit behind a desk at Cal's office. I couldn't imagine working a physically demanding job all day and heading straight to Karma after.

He shrugged. "I'm getting the hang of it. Lauren keeps telling me I should cut back at the café, but I like sending the extra money home to my family."

"That's really sweet of you," I said, pretending I didn't already know. I studied him while he rinsed off our plates and put them in the ancient dishwasher, which, despite its age, was a luxury to me. He looked tired, though not like he was about to collapse on the floor and sleep a full day. Maybe he was one of those people with endless energy.

I bet he could go all night.

My cheeks reddened at the inappropriate thought and the images it created. "Thanks for dinner," I said in a rush. "I'm going to read in my room, so I won't keep you up."

"You can stay out here and watch TV if you want," he said, drying his hands.

"I'm good," I said, practically sprinting to Lauren's room. "Night."

I closed the door softly and debated pushing in the flimsy lock on the knob before deciding to wait a few minutes, so he didn't hear me. Not that it mattered. Locks like these could be popped with an ink pen. How Lauren emerged from her childhood without obsessing over security measures was beyond me.

I sighed and crossed the room to my guitar. Lauren had placed it in the corner, making the space feel a little more like mine and not my dear friend's. Though I'd never told her the guitar had been my mother's, Lauren had been extremely careful when she carried it from my apartment. She'd put it in her own car for the drive to the farmhouse, carried it into her bedroom, and insisted on bringing it to Karma with her in the morning.

I let out a short laugh when I realized she'd held the instrument hostage, assuming, rightly, that I wouldn't run without it. She didn't want me to make any knee-jerk decisions before she'd given it back and done everything she could to make sure I'd be comfortable in her apartment. The bedding smelled like fresh lavender, and she told me she'd cleared out her pre-pregnancy wardrobe from her dresser and closet to give me space. She'd also cleaned the room to hospital standards and written me lots of sticky notes.

I pulled the one off the dresser that read *Bottom drawer can stick* and tossed it in the trashcan. A note by the window let me know I'd need to prop it open with something because the sash was broken (no doubt she hadn't mentioned that to Aiden) and another in the bathroom advised not to flush the toilet or run the dishwasher while taking a shower. I smiled at each of them until I found the one on her nightstand.

Use if needed.

I studied the table. It held a lamp, which I'd definitely use. I'd probably put my book on the table itself. The note didn't make sense until I realized it was stuck on the table's single drawer. I pulled it open before slamming it shut.

"Seriously, Lauren." I yanked my phone from my pocket, opened the drawer again, and snapped a picture of the massive box of condoms inside.

You forgot something.

Lauren

I'm in a monogamous relationship and pregnant. What use are they to me?

They're no use to me either.

Lauren

Fine. Give them to Wyatt.

My stomach dropped. I hadn't considered the possibility that Wyatt might bring people back to the apartment. After I turned him down, I figured he'd start dating one of the college students in town. He was kind and thoughtful and incredibly hot. Men like him didn't stay single unless they wanted to be, yet Wyatt hadn't mentioned dating anyone to me or Lauren, to my knowledge. He must just hook up with randoms. The thought made me sad and something else. It couldn't be jealousy. If I didn't want to date Wyatt, I had no reason to feel territorial. Still, as I stared at the condoms, my stomach ached thinking of him with someone else.

OK

It was not OK. And I would not be giving Lauren's castoff condoms to Wyatt anytime soon.

Lauren

You lie better in person.

I smiled.

Goodnight, Lauren.

Lauren

> *Good night, Cam. Try to get some sleep.*

Fat chance of that.

Before I could plug my phone in by the bed, it buzzed again. I braced when I saw the group text with Lauren and Stevens sisters.

Rowan

> *You're living with Wyatt!*

Lauren

> *I didn't tell her.*

Poppy

> *Aiden told me when he stopped by to fix something at the house. But I didn't tell Rowan either.*

Rowan

> *You knew, and you didn't tell me!*

Poppy

> *Figured she'd say something if she wanted us to know. Just because Aiden's chatty doesn't mean I have to be. He knows that mold excuse is bullshit by the way.*

Lauren

> *Why would he think that?*

Poppy

> *How would I know? You live with the guy. Ask him.*

Rowan

> *What's going on Cammie?*

I didn't want to lie to Rowan. She'd become a really good friend in the past year. Plus, anything I told her was bound to get back to Cal.

Lauren

> *I still want to know how you found out.*

Rowan

> *Aiden told Cal.*

Crud. I'd have a lot of explaining to do at work tomorrow if I didn't come up with something fast. I couldn't say I was trying to save money because it'd make Cal feel bad, and he already paid me well above market rate for a practice manager. Realistic or not, the mold excuse fit.

Lauren

> *Her apartment is a hazard to her health. End of story.*

And thank you, Lauren.

Poppy

> *What do you think of something like this for the wedding?*

A picture of Poppy holding a metal flower followed. I couldn't stop the smile on my face at her obvious attempt at changing the subject.

> *It's perfect.*

Rowan

> *Cam! Are you comfortable staying with Wyatt? You're welcome here.*

Poppy

> *Read the subtext, sis. If she wanted to stay with you, she'd have told you about the mold. Let it go.*

> *I'm fine. I'm sorry I didn't tell you or Cal. It all happened so fast. I didn't want either of you to worry.*

Lauren

> *Are you going to paint those flowers?*

Poppy

> *Different shades of red.*

Rowan

> *Oh, I like that idea.*

I silenced the chat. Now that the conversation was off of me, I could only bring it back by contributing. Rowan's surprise reminded me that I hadn't yet told my dad I'd left my apartment. I quickly sent him an email, keeping the details vague in case someone read it over his shoulder. I also had no intention of mentioning I'd be living with a man since that would likely send my dad into a worry spiral for different reasons.

After I got ready for bed, I climbed under the freshly washed sheets to read, but every time my eyes grew heavy, a car would zip by on Main Street or some other noise would snap me awake. I caught sleep in tiny spurts, waking to the sound of the cats in the living room or a pipe groaning in the unfamiliar building.

By the time I heard Wyatt shuffle into the kitchen, my nerves were frayed. I listened to him open the fridge and light the burner on the stove. My last thought before I drifted into the best hour of sleep I'd had in a while was how relieved I was to hear him.

Chapter Ten

Wyatt

By the time Saturday afternoon rolled around, I was exhausted and looking forward to an evening off. Hopefully, with Cammie. Apart from the thirty minutes a day when we shared food before I crashed, I hadn't spent much time with her in the apartment. I was long gone every morning before she woke. She was already working downstairs when I took a quick break to shower, eat, and get ready for my shift at Karma.

I'd learned that eating four or five small meals a day helped me better manage my blood sugar. So while Cammie thought we were sharing a very late dinner, I was eating my pre-bed mini meal in the hopes I wouldn't wake up low in the middle of the night. This evening would be the first we had dinner at a normal time, assuming she wasn't fleeing the building right after closing.

I'd been working beside Cam for hours and hadn't yet asked about her plans. First and foremost, I didn't want to scare her by suggesting we spend Saturday night together, which screamed date night. Second, I wanted to minimize the time I had to pretend not to be disappointed if she planned to ditch me.

"Thanks again for putting my suitcase on the top shelf of the closet," she said, dumping a filter of used grounds in the trash. "I'm usually tall enough to reach anything I need, but the ceilings in this building are insanely high. I don't think I could have wedged it up there without dragging a chair from the kitchen."

When I showered in her bathroom, I'd noticed she kept her suitcase in the corner. I knew her stay in the apartment was temporary, but the suitcase was a daily reminder I didn't want. It bothered me a little more each day. Last night I'd finally broken down and asked if she needed help with putting it away, which I should have done the first time I saw it.

"You're welcome," I said, shoving my hands in my pockets and letting the silence stretch between us.

Typically, I jump-started our conversations, Today, Cammie had been the one filling the awkward silence that formed every time I wanted to ask about her plans and convinced myself to wait. With only twenty minutes left until closing, it'd almost be weird if I didn't ask now. I watched her arrange the baked goods that Rowan delivered earlier, trying to work up the nerve to ask her, when the front door opened and one of my favorite customers hurried inside.

"Doña Valentina," I called, walking around the counter with my arms opened wide.

She was about the size and age of my *abuela* and her hugs felt a little like home.

"*Niño dulce*," she said, cupping my cheek affectionately with her weathered hand after we embraced. "Do you have time to help me with a form?" she asked in Spanish.

"Always," I said, pulling out a chair for her at the nearest table.

She straightened her tiny frame. "I pay first," she said in English.

Cammie looked between us with obvious confusion before Doña Valentina shuffled to the counter and ordered. "One small coffee, please.

Black." She handed Cammie a five-dollar bill and dumped all her change in the tip jar before returning to me with her coffee in hand.

"You don't have to buy anything," I said, switching back to Spanish.

She shook her head. "Your boss is too nice. She pays for your time, so it's only right I pay her for a coffee."

I nodded. I understood how important it was for her not to feel like she was taking advantage.

"And I pay you in tamales," she said, reaching into her purse and taking out a huge plastic zipper bag filled with tightly wrapped foil bundles.

"You spoil me," I said, accepting her gift.

"They're still warm," she said. "Eat while you help me."

I shook my head. "Tamales should be savored, especially yours."

It's true tamales were a time-intensive labor of love, but I also couldn't eat them without taking my insulin. And these little foil-wrapped packets just made it easy to ask Cammie to have dinner with me.

Doña Valentina's face brightened before she flapped her hand as if to push my compliment aside. "You're too charming. You would be a dangerous man if I was fifty years younger."

I laughed. "What did you need help with?"

She pulled a paper from her purse and slid it across the table to me. "My doctor wants me to switch to a different medication. Of course, my insurance won't cover it. There's an assistance program, but the form is in English."

I nodded and read through the form.

"Apparently, I'll get it for free if I filled this out." She shook her head. "I could have paid what I was paying for the other medicine, but if they're giving it away, I'd be a fool not to take it."

My eyes widened. "Really?"

She nodded. I'd never looked into assistance programs for my insulin, though I would now. Perhaps there was even a program for pumps.

"How did you find out about it?" I asked.

"They gave me the form at my doctor's office. But you know how busy they are. I couldn't ask the nurse who translates for me to help fill it out."

"I'm happy to do it," I said, pulling a pen from my apron. I smiled when I saw that she'd already filled in as much of the form as she could herself. Her husband had translated for her before he passed last year, and she'd made a genuine effort since to learn English. Even so, there were questions that required fluency to answer. I asked her the requested specifics about her dosage, other medications, and her known allergies. She watched closely while I wrote her answers in English.

"You can mail it, or I can take a picture and upload it to the online portal."

"I'll mail it. Thank you, *niño dulce*." She folded the paper neatly and put it back in her purse before standing. I hugged her goodbye and held the door for her as she left.

When I turned back toward the coffee bar, Cammie was standing at the counter with a huge smile on her face. "I love watching you translate for people. It's fascinating how easily you slip between two languages."

Not for the first time, I thanked my parents for insisting we speak Spanish at home. "You're going to love it even more once you've tried Doña Valentina's tamales," I said, holding up the zipper bag.

"You don't mind sharing?" she asked, eyeing the foil packets.

"Pretty sure we're down to beef jerky and oatmeal upstairs. Unless you had plans to go out?"

Cammie shook her head and the tension I'd been carrying through our entire shift eased. "I limit my restaurant spending to coffee and nights out with friends. I was going to drag myself to the grocery store later."

"Well, no need now."

By the time we'd closed and cleaned up, the tamales were only slightly warm.

"Let me pop these in the oven for a few minutes," I said, opening the plastic bag and pulling out each tightly wrapped packet.

"Would it be weird if I change into my pjs?" Cammie asked, worrying her bottom lip. "I smell like burned coffee, but I'm not going anywhere, so I don't want to put on a whole other outfit." Her cheeks turned an adorable red. "Like telling you my entire thought process isn't weird enough."

It wasn't weird. It was amazing. Not only was she talking around me, she was rambling. "I'll put on mine too while the tamales reheat."

She tilted her head to the side. "I wouldn't take you for a pjs kind of guy."

"What do you think I sleep in?"

"Nothing." Her eyes widened, and I knew I had about two seconds to put her at ease before she scurried into her room and hid the rest of the night.

"I got in the habit of wearing a t-shirt and gym shorts when I shared a dorm room freshman year."

"Well, that's disappointing," she said, the flush in her cheeks draining with her embarrassment. "I was picturing those striped matching sets grandpas always seem to wear in movies. You might as well keep on what you're wearing now."

"Go change," I said, trying not to laugh. "I'll get everything ready."

I slid six of the foil packets into the oven and left the rest to finish cooling on the counter before I headed to my room. When I learned Cammie was moving in, I ran out on my lunch break and got the smallest, cheapest mini fridge I could find to store my medicine. While I was in my room, I went ahead and changed since it was the best excuse for being behind a closed door. Then I measured the amount of insulin I estimated I'd need, wiped my stomach with an alcohol wipe, and injected myself. I pulled out the red plastic container from under my bed where I disposed of needles and shoved the one I'd just used inside. By the time I returned to the kitchen, Cammie was setting the table.

And fuck me, her pajamas were far from the oversized sweats I was expecting. Not that they were overtly sexy. They just showed off her body in a way I'd never seen before. Her pink gym shorts left most of her toned legs bare and hugged her firm ass, especially when she bent over the table to place a plate on the other side. Her loose t-shirt fell off one of her shoulders, revealing her purple bra strap. I was both relieved and disappointed she was still wearing one. She tensed, as though sensing my presence, and turned.

I swallowed hard as her eyes quickly traveled down my body and back again. She blushed and spun back to face the table. Encouraged by her perusal, my dick swelled in my shorts. I walked as fast as I could to the sink and started washing my hands while I got my body under control.

"Do you think they're hot enough?" she asked, her voice slightly higher than usual.

"Should be." I placed a cookie sheet on top of the stove before I pulled the foil packets out with oven mitts and spread them across the sheet. "If you ever repeat this," I said, carrying the food to the table, "I'll deny it to my dying breath, but Doña Valentina's tamales are better than my mom's."

She watched me peel back the foil and place a husk-wrapped tamale on her plate. She studied it while I served myself, then picked up a knife and fork and started cutting at the corner of the husk.

I gaped at her. "Have you ever had one before?" I knew she wasn't Latina, but I couldn't imagine living twenty plus years without ever trying a tamale.

She hovered her utensils over her plate. "Um," she said before looking up at me through her thick lashes. "Is it that obvious?

Instead of answering, I picked up my tamale, peeled back the corn husk and took a large enough bite of the savory masa to reach the pork and cheese filling. She mimicked what I'd done and let out a groan with her first bite that made my cock stir again.

"Oh my stars," she said after she swallowed. "Where have you been all my life?"

I smiled at her and took another bite of my tamale, thankful there was a table to hide my reaction to her. "Good aren't they?"

"Good doesn't do them justice. I'm surprised I've never had one before."

"A lot of Mexican restaurants don't serve them. They're time intensive, a real labor of love."

"And Doña Valentina made them to thank you," she said, smiling. "Sweet boy."

I almost choked on the food in my mouth. Cammie jumped from her chair and grabbed me a cup of tap water. Once I finished coughing and gulped half the glass, I set it on the table carefully. "I didn't realize you spoke Spanish." Which wouldn't have surprised me or made me cough. Hearing her call me sweet boy did something to me. Maybe it was her soft tone or the way she'd looked at me when she spoke, but there was a very real possibility I was developing a praise kink to go along with my infatuation for this woman.

Cammie shook her head. "I don't. I Google translated it. I thought she said *dolce*, which is what Antonio's had on their menu for dessert the one time I went there." She shrugged. "I was curious. I didn't think she'd call you a dessert."

"*Postre*. That's dessert in Spanish."

"*Postre*," she repeated, her accent near perfect.

"Very good."

She smiled and reached for a second tamale.

"If you want me to heat more, just let me know. Otherwise, we can have them for dinner tomorrow."

"No, two is plenty for me, but that reminds me," she said, her eyes brightening. "I pulled the store circular from the mail if you want to go over the sales and make a grocery list with me. We can go after work tomorrow if you're free. I'm buying since I ate all your food this week."

I just wanted to be with her, and if grocery shopping and meal prepping didn't spook her, I was all in. Making the list together made sense, but grocery shopping didn't require company. It was ridiculous how pleased I was that she'd asked me to tag along with her to the store. "Sounds great."

Chapter Eleven

Cammie

I CHECKED THE TIME on the wall clock by the door and frowned. Since the heat finally broke this week, Cal and I went back to our usual schedule, which meant Wyatt was typically at Karma before I arrived. As much as I liked the extra money, I loved sleeping in an hour and knowing I wouldn't have to work alone if I convinced Lauren to go home. But today, it was nearing six with no sign of Wyatt. Lauren didn't seem the least bit concerned or the least bit eager to leave, which probably meant Aiden had texted her to say they were working late. I'd been fighting the urge to ask about Wyatt ever since I clocked in.

"I have an idea for Poppy's bachelorette party," Lauren said with a devilish smile on her face.

"Does Poppy even want one? It was hard enough convincing her to have a wedding," I said, emptying the grounds in the drip brewers.

"If you asked her, she'd say no, which is why we aren't asking. We're just going to plan it for when she least expects it and kidnap her."

I raised my eyebrows. "I'm not kidnapping anyone."

Lauren waved her hand. "Don't worry. Aiden's got that part covered."

"OK," I said cautiously. "What exactly are you planning that would require a kidnapping?"

"A high tea limo ride on the Skyline drive," she said, clapping her hands. "Scones. Tiny sandwiches cut into shapes—I have a penis cookie cutter. She'll wear an enormous hat and frilly dress. Floral everything. I even found a company that will rent us a pink limousine."

Poppy looked like a singer in an emo-punk band. I couldn't imagine her being comfortable in something so opposite to her aesthetic. "That doesn't sound like Poppy at all."

"Exactly," Lauren said, rubbing her hands together. "And the best part is, you, me, and Rowan will be in full goth. All black, eyeliner, skulls. The whole shebang."

"That actually sounds fun," I said. "If you let Poppy wear her own clothes too. Kidnapping her is one thing. Stripping her and forcing her into florals is another. She'd probably get a kick out of everyone dressing like her, though."

Lauren's eyes became unfocused, like she was deep in thought. "Would we go full dark on the tea stuff too or keep that girlie?"

"I'm all for a penis sandwich," I said, a little too loud.

The guy at the bistro table nearest the counter choked on his drink.

"I mean, I think you could go pink and frilly for the decorations and have Rowan plan a menu of Poppy's favorite foods and plan to stop for a picnic. We could have whiskey to add to the tea, obviously not yours. That's her favorite drink, right?"

Lauren chuckled. "I doubt it. That stuff just tastes so bad she doesn't overdo it. She's a complete lightweight."

I motioned to her pregnant belly. "Says the woman who was drunk on whisky when she conceived a baby with the man she claimed to despise."

Lauren shrugged. "We were taking shots. And I'm pretty sure the universe took over that day."

"Well," I said, wrapping my arm around her shoulder. "Aren't you glad it did?"

She smiled sweetly. I started to pull my phone from my pocket and take a picture for Aiden, but the moment passed, as beautiful ones often do, before I could capture it.

"Can I get a warmup?" asked the man who'd heard my penis sandwich comment. He held up his ceramic mug and smiled at us.

"Sure," Lauren said, taking his cup and refilling it. He kept smiling at me after Lauren handed him the refill. I pretended not to notice.

"When should we plan this sneak-attack party?" I asked, keeping my eye on the guy as he walked back to his table.

"I'll need to loop in Rowan. She knows Poppy's schedule better than anyone. Oh," she said, her face lighting up. "I should take her the cookie cutter on my way home, so she can start planning the menu."

"Is there a reason why you have a penis cookie cutter handy?"

"I wanted to do something special for the first meeting of the Torrid Tuesdays Book Club. I hope Wyatt gets here soon. My feet are tired."

"Here," I said, pulling out the stool I insisted Lauren keep behind the counter when she worked. "Tell me where the cookie cutter is. I'll run upstairs and grab it."

"In the kitchen. Bottom drawer, closest to the fridge," she said, sinking onto the stool with a sigh.

I walked through the back and up the stairs to the apartment. Just as I crossed the living room, Wyatt stepped from my bedroom wearing nothing but a towel around his waist.

We both froze.

I should have moved aside and let him pass through to his room. Instead, my eyes ate up every inch of his delicious torso. I'd never seen anyone in real life with a chest and abs as chiseled as his. Maybe in photos of body builders that made their way onto Insta, but never on a man standing two feet from me. He was still wet from the shower, the water droplets emphasizing each tight muscle as they dripped down his body.

If Wyatt and I had a different relationship, I'd have licked his stomach dry. When I finally moved my eyes up to his face, his expression snapped me from my ogling. He looked mortified, which didn't make sense given the incredible state of his body. I forced my mouth closed and spun to face the sofa.

"Sorry," I squeaked. "Lauren asked me to grab something, and I didn't think to knock because I live here. Of course, you live here too and have to shower sometimes. And you should, anytime you need."

Wyatt cleared his throat. "I'm going to get dressed."

I kept facing the sofa but could feel him walk behind me, so close I could smell the woodsy scent of his soap, the soap he left on the side of the tub and which I may or may not have sniffed once.

As soon as I heard his door shut, I buried my warm face in my hands. I needed to pull myself together before I went downstairs, or Lauren would ask why my cheeks were fire-engine red. I also couldn't linger so long that Wyatt had time to cover his glorious body and find me standing in the living room as if his hotness had seared my feet to the carpet. Since Lauren was the lesser of two evils, I hurried to the kitchen, dug through a hodge podge of crap in the drawer until I found the penis cookie cutter, and bolted. Lauren gave me a curious look when I held up the metal phallus.

"Wyatt's here," I said, shocked at how breathless I sounded. "You should head out."

She stood and held out her hand for the cookie cutter. "No wonder you look flustered. Did he see you carrying this?"

"It's OK," I said, which wasn't a lie or an answer. More like a mantra I'd be repeating to myself for the rest of the day. It's OK I saw Wyatt half naked. It's OK the sight of him made me ache with need. It's OK because nothing happened. Nothing at all.

"I'll wait to say hello to Wyatt," Lauren said, shoving the cookie cutter into her tote bag.

As if summoned, he pushed through the swinging door into the already crowded space behind the counter. Our eyes locked a moment before his slid to Lauren.

"Hey, Wy," she said, pulling him into a hug.

While they embraced, I allowed myself another look at him. His hair was still damp, like it always was at the start of his shift, but his clothes clung tighter to his body as though he hadn't dried off completely in his haste to get downstairs. Or maybe I was just noticing his body more now that I knew what he was hiding under his shirt.

He stepped back from Lauren and reached for one of the aprons hanging on the back wall. "You heading out?" he asked her.

"Yeah, I'll see you both soon." She gave me a quick squeeze before pushing through the door, leaving Wyatt and me standing on opposite sides of the coffee bar. The only way he could get farther from me would be to hop over the counter.

"Sorry about earlier," he said, starting his daily check of the espresso machine. Though he'd spoken to me, he hadn't taken his eyes from the machine. "I should have brought my clothes into the bathroom."

"No need to apologize." If anything, I should thank you for the show. That's what I wanted to say. If I wasn't still so messed up from Bishop, I would have.

The more time I spent with Wyatt, the more I liked him. Whether we were working together or hanging out in the apartment, every minute with him was fun, easy. But given the heat in his gaze when he saw me in my pajamas on Saturday, the lust I felt for him was mutual. And, therefore, dangerous. I was still dealing with the aftermath of my last relationship. I sure as heck didn't need to start another.

"Excuse me," a male voice said behind me.

I plastered a customer-service smile on my face and turned. When I saw who was on the other side of the counter, my stomach sank. No way could refill man need another already.

"Can I help you?" I asked.

"I think you can," he said, smiling at me.

Here we go. I waited for him to elaborate, since I had no intention of engaging with him any more than necessary.

"I'm looking for someone to join me for dinner tonight."

Well, at least he lobbed something I could easily turn down. Not that he'd even bothered to ask it as a question. "I'm working," I said, proud of myself for not freezing.

"A woman as beautiful as you is worth waiting for."

So, a simple no wouldn't work for this one. I choked on the red flag he'd just waved, my pulse ticking up every second that passed in silence. Why couldn't I just tell him no again or however many times it took to sink in that I wasn't interested? The moment a guy seemed the least bit problematic, I clammed up so tight I could barely breathe.

"Hey, Angel," Wyatt said behind me. He placed his thick arms on either side of mine. It should have felt like he was caging me in, but though he'd stepped close enough I could feel the heat of his body, he kept a respectable distance between us. "This *cretino* bothering you?"

I had no idea what *cretino* meant, but judging by the look on the guy's face, he did.

The guy held up his hands and said something in Spanish. Wyatt laughed behind me, and before I could stop myself, I leaned back onto him. He wrapped his muscular arms around my waist, like it was the most natural thing in the world to do. I placed my hands over his, and we stood pretzelled together like a longtime couple finding home in each other's arms.

"Enjoy your night," the guy said to me before turning and walking out of the café.

Wyatt stepped back, and I lifted my hands from his.

"You OK?" he asked.

"Wishing I hadn't taken German in high school."

Wyatt smiled. "I bet you understood more of that than you think."

"What does *cretino* mean?"

"Your pronunciation is really good for someone who doesn't speak Spanish."

I waited.

He gave me a sheepish smile that made my stomach dip. "Honestly, I didn't think he spoke Spanish either. I basically called him a dick."

"Oh my word," I said, covering my mouth with my hands. "You could have made him angry."

Wyatt shrugged. "He apologized, which honestly pissed me off. You'd clearly turned him down already. I shouldn't have had to claim you to make him back off."

My stomach bottomed out at the realization that I wanted him to claim me. Hard and often. "Some guys are persistent."

A tiny crease formed between his eyes. "You get pestered more than any woman I know."

I shook my head. "You just notice because I'm so weird about it. I'm sure people hit on Lauren all the time when you two worked together. She just doesn't freeze up like I do."

He nodded, but the tension remained on his face. "I'm sorry that happens to you."

"Trust me, you're the last man on earth who should be apologizing."

For a second, he looked as embarrassed as he had when I stumbled upon him in his towel. He opened his mouth before pressing his full lips together.

He clearly wanted to ask me a question. I replayed what I'd said. It was a compliment, right? He wasn't a creep. Sure, he'd asked me out before, but he'd respected my refusal. Which I was regretting more and more each day. "Whatever's on your mind, you can ask me."

"Why do you freeze around some men but not others?" he asked gently.

The first part was exactly the question I was expecting. The last bit wasn't. It was also the hardest to explain. "I left a really bad relationship when I moved here."

He nodded as though he'd already assumed that part of my story.

"That's it," I said with a shrug. I wished that was everything. Bishop wrecked the girl I was before I met him, and if he found me, he could wreck the woman I'd been trying to become.

"But you're comfortable around Cal, Aiden, and Theo," he said. His tone was curious, not challenging, and I could see how my ease around those three might be confusing, given my reaction to every other guy.

"I know they aren't interested in me." True. Also true: I wasn't interested in them.

He cleared his throat. "You seem comfortable around me now."

My heart pounded in my chest. He hadn't flat out said he was still interested in me, yet the implication was there. And unlike Cal, Aiden, and Theo, I was attracted to Wyatt. I could brush him off, say he was my friend, and make an excuse to hide in the book stacks for the rest of the night. But the way he looked at me, so calm, so open, made me want to tell him the truth. Or at least part of it.

"Because you're Wyatt," I said. "And there's no one else like you."

He smiled and cast his eyes down before biting his full bottom lip. When he looked up at me again, his eyes were filled with heat. "Just to be clear," he said slowly, in a voice so deep and gravely my breath caught. Sweet, shy Wyatt had left the building. "When a woman tells me no, I listen. If she ever changes her mind, she has to tell me. Or, better yet, show me."

I felt my head bob up and down. "Good to know," I squeaked out. It was incredible I'd spoken three words with how dry my mouth felt.

"I'm going to unbox some inventory," he said, smiling. "I'll bring the boxes to the stacks in case another *cretino* tries to bother you." He winked at me and pushed through the swinging door. Like the conversation hadn't turned him into a quivering puddle of hormones. Or if it had, he hid it a heck of a lot better than me.

Chapter Twelve

Cammie

"Are you sure you don't mind working alone?" Lauren asked, worrying her bottom lip. "I can wait until Wyatt gets here."

"No, you can't," I said. "As someone who works the front desk at a doctor's office, I cannot make you late for your appointment. Especially at the end of the day. Everyone just wants to go home. Now, get."

"I don't like it," Lauren said, making no effort to move. "Especially now."

"My dad checks in almost every day to ask how I've been and to keep me updated on Bishop's brother. So far, so good."

Lauren glanced at her phone again and sighed. "Text me when he gets here, OK?"

I nodded. "Go. I'm fine."

If Karma had been empty or filled with single men, I wouldn't have pushed her so hard to leave. Besides whomever was browsing the book section, the café was packed with couples and groups. A few solo women were either buried in a book or typing on their laptops, like Maddie. I still couldn't wait for Wyatt to arrive.

We shared dinner last night as if he hadn't just flung open the door to the possibility of *us*. I should have been scared out of my mind when he admitted he still wanted me, yet I trusted Wyatt not to push. Part of me wished he would. Because as much as I liked him, I questioned whether I'd ever be able to tell him. Or *show* him.

Between his post-shower smoke show and that little invitation, I couldn't sleep until I'd slid my hand to my aching clit and came twice while imagining my fingers were his. I still woke wound tight and desperate for his touch.

I wanted him. Plain and simple. But wanting someone and acting on it were two very different things. I may never be ready to be with a man again. The thought stung more now because it wasn't just any man. It was Wyatt. Kind, patient, incredibly sexy, Wyatt. Who I lived with because my psychotic ex might know where I'd run off to and want to hurt me. Thinking of Bishop zapped my lust right quick, replacing all my longing with fear. Wyatt still didn't know why I'd moved in. If he'd called me Angel to "claim me" in front of Bishop, no doubt it would have ended with bruises.

Wyatt shoved through the door so hard I jumped.

"Sorry," he said, running his hand through his wet hair. "We were in the middle of something we couldn't leave until tomorrow. Were you here by yourself long?"

He seemed flustered, fumbling with the ties of his aprons as he secured it around his waist.

"Not at all," I said, studying him. He hadn't seemed nervous around me yesterday. Perhaps, like me, he'd been thinking about our conversation all day, but he was typically so easy going.

"That's good," he said, sounding slightly distracted. Without another word to me, he walked to the espresso machine and checked it like he usually did. Then he just stood there, staring at the diva beast.

"You OK?" I asked, taking a step toward him.

"I'm fine," he snapped.

Adrenaline shot through my body. I'd never heard him sound angry. Even when he was talking with the guy who'd hit on me, he'd been levelheaded.

"Where the fuck is the brush I use to clean the portafilter?" he asked, ripping open the drawer under the machine.

I stepped back until my body hit the swinging door. Given his current mood, I'd think of something to do in the stacks until we closed and keep my distance.

He gripped the counter and hung his head. "Cam," he said, his voice shaky.

But it wasn't just his voice. His hands shook on the glass countertop. He turned, and I watched in horror as all the color drained from his face, and he slumped to the floor with his head against the bakery case.

"Wyatt," I shouted, kneeling beside him.

His eyes fluttered open and locked on mine. "Sorry," he said, weakly.

I grabbed his trembling hand and gave it a squeeze. His skin felt cold and sweaty, and I realized, far later than I should have, that he was having some sort of medical event. I grew up watching my mom have seizures. Each one was terrifying, yet at least I had some idea what to do. I didn't have a clue what was happening with Wyatt or how to help him.

I was about to shout for help when my phone buzzed in my pocket. Over and over. I yanked it from my apron. Whatever was happening, I needed to call 911, but before I could, a text came through from Lauren.

> *Give him juice!*

"Juice?" I said out loud as I swiped her text away.

Wyatt gave my hand a weak squeeze.

"You need juice?"

He squeezed my hand again. I jumped up, ran to the drink cooler, and pulled out a bottle of orange juice. By the time I got back to Wyatt, his hands were curled into fists, and his body was rigid.

My phone buzzed in my pocket again as I opened the cap and held the bottle out for him. When he didn't uncurl his hands or open his eyes, I held it to his mouth. "Drink, Wyatt," I shouted. He didn't move.

By this time, I'd drawn the attention of several café customers.

"Force his mouth open and pour it in," Maddie said, leaning over the counter.

I must have looked as helpless as I felt because she hurried around the counter and grabbed the juice from me. She pushed his mouth open and poured in a mouthful, telling him to swallow.

"What's his blood sugar?" she asked when he coughed out what little juice she'd put in his mouth.

"I don't—" My phone buzzed again, and I didn't even bother to check if it was Lauren before I answered.

"Do you know his blood sugar?" I asked, sitting on the floor beside Wyatt and taking his limp hand.

"44," Lauren yelled, sounding out of breath.

"Guy in the blue shirt," Maddie said. "Call 911 and tell them we need help for a severely hypoglycemic male, around 180 pounds." She poured more juice into Wyatt's mouth, and this time, he swallowed. "Where does he keep his glucagon?"

"I don't even know what that is," I said, fumbling to put the phone on speaker and lay it on the floor. "Lauren, where does Wyatt keep his glucagon?"

"Oh fuck," Lauren said, her voice almost a whisper.

"Lauren, it's Maddie," she said calmly. "Do you know where he keeps his medication?"

"No," Lauren said through a sob.

"I want you to call out his blood sugar as it changes," Maddie said. The entire time she spoke, she kept pouring juice into Wyatt's mouth, increasing the rate as he swallowed more and more.

"50," Lauren said, her voice shaky but not nearly as panicked. "It's going up."

"Blue shirt," Maddie said without taking her eyes from Wyatt. "How long until EMTs get here?"

He repeated her question, then said, "Two minutes."

"Clear a path for them. Move any tables or people in the way."

"52," Lauren said and took a deep breath.

Wyatt's hand curled around mine weakly. He reached up with the other hand and took the bottle from Maddie, chugging the rest before he opened his eyes. He glanced at the phone on the floor and leaned his head on my shoulder. "I'm fine," he mumbled.

Maddie rolled her eyes. "Where's your glucagon, tough guy? Just in case you're not."

"In my room," he said weakly.

"Lot of good that will do you," Maddie said.

"He lives upstairs," Lauren said.

Maddie looked at me, and I realized I needed to get whatever they were talking about.

"I'll be right back," I said, lifting Wyatt's head off my shoulder before I ran. I'd never been in Wyatt's room, but it only took a second to find a bright red case on his dresser with Glucagon Emergency Kit stamped across the front.

By the time I returned downstairs, a pair of Peace Falls EMTs surrounded Wyatt, taking his vitals. He no longer looked near death, but his shoulders were hitched up around his ears. If I had to guess, I'd say he wished the floor would swallow him whole.

"I got it," I said, holding up the shot kit. "I think."

Wyatt nodded and said, "I'm fine."

He did actually sound better, which seemed weird given all he'd done was chug a bottle of orange juice.

The EMT glanced over his shoulder at me. "Yeah, he won't need that. Just dinner and some common sense."

Wyatt's face burned red, and he stared down at his lap.

"He's got plenty of common sense," I said. "There's no need to make him feel worse than he already does."

With that, I walked around the EMT, plopped my butt on the floor next to Wyatt, and gripped his hand. I sent the EMT the meanest glare I could muster. His cheeks pinked, and he let out a mumbled apology before getting back to work. I continued to stare him down, not giving a fig that he could probably bench press two of me.

Chapter Thirteen

Wyatt

I've done a lot of embarrassing shit in my life. That time I called my math teacher Mamá in middle school. Stalling out my dad's manual transmission on a first date. Anytime I've ever been forced onto a dance floor. But having my blood sugar tank in front of Cammie and a full café was the pinnacle of embarrassment. It was the exact scenario I had nightmares about. Only worse.

By the time I started to really come around, a pair of EMTs had arrived and were measuring everything from my blood sugar to my oxygen levels. One look at Cammie's terrified face as she ran through the swinging door with my emergency shot kit, and I wanted to disappear into the floor.

I kept hoping I'd wake up and find out I'd dreamed the entire terrible thing, but the squeeze of the blood pressure cuff on my arm suggested otherwise.

"I got it," she said, sounding like she'd sprinted a mile. "I think."

I forced myself to smile. "I'm fine."

The EMT checking my blood sugar glanced at her. "Yeah, he won't need that. Just dinner and some common sense."

Forget it. I'd unlocked a new level of peak embarrassment.

"He's got plenty of common sense," Cammie said, glaring at the EMT. "There's no need to make him feel worse than he already does."

I'd never heard so much fire in her voice. I wished she could summon that heat for herself when she needed it. Still, it made my chest warm that she'd stood up for my dumb ass. Before I could thank her, Cammie sank to the floor next to me and grabbed my hand. Her fingers trembled even as she caressed my thumb with hers. The EMT mumbled something, but I was too focused on Cammie's touch to pay attention to him.

Fuck. I hadn't realized how scared I was until she grabbed my hand. I couldn't remember much of what happened after I walked to the espresso machine. Judging by the presence of the EMTs and the black hole in my memory, I must have passed out.

"You staying with him awhile?" the EMT monitoring my sugar levels asked Cammie.

"Yes," she said in the same assertive voice she'd used before. "I'll make sure he eats and keep an eye on his blood sugar." She turned to me and frowned. "Or do you need Lauren for that?"

"Not if he has his phone," Lauren snapped from the other side of the counter.

I closed my eyes and leaned against the bakery case. Fuck. I really did need common sense. "I must have left it upstairs."

Lauren walked into the crowded space behind the counter and threw her arms around the young woman who'd poured juice down my throat, though the memory was a little hazy. I'd seen her in the café plenty of times, but I couldn't remember her name.

"Could you check her blood pressure before you go?" I asked the EMT who was taking the cuff from my arm. I lifted my chin at Lauren, and he nodded after seeing her pregnant belly.

"Ma'am, I'm going to need you to step around the counter and take a seat," he said, standing and placing a gentle hand on her shoulder.

Lauren looked like she was building up steam for the longest tell off in history when the young woman she'd been hugging grabbed her hand. "Come on, Lauren. Aiden is already going to lose his shit. Let's not make it worse."

Guess I was getting fired. Technically, I wasn't on a job site, but I doubt Aiden would care.

"You're lucky," the second EMT said without taking his eyes from the monitor. "Any lower and you could have fallen into a coma."

Cammie sucked in a breath next to me, and when I turned to face her, her eyes were filled with tears.

"Dude, you need to work on your bedside manners," I said, putting my arm around Cammie. She melted against me. The warmth of her body next to mine, coupled with the adrenaline crash, made me want to fall asleep right on the floor.

"You need to work on your blood sugar maintenance," the EMT said, shaking his head. "You should know better by now. You aren't some five-year-old figuring it out."

"I was diagnosed last fall."

His eyes filled with the sympathy I'd tried so hard to avoid. "Well, now I feel like an asshole."

"Nah, you're right. This crash hit me faster than anything has before, but there's no excuse for not having my phone on me."

I was rushing, plain and simple. I knew Lauren had a doctor's appointment and didn't want Cammie to be alone. Instead of eating my usual between-shifts meal, I'd shoved a few pieces of beef jerky in my pockets and left the apartment without my phone.

The EMT nodded. "OK. You're at 67. Unless you want an expensive ride to the ER, we can leave now."

"Thank you," I said, holding out my hand for him to shake. "I'm good."

He shook it and glanced at Cammie before looking back at me. "The more people who know how to help you while you're figuring this out, the better. Take it easy tonight. Eat dinner. Keep monitoring your blood sugar in case it spikes. I hope I don't see you anytime soon unless I'm getting coffee."

I nodded and he walked around the counter, disappearing into the noise of the café.

"Do you need help standing?" Cammie asked, staring up at me with her gorgeous eyes. They looked impossibly bluer with tears, and seeing the concern on her face filled me with something so bittersweet. I loved that she cared. I hated that I'd scared her.

"I really am good now," I said.

She frowned. "Baloney."

I smiled at her and some of the weight of my embarrassment lifted from my chest. "Maybe you should come up to the apartment with me in case I get dizzy on the stairs." Or tank again before I eat or find my fucking phone.

"Of course," she said, straightening her body away from mine.

There's no graceful way to get off the floor where you almost went into a coma, so I just rolled to my knees and stood while she did the same.

Lauren leaped from the bistro chair where she was sitting and stormed around the counter to pull me into a hug. "If you ever do that again, I will kill you myself."

I leaned down to tighten the hug before I kissed the top of her head. "I'm so sorry. Let me eat something, and I'll get back to work so you can go home and rest."

"Did you hit your head?" she snapped. "Get upstairs and take Cammie with you. She looks as pale as you did when I got here."

Cammie did, in fact, look drained now that she was standing.

"I'm Maddie," the young woman beside Lauren said. "I'll stay and help until Aiden gets here."

Lauren closed her eyes and let out a breath. "Sorry," she said to me when she opened them. "He called when I wasn't at the doctor's office to meet him. I'll make sure you have a job tomorrow."

"Here or with Aiden?" I asked.

"Not here if you don't go upstairs and eat," she said, swatting my arm.

"Pleasure meeting you, officially, Maddie," I said. "Thanks for saving my ass."

She beamed at me. "You're the first person I've saved."

"Med student," Lauren said, gripping Maddie's shoulders. "Don't make her save you again. Go eat."

I nodded and Cammie followed me through the swinging door, across the back room, and up the stairs to the apartment.

"Sit," she said, pointing to my usual chair at the table. "Where's your phone?"

I rubbed my forehead. "I think I left it on the counter in your bathroom when I took a shower."

She quickly retrieved my phone and put it on the table in front of me. Without a word, she went to the fridge and pulled out a carton of eggs and a package of shredded cheese. We'd prepped a Cobb salad for dinner, but a glance at my phone told me I could wait a couple minutes. Shit, there were a lot of missed alerts. My eyes widened when I saw that my blood sugar had dipped to 44 at one point.

"I'm making an omelet because I'm not eating a cold salad after that. You might as well start with it," she said, pulling the massive bowl we'd prepped earlier from the fridge. She set it in the middle of the table and brought over a pair of salad tongs, two plates, and a pair of forks before walking back to the stove.

I started to stand but stopped when she glared at me.

"What do you need?" she asked.

You, not to be mad at me. To trust me. Clearly, I needed to do some damage control after what just went down. "The dressing."

She hurried to the fridge and grabbed the measuring cup I'd used to make and store a low-carb salad dressing. When she set it on the table, I placed my hand over hers. "I'm sorry I didn't tell you."

She nodded, but her bottom lip quivered, and her eyes filled with tears.

Damn it. Had I hurt her feelings? There was plenty about her I still didn't know. Like what her asshole ex did to make her so afraid.

"My own parents don't know," I said, hoping to put her at ease.

Her eyes widened, and a single tear slid down her cheek. She pulled her hand from under mine and wiped her face. "Eat, please," she said softly.

She turned her back to me and started cracking eggs into a bowl. I shoved a forkful of salad into my mouth and started chewing. For a while, the only sounds were the crunch of eggshells and the scrape of my fork against the plate.

"My mom had epilepsy," she said as she whisked the eggs with force.

My fork paused halfway to my mouth. People didn't get over epilepsy. The past tense meant she'd probably passed. Seizures were common in people with CP. Luckily, Wade had yet to experience one, but I lived in fear of what might happen if he did.

"I watched her have several seizures before the one that took her in her sleep," Cammie said in a small voice. "I was ten when we lost her." She blew out a breath. "I thought you were having one earlier."

My chest ached. I wanted to wrap my arms around her, yet I could tell she'd fall apart if I did, and I wanted to know everything she was willing to tell me. "I'm sorry, Cam."

She stopped whisking and nodded, the slight dip of her chin the only acknowledgement that I'd spoken. She poured the egg mixture into the pan she'd preheated on the stove, and the sizzle and hiss filled the silence between us.

"There wasn't much I could do for her," she said, pushing the eggs around the skillet with a spatula as they cooked. "But I did everything I could. I would have helped you downstairs. If I'd known what to do."

"I can teach you."

"That's a given," she said, reaching for the bag of cheese and tossing a handful into the skillet, her movements sharp and quick, not at all like the graceful way she usually worked. I finished up my salad in silence while she finished cooking. After she snapped off the stove, she brought the skillet to the table, hacked the omelet in half with the spatula, and slid a piece onto my plate before filling her own and placing the pan back on the stove.

"Thank you for this," I said, cutting off a piece of steaming omelet.

She shrugged as she sat down across from me. "It's no tamale, but salad isn't comfort food."

She stared at her plate instead of eating. I put my fork down, reached across the table, and took her hand. "Please don't be mad."

She looked up at me with tear-filled eyes. "I'm not mad," she said. "I'm scared."

"Hey," I said, sliding out of my chair to kneel next to hers. "I'm OK now. All I need is dinner."

She nodded, but the tears kept falling down her cheeks.

"I'm so sorry," I said, wrapping her in my arms.

She leaned in closer and buried her face against my neck. I wished it hadn't taken a life-threatening experience to hold her again, though I was going to enjoy it all the same. Since I wasn't about to end it, we stayed locked in the embrace long enough for my body to react. Fuck, I wanted her. When I felt her lips graze my skin, my breath hitched. I told myself it was nothing. She was upset and her lips just happened to touch my neck. But then she lifted her face and placed a gentle kiss on my jaw.

"Wyatt," she said, her voice breathy and soft, before she pressed her lips to mine.

I should have let her take the lead, but fuck Cammie Gibson was kissing me. I threaded my hands in her soft hair and kissed her like I'd never get another chance. Our breathing became ragged as the kiss deepened, my tongue caressing hers, her fingers gripping my shirt above my pounding heart.

She pulled away suddenly, her lips swollen, eyes wide. "I better go check on Lauren," she said, panting. Before I could stop her, she pushed her chair back from the table and was gone.

Chapter Fourteen

Cammie

I kissed him.

I can't believe I kissed him.

I can't believe how good it was.

It'd been over two years since I'd last locked lips with anyone, though kissing Bishop had never felt like *that*. I practically tripped over my feet as I ran down the stairs from the apartment. From Wyatt.

When I pushed through the swinging door, the café was eerily quiet.

"Is Wyatt OK?" Lauren asked.

Wyatt was more than OK. Wyatt was mind-numbing, forget-why-you-don't-do-relationships good.

She had a bottle of cleaner in her hand, scrubbing down the counter like we did at closing. I took a second to scan the café and found Aiden holding a chair, staring at me. He'd already flipped over half the seating.

"Are we closed?" I asked, even though it was obvious to anyone with half a brain. See, mind-numbing.

"Cammie," Lauren said, putting down the spray bottle and taking a step toward me. "What's wrong?"

"I kissed Wyatt," I yelled. Her eyes widened, and she slapped her hand over her mouth. "Me," I said, jabbing myself in the chest. "I started it."

"Wyatt's having one hell of a day," Aiden said.

Lauren lowered her hand from her mouth and glared at him. He smiled at her and a look passed between them that seemed to contain an entire argument and agreement. I'd have smiled if I wasn't freaking out.

"I'll be upstairs," he said, putting down the chair in his hands.

"I'll finish with the chairs and mop," I said because, so help me, I needed to be doing something. Lauren followed me into the café seating area, but I slapped her hand when she reached for a chair. "You don't need to be lifting anything."

"The chairs aren't that heavy," she said, rubbing her hand. "And I can't stand over there cleaning the counters, pretending you didn't just drop an epic piece of info."

Which reminded me. Talk about an epic piece of missing information. "Why didn't you tell me Wyatt's diabetic?"

She rested her hands on her stomach. "The same reason I didn't tell him you're hiding from your ex."

I shook my head. "You said you'd tell everyone about Bishop if you thought I was in danger. Wyatt was clearly in danger today, Lauren. The EMT said he could have—" I choked on a sob before I could repeat the lovely little tidbit about Wyatt slipping into a coma. I knew the situation was serious, yet now that I wasn't in the moment, the reality of what could have happened hit me hard.

"I know," Lauren said, wrapping me in a hug. "Believe me, I regret not telling you. Truth is, one reason I wanted you to move in here was to keep an eye on him, which was pretty impossible to do when you didn't know what to look for. I wanted him to tell you, but for some reason, he doesn't like people to know."

"He said he hasn't even told his parents," I said, hiccupping as I tried to talk through my tears. "Why wouldn't he tell them?"

"That's something you'd have to ask Wyatt," she said, rubbing soothing circles on my back. "I suspect he didn't tell you because he didn't want you to think less of him."

"That's ridiculous," I said, standing back.

She shrugged. "Yeah, but he likes you, always has."

"I like him too," I whispered.

Lauren beamed at me.

"Oh my goodness," I said. "I kissed Wyatt."

"Yeah, I hadn't forgotten," she said with a smirk.

"No, I mean, how am I supposed to go back up there? I can't live with him now."

"Was the kiss that bad?" she asked, tilting her head to the side.

"No, it was that good."

She pressed her lips together, but the smile she attempted to hide shone in her eyes.

"I'm serious, Lauren. This is a real problem. The other day he basically told me if I wanted to be with him, I just had to make the first move."

"And you did," she said, finally allowing a huge smile to spread across her face.

"I shouldn't have," I said, slumping into the chair that I should have been flipping onto the table. "I was upset, and he hugged me and watching him collapse —"

When my voice trailed off, Lauren took a seat. "You care about him."

"I shouldn't," I said around the lump in my throat. "Kissing him was a mistake."

"Did it feel like a mistake?" Lauren asked gently.

"No," I said, burying my face in my hands. "It felt incredible. I didn't know kissing could make my toes tingle."

Lauren laughed.

"But it also felt like I'd been kissing him my whole life, which doesn't make a lick of sense."

"Sure it does," she said, peeling my hands from my face. "It means you're comfortable being physical with him. And after what you've been through, *that's* pretty incredible."

I shook my head. "It's dangerous. When I'm around Wyatt, I don't think about all the reasons I vowed to never get into another relationship. The last thing I want to do is hurt his feelings, but he weakens my self-control, and that's terrifying. He must think I'm insane. I kissed him and then bolted."

Lauren blew out a breath. "Let's get this place straightened up. Then I'll go upstairs with you to get Aiden. After we leave, you should tell Wyatt about Bishop."

"I'll think about it." Hard pass. I didn't want to think about Bishop, let alone rehash the horrors of the years I spent with him. Not to mention, I wasn't sure I could face Wyatt to even have the conversation.

It didn't take us nearly long enough to clean the café. I still wasn't ready to see Wyatt as I followed Lauren up the stairs to the apartment. I could hear Aiden's voice from the stairway, and Wyatt's responding laughter lifted some of the weight from my chest.

"Hey guys," Lauren said, opening the door to the apartment without knocking.

Aiden and Wyatt were both sitting on the couch with Aiden balancing an empty plate on his leg. Desdemona and Medusa were perched on the back of the couch on either side of Wyatt's head, like a pair of Sphinxes keeping tabs on him. Both men and cats turned to face us as we walked in, and my stomach felt like it fell to my feet.

One look at Wyatt, and I knew a conversation wouldn't be necessary. At least not tonight. Though his eyes were sad, he gave me a small smile. He knew I regretted the kiss, yet what struck me was how at ease he looked. It's like he understood, without me saying a word, that I was scared of hurting him but more terrified of being with him.

"Sorry, I ate your omelet," Aiden said to me. "Figured you wouldn't want cold eggs."

"I'm glad you did," I said. "I'm not even hungry." I held out my hand for the empty plate.

"How you feeling, Wy?" Lauren asked, squeezing between the two men on the small couch.

"My blood sugar has leveled off," he said after I turned and walked to the kitchen area. I put the plate in the dishwasher, then started on the skillet I'd used to make the omelet, keeping my eyes from the living room but my ears on the conversation.

"I was so scared," Lauren said, her voice breaking.

"It's OK," Wyatt said. "I'm fine now."

Wyatt had been the one in danger, but since he regained the ability to speak, he'd been assuring everyone around him. It was like his default setting was to help any way he could. Even Lauren, who was practically saint-like when it came to supporting others, had moments of self-indulgence. Did Wyatt ever put himself first?

"We should get going," Lauren said.

Which meant in a few moments, I'd be alone with Wyatt with no clue what to say to him.

"Night everyone," I said, heading to my room without turning to see them. I closed the door and leaned against it. The conversation in the living room continued, too hushed to hear. For the first time since I moved in, I pushed the lock on the door. Then, I headed to the bathroom and took the longest everything shower of my life to avoid hearing anyone knock. By the time I'd finished blow drying my hair, the living room was quiet.

My stomach growled. I'd gone to bed hungry plenty of times in my childhood. Doing it now felt like a huge step back in the progress I'd made in life. The lock made an obnoxiously loud click when it popped. I winced, and pushed the door open all the way. The living room was completely dark. Desdemona looked up at me from her place on the sofa before laying her head back down beside Medusa.

I tiptoed to the fridge and pulled out what was left of the salad, dumped a healthy amount of dressing on it, grabbed a fork, and hurried back to my room where I ate alone, missing Wyatt with every bite.

Chapter Fifteen

Wyatt

When I asked Lauren to cover my next shift at Karma, she refused at first. She didn't want Cammie to think I was avoiding her, and that pretty much confirmed Cammie had told Lauren about the kiss. I assured Lauren I just wanted to wait until Cam and I were alone to talk, which was why I was idling in the grocery store parking lot on a Friday night, video calling my twin.

"Why aren't you more excited?" Wade asked. "You've been crushing on this woman for over a year and she kissed you."

"And ran off after," I reminded him. "And avoided me the rest of the night."

Wade shrugged. "You said she was skittish. She probably just freaked out. Unless you suck at kissing."

I glared at him and he laughed.

"I called you to help talk me through this."

"Sorry," he said, forcing the smile from his face. "Go on."

"I took tonight off so our first interaction wouldn't be behind the coffee bar."

Wade nodded. "Good, make her stew a little."

"What? No. I just wanted to be alone with her when we talked. I didn't want to pretend like nothing happened for an entire shift."

"So you're hiding from her in your car, talking to me. Got it. Go on."

I rubbed my forehead. "I don't know why I bothered calling you."

"Because you know I'll tell you exactly what you need to do."

I raised my eyebrows and waited.

"Kiss her again. Forget whatever thoughtful conversation you've been rehearsing in your head all day. The second you see her, just lay one on her."

"I can't just walk up to her and kiss her. She ran away from me, for fuck's sake."

"After kissing the shit out of you."

"I didn't tell you that."

Wade smirked. "Didn't have to. If it was a peck on the lips, we wouldn't be having this conversation. It wasn't a little lip smack that could be taken as something friendly. She kissed you because she's attracted to you. And you're attracted to her. Ergo, just kiss her again."

"Ergo?"

"He's right," a woman's voice said. Wade's girlfriend leaned into the frame and waved at me.

"Hey, Megan. Wade didn't tell me I was interrupting a date."

I shot Wade a look. It's one thing to spill my embarrassing story to my twin. It's another to tell his girlfriend, who I'd only met once before on a video call.

The fucker smiled. "I didn't want to make you feel more pathetic."

Megan rolled her eyes at him, then turned her attention back to me. "From what you've said, she likes you, but she's too in her head. Kiss her stupid."

Wade beamed at her, and when she beamed back at him, a feeling grabbed me so hard it took me a second to realize I was jealous. I should be ecstatic that Wade had found another piece of happiness. All I felt was envy.

"Thanks, guys. I won't take up any more of your night."

"You sure you're good?" Wade asked, looking serious for the first time in the conversation.

"Yeah, I'm going to grab some groceries. I've burned enough gas sitting here already."

"Good luck!" Megan said.

"Text me later," Wade said before ending the call.

I shoved my phone in my pocket and blew out a breath. Wade and I shared practically every moment of our childhoods. We'd been in the same classes, had the same friends, and spent all our free time together. When I first moved to Peace Falls, forming an identity apart from being one half of the Romero twins had been exhilarating. Wade might have stayed at home, but he attended a local college, got a job, and started building relationships on his own as well. It still felt strange that he knew people I didn't and vice versa. Especially as those people became significant, like Megan. And hopefully Cammie.

I pushed the thought aside and climbed out of my car. Grocery shopping could have waited until Sunday, but I figured I'd at least do something productive while Cam finished her shift. I walked through the aisles, grabbing shit at random. It wasn't like me not to have a list, and after planning out last week's meals with Cammie and shopping together, being back at the store alone sucked. I tossed enough meat and veggies into the cart to put together meals for at least a couple days, checked out, and headed back to Karma.

The café lights were on when I drove around the building to park. After looping all the bags on my arms, I started up the stairs to the apartment. I was so determined to get everything inside before I dropped something that I didn't notice the music at first. I paused halfway to the kitchen when

I realized the sound was coming from behind Cammie's closed door. When the song stopped and started in a different key, I placed the bags quietly on the floor and walked closer to listen.

Cammie was singing. Not humming along to the radio or belting out something in the shower, but singing in a clear, controlled voice while she strummed a guitar. She sounded like a professional. I waited until she finished the song before I raised my hand and knocked on the door.

She was quiet for so long, I thought she planned to ignore me. Then slowly the door swung open, and she stood before me in a pair of cut-off jean shorts and a bright pink tank top, clutching a guitar.

"You're incredible," I said.

Her cheeks flushed, and she smiled before ducking her chin shyly. "Thank you. I didn't know you were here."

"I just got back. I didn't expect you for a while. It's a nice surprise."

"Lauren," she said simply.

I should have seen that coming. Of course, Lauren would staff the café for the evening and send Cammie to the apartment to talk with me ASAP.

"Have you eaten?" I asked, pointing behind me to the pile of grocery bags I'd abandoned on the living room carpet. "We could throw something together."

She shook her head. "No need. I already have a casserole in the oven. I tried to make it low carb by substituting the potatoes with cauliflower."

My chest warmed. I told myself to get a grip. She'd swapped vegetables for me, not offered herself for dinner. "Sounds great."

"I thought maybe you could teach me how I can help you," she said, running her bare foot across the carpet. "I read some things online, but I'd really like you to show me where you keep your medicine and how to use your monitoring app."

She looked as nervous as I felt. And sexy as hell. Her toes were painted a bright red and the amount of toned leg she showed in those shorts made me want to pick her up and wrap them around my waist

"Sure," I said. "I just have to handle the groceries. Want to play for me while I get everything put away?"

Her eyes widened. "Oh, no. That's OK."

"I'd love to hear you play."

She shook her head. "I don't like performing."

"I don't like talking about my diabetes," I said and smiled to lighten the comeback.

"OK, one song," she said, blushing.

She settled on the couch with her guitar as I moved all the bags to the kitchen counter. I started unpacking the first bag as she strummed a few notes. Once her voice filled the room, my hand stilled, and I stood like a statue, listening. Her voice was lower than I'd expected given her speaking pitch, sultry with a slight grit that made every note a punch to my stomach. I didn't recognize the music, though it sounded like something country.

When she finished the song, I turned and clapped. "That was so good, I forgot to put away the groceries."

She smiled and looked down at her hands, strumming a few chords.

"Did you write that?"

She looked up at me and burst out laughing. "That was Patsy Cline."

I shrugged.

"Oh my word. You've never heard of Patsy Cline? She's from Virginia."

"Huh, I've never heard of her performing."

Cammie's eyes widened in horror. "Wyatt, she's been dead since the early '60s. Didn't they teach you about her in your state history class?"

"They focused on the founding fathers and the Civil War."

Cammie shook her head and kept strumming. "That one was called *You're Stronger Than Me*. It's not as popular as some of her others. You've probably heard this one."

I watched as she closed her eyes and began to sing. I still didn't recognize the song, but I felt every word of the lyrics. I was certifiably crazy for this woman and as she sang, it was getting harder and harder not to walk across the room, take her face in my hands, and kiss her senseless, like Wade suggested.

"That one was even better," I said when she finished.

Her mouth dropped open. "You haven't heard it before."

I shook my head.

"My mom played it all the time. It's the first song she taught me on this guitar."

She placed the instrument down gently beside the sofa and crossed the room to me. My breath caught when she stepped close to reach for a bag of lettuce and a carton of milk before turning to the fridge. We worked together putting everything away much like we handled a rush in the café, seamlessly, anticipating the other's steps before they happened in the tiny kitchen.

I could smell the delicate floral scent of her perfume. She used so little, I hadn't noticed it until she'd allowed herself to get closer to me. Her scent lingered on my shirt last night long after she kissed me. Having her so close again brought back every feeling from that kiss. Fuck, I'd never wanted someone more. But Cam had been hurt in the past, and I knew without asking, I'd have to let her set the pace if I wanted a chance to be with her.

"So, your mom was a musician too?" I asked as I folded up the empty shopping bags.

"Yeah," Cammie said, smiling. "She was incredible. She never sang professionally or anything, but she'd sing for Daddy and me all the time. When

I got old enough, I joined her." She let out a little laugh. "My father is hopelessly tone deaf."

"Have you ever thought about singing professionally?"

She shook her head. "It's just a hobby."

"Nah, not with the way your eyes light up when you talk about it. That's passion."

Her breath caught, and for a moment, we stood staring at each other. Wade's voice screamed in my head to "Fucking kiss her already!" I took a step towards her but stopped when she took a step back.

She turned and peeked into the oven, filling the kitchen with a rich smell. "This has a few minutes to go," she said, closing the door. "Do you need to eat something while it cooks?"

"Want to check with me?"

She nodded and followed me to the couch, where she sat as far from me as physically possible. I pulled out my phone and opened my monitoring app.

"Normal range for me is 80 to 130. After what happened yesterday, I've been trying to keep it on the higher end." I turned the phone and showed her the 140 reading, and she nodded. "Anything lower than 70 is low and means I need to eat to raise it. If it's over 180, it's too high, and I need to take more insulin."

"I saw what happens when it gets too low. What happens if it gets too high?"

"Long term, it can hurt my kidneys, eyesight, and a bunch of other things. Short term, my body can start producing something called ketones. If those build up, I can go into diabetic ketoacidosis."

"That sounds serious," she said, paling. "What are the symptoms?"

"I've never experienced it before. I do know my face gets flushed when my blood sugar is high."

"And when you're low, you get pale and cranky."

I nodded. "Was I cranky yesterday? I honestly don't remember much of what happened."

"Yeah," she said, looking down at her hands in her lap. "If I'm being honest, you scared me. You were really angry."

"I'm so sorry," I said, sliding closer and grabbing her hand. Fuck, no wonder she was skittish.

"I read people can become violent when their sugar levels dropped," she said in a near whisper before looking up at me with eyes filled with fear.

As much as I wished it wasn't true, I nodded. The thought of that ever happening around Cammie or Lauren made my stomach ache. So far, I'd just gotten irritated, but if yesterday taught me anything, it's that I could completely lose control if my blood sugar went too low. "I'm doing everything I can to make sure it never drops that low again."

"Are you?" she asked, raising an eyebrow. "Do you have a pump linked to your continuous monitor?"

Something told me she already knew the answer. Hell, she'd probably read more on late-onset type 1 diabetes in the past twenty-four hours than I'd read since I'd been diagnosed. Cammie was the best at finding information online. When Lauren was suffering with hyperemesis gravidarum, Cammie looked up every possible way to help. It didn't surprise me at all that she'd researched ways to better manage my blood sugar.

"Pumps are really expensive," I said, "so I just have the sensor for monitoring now. It helps though. If I'd been diagnosed as a kid, I'd have had to prick my finger every time I wanted to test my blood sugar."

"Where's the sensor?" she asked, blushing.

"It's on my upper arm. You didn't see it when you caught me coming from the shower?"

Her eyes filled with a heat that made my cock press against my jeans. "I wasn't looking at your arms." She pulled her hand from mine and cleared her throat.

I fought the urge to pull off my shirt and give her another look at whatever had captured her attention. Instead, I pushed up my sleeve like she hadn't just made me hard as steel with one look and angled my body so she could see the sensor.

Her eyes instantly went to the small white disc on my arm. "Does it use needles?"

"Yes," I said, pulling my sleeve back down. "Tiny ones. It doesn't hurt."

"Can I see the app again?"

I opened it and handed her my phone.

She studied it a moment and then looked up at me. "Does anyone other than Lauren monitor your sugar levels?"

I shook my head, dreading where the conversation was heading. I didn't want Cammie focused on my blood sugar like Lauren was. I waited for her to ask if she could install the app on her phone. Instead, she looked back at the screen and laughed. "You just got a notification that one of the cat's tags has a low battery. You track Desdemona and Medusa too?"

"I made Lauren take the app off her phone. If she insists on tracking me, I told her I'd handle the cats. I got the better end of that deal, since my app alerts more than theirs."

She handed back my phone with a smile. "Well, FYI, you have some batteries to change."

I nodded, waiting for her to ask about adding the app to her phone. To my surprise, she stood and walked back to the kitchen.

"OK," she said, pulling the casserole dish from the oven. "There's about five grams of carbs per cup of cauliflower and a gram for all the garlic in the entire dish, but that's it. I used lactose-free cheddar cheese and cream since it has zero carbs. I checked. And then just the chicken, salt, and pepper."

Yep, she'd definitely done some research. I smiled at her and joined her in the kitchen. "That was really thoughtful of you," I said, reaching for the plates in the cabinets.

She shrugged as I put the plates on the counter by the stove. "I'd noticed you don't eat a ton of carbs, but I thought you were on some Keto diet."

If only. "I'll just take my insulin, and we can eat."

She nodded and started scooping out portions of the casserole onto the plates. She didn't ask to watch me fill and take the shot, which I appreciated more than she knew. It was strange enough talking so openly about diabetes without adding in needles and the importance of air bubble removal. The space she allowed me made me want to tell her more, to show her more. But not tonight. Not when the kiss still loomed between us.

"Cam." When she turned and looked at me, I cupped her chin in my hand, placed a gentle kiss on her lips, and walked back to my room before she could say a word.

CHAPTER SIXTEEN

Cammie

BY THE TIME WYATT returned to the kitchen, I'd gotten myself under control. Sort of. His brief kiss had left me speechless. Not only had it caught me completely off guard, but it was tender in a way I'd never experienced before. In one small moment, he'd acknowledged the line I'd crossed last night, let me know he'd be fine with it happening again, and kept it just innocent enough that I understood he wouldn't pressure me for more if that wasn't something I wanted.

Unfortunately, I wanted.

My legs shook as I made my way to the table with the plates and took my seat to wait for him. I tried to calm down, but my stomach dipped the moment he started walking toward me.

"This looks delicious," he said, pulling out his chair and taking a seat with zero acknowledgement of the kiss. He looked up from his plate and smiled, and my heart stuttered in my chest.

I'd seen that look before, though never directed at me. It was exactly the way my dad looked at my mom every day until she died. Had Wyatt always looked at me like that and I'd never noticed, or had everything suddenly shifted? His smile dimmed, and I realized he'd been waiting for me to speak.

"I found a website with diabetic-friendly recipes," I said, sticking my fork into a piece of chicken. "I figure we could try a new one every week."

"Good idea," he said, the relief obvious on his face. He wasn't as calm as he was trying to appear, which, for some reason, put me at ease. "As long as we keep the rotisserie chicken in the rotation."

"What do you think is in this casserole?"

"Well, it's delicious," he said in a tone that made an ache form between my legs. I'd never been this turned on while trying to eat. I pushed the food around my plate as I tried to get my body under control.

"You really are an incredible singer," he said, not taking his eyes from his casserole. "I'm surprised you don't do the open mic nights in town."

"I avoid singing for people. It scares me."

"You get stage fright?" he asked, resting his fork on his plate and giving me his full attention.

"You could say that." But it'd be a lie. I loved performing. Nothing filled me with joy quite like the applause that followed, knowing people enjoyed my voice. Basking in Wyatt's admiration without the nausea that usually accompanied it had me equal parts confused and relieved. I'd sung the second song to confirm it hadn't been a one-off.

"It's a shame," Wyatt said, picking up his fork again. "It's clearly your passion."

"What are you passionate about?" I asked, my voice sounding far too breathy. I was like Pavlov's dog with a bell every time he said the word passion.

His eyes darkened a moment before he dropped them to his plate. "Architecture," he said quietly. "Ever since I was little, I've wanted to design homes. When it's done right, it's like living in a piece of art, functional, yet beautiful. So much of life happens where a person lives, and to be the one who creates that space feels special. I moved to Peace Falls for college, but

I had to stop taking classes when I got sick. It was too much to balance, trying to pay for everything I needed and tuition."

"Do you think you'll go back?"

He nodded, then looked up at me with so much determination in his eyes my breath caught. "It's what I want. I like working for Aiden and learning how to build things firsthand, but I want to go back to school and finish what I started."

"You will," I said with a certainty I rarely felt in my life. "It's obvious you love it."

"Kind of like your singing," he said, with a sad smile. "Do you think you'll ever get over your fear of being the center of attention?"

"That's a complicated question. It's not all the attention. Remember how I told you I'm afraid of most men?"

Wyatt nodded.

"Men always hit on me after I perform."

Though I could tell he wanted to ask more, as usual, he didn't push the subject, which made me want to say more. "I have a terrible picker."

"Picker?" he asked, his confusion clear on his face.

"I can't distinguish the good guys from the bad. Everyone I've dated seemed nice at the start. Then at some point, they turned. My parents adored each other, so I know exactly what love is supposed to be like. They were always laughing and snuggling like giddy teenagers. My mom and I would take turns playing for my dad every night, and he'd spin whichever of us wasn't singing around the living room. Daddy hasn't been the same since she died, so in a way, I lost him too. I guess I was so desperate to find love for myself that I ignored every red flag waved in my face and made all the wrong choices. I've only had a few relationships in my life, but they were all with guys who mistreated me, each one worse than the last. The last one hit, so I've just avoided men since I'm a terrible judge of them."

Wyatt sat so still after I finished my impromptu monologue, I wondered if he'd heard what I'd said about being abused. It wasn't something I shared often. Even Cal and the Stevens sisters didn't know the specifics of my past, though I had a feeling they'd put enough pieces together to draw a fairly accurate picture. Eventually, Wyatt pressed his lips in a hard line, shoved back from the table, and walked down the hall into his room with his shoulders bunched to his ears, leaving the door open.

Had I offended him? I wasn't sure what I said that could have pissed him off. He'd have slammed the door if I'd made him angry. Wouldn't he?

I listened, and all I could hear down the hall was the whirl of the window unit in Wyatt's room. I waited. When Wyatt didn't return after a minute, I looked down at the food on my plate and decided I couldn't eat. I was torn between giving him the privacy he'd sought by leaving the table and checking on him.

The open door taunted me like a silent invitation. He'd been in his room long enough to close it if he'd forgotten, which must mean he didn't mind if I went to him.

I pushed back from the table and made my way down the hall. "Wyatt," I said before I reached his doorway. I waited for him to tell me to go away. When he remained silent, I walked into his room.

Wyatt stood at the window without the air conditioner. The view of the parking lot was nothing special, but he didn't turn when I entered the room. His hands gripped either side of the window frame, the thick muscles in his arms taunt.

"Wyatt," I said again.

His grip tightened before he blew out a long breath and turned. His expression remained tense as he walked slowly toward me. "Can I hold you?"

The question caught me completely off guard, and I nodded before I could stop myself. He erased the small distance between us and pulled me into a tight embrace, bending to rest his head on my shoulder. He was breathing hard, yet his touch was soft as he ran his hands up and down my back. "I can't—". His heart was beating so hard, I could feel it against my chest.

"Talk to me," I said, stepping from his arms. I couldn't read his expression. I only knew I'd never seen it before.

Wyatt shook his head and gripped his hair. "Something terrible happened to you, and you're trying to comfort me after I heard about it. I'm sorry I made you worry," he said taking my hand. "I just needed a minute to calm down. I can't imagine hurting any woman, let alone one I cared about."

"You're angry," I said. A statement, not a question, though his reaction had left me perplexed. I was used to people raising their voice when upset. Even Daddy could holler up a storm when he was pissed. The guys I'd dated threw things, sometimes at me, sometimes at the wall.

Wyatt nodded.

"But you're so quiet."

His eye's softened as he ran his thumb across the back of my hand. "I've always tried to keep my temper in check. Even the thought of hurting another person makes me feel sick. Don't get me wrong, I'll fight back if someone hits me, but I prefer to talk things out like I did with that *cretino* in the café."

I believed him, yet I couldn't stop the words that came out of my mouth. "What would you do if I slapped you right now?"

He raised his eyebrows at me. "Like I said, I'd never hit a woman, but what I did next would depend on why you slapped me."

"Because I was mad at you."

He stepped closer and lifted his hand to brush my hair back from my cheek, his fingers lingering. "Depends on why you're mad at me," he said softly.

His fingers were callused, the roughness a stark contrast to the gentle way he swiped my skin. For a moment, I forgot what we were talking about and simply enjoyed his touch. "Um, just imagine we're arguing about something."

"You and me," he said, gesturing between us.

"Yes, you and me."

He leaned down and whispered in my ear. "If you were heated enough to slap me, I'd assume you were very frustrated, and I'd offer to relieve that frustration in a much more enjoyable way for us both."

Oh. This was dangerous. He was dangerous, yet being close to him felt so good.

"Wyatt," I said. "Please don't say things like that. You have no idea how long it's been since I've had sex."

He took a step back, and I ached for the solid feel of his body close to mine.

"Same," he said, running his hand through his thick black hair. "And damn I miss it."

"I doubt you'd have trouble finding someone." The thought made me angry, as if I had any claim to him.

His face flushed and for a moment I thought maybe his blood sugar had spiked until he cleared his throat and said, "I haven't been with anyone since I was diagnosed."

"Why not?"

He shrugged.

"Wyatt," I said, taking a step closer. "I promise I won't judge you."

He looked at me with that same warm expression that had made my heart skip a beat earlier, before he glanced away and said, "I'd have to explain the sensor in my arm."

"That wouldn't deter anyone, if they even noticed. I sure didn't when I saw you with your shirt off."

His eyes snapped back to mine with a flash of heat before they washed with sadness. "What if my blood sugar crashes during sex? I don't want to think about whether I'm being too physical when I fuck."

He didn't sleep with someone or make love. He fucked. Hearing him say that word made my body super aware of how close we were standing. It also seemed at odds with everything I knew him to be. Wyatt was sweet, kind, and gentle. Yet, he was apparently such an animal in bed he worried it'd make his blood sugar crash. The man did manual labor all day. His idea of "being too physical" must be beyond my comprehension of sex. "Sounds like we both need to rip off the Band-Aid."

He threw his head back and laughed before I even registered the words that had poured from my mouth and the invitation it implied.

"Happy to help you with that any time," he said, his voice dropping low. "But you'd have to be on top."

My mouth fell open. When I left my casserole cooling on my plate, this wasn't the conversation I expected. *But it was a long time coming.* The truth felt like a shot of espresso, setting my nerves on end. Wyatt found me attractive. And despite all my reservations about opening myself to a man again, I felt the same. We were both single, living together, and apparently longing for sex.

"I've never been on top," I said, forcing my voice to sound as matter of fact as his, despite the nerves in my stomach. "I'm probably terrible."

He studied me a moment before he replied. "I doubt you'd be terrible, and I've got no problem topping from the bottom."

We burst out laughing. I'd never felt so light talking about sex before. Heck, I'd never talked about sex with a man, period. At least not until after we'd already had it. The few men I'd been with had touched me and kept going until we were both naked. Sex felt like an inevitable conclusion, not something to be discussed. Having an actual conversation beforehand felt odd, yet strangely exhilarating.

"If I were on top," I said, "it'd probably make it less likely that your blood sugar would crash."

He nodded. "And you'd be in control, so you could stop anytime you wanted."

I narrowed my eyes at him. "And you'd just say 'Well, we tried but that Band-Aid was glued on.' Yeah right. I doubt once we got started, you'd be OK with that."

"You want to stop. We stop," he said in a voice so firm my breath caught.

He sounded angry. No, he sounded commanding, which didn't make a lick of sense because he was telling me to take control.

"That goes no matter what position we worked ourselves into," he said in a low voice, running his hand down my arm and leaving a trail of goosebumps.

"I believe you," I said. And what's even more shocking, I did.

He lowered his mouth to my neck and placed a soft kiss just below my ear. "Whenever you're ready. Just let me know." He straightened and stepped away, but every muscle in his body looked tense. He was holding himself back, waiting for me to agree. Not just agree. Initiate.

Physically, he was stronger than Bishop, yet I believed with a certainty deep in my mind, body, and soul, Wyatt would never hurt me.

"How about now?" I asked, placing my hands on his chest and rising on my toes to kiss him.

Chapter Seventeen

Wyatt

CAMMIE GIBSON, THE GIRL I'd wanted since I laid eyes on her a year ago, was kissing me. She lifted her hands from my chest and threaded her fingers in my hair as she kissed me like her life depended on it. I knew she needed to be in control to feel safe, but fuck, when she kissed me with so much passion, I snapped.

I put my hands on her hips and pulled her closer. She gasped when she felt how hard she'd made me, and I deepened the kiss, tasting her until we were both breathless.

She grabbed my hand and lifted it to her breast, granting me permission to touch her. Her nipple hardened with each pass of my thumb, and she arched against my cock, igniting sparks of pleasure that tested my control. She was so fucking responsive. I wanted to slide my other hand into her shorts to feel her there, to know without question that she wanted this, wanted me. But I had to let her lead.

She surprised me with how fast she propelled us forward, reaching between us and cupping me. I threw my head back and groaned as her fingers traced my hard length. Shit, if she kept doing that, I wasn't going to be able to hold back.

"Angel," I said, grabbing her hand and placing a gentle kiss on the pad of each finger. "If you keep touching me like that, I'm going to fuck you against the wall before we get our clothes off. Let's focus on you first."

Her eyes darkened like half-dressed wall sex was exactly what she wanted, but she nodded, her breath coming in short bursts. "What did you have in mind?"

"Whatever you need to come," I said, rubbing slow circles on her soft skin above the waistband of her shorts. "However many times you need before you lower that sweet pussy on my cock and ride me until I come so hard I black out."

"Oh," she breathed. "Maybe we can start with you taking your shirt off?"

I smiled at her before I pulled my t-shirt over my head and tossed it on the floor. Her eyes immediately went to the plastic disc in my arm, but didn't linger long enough for me to get self-conscious. Instead, her hands followed her eyes to my chest as she ran her fingers across my pecks and down my abs. I'd packed on muscle since I started working construction full time.

"Your body is unreal," she said, raising her eyes to mine. "I mean, it's obviously real," she added, blushing.

"And all yours," I said, which made her suck in a tiny breath.

"I'm not really sure how to do this," she said. "I've never been in charge before."

"Easy," I said. "Just tell me exactly what you're thinking."

She shook her head. "Way too many demons in there to share."

My chest ached. I wanted her to be in the moment, not triggered and thinking about whoever hurt her. "How about this," I said, leaning in to kiss the spot on her neck she'd liked earlier, "you tell me when something feels good or doesn't?"

"Pretty sure anything you do will feel good," she said in a breathy voice that made me want to bury my face between her legs.

"When you want more of something then," I said, sliding my hand down her sides to the hem of her tank top. My fingers itched to pull it from her body with the rest of her clothes, but I stopped myself and stood back to look her in the eyes. "You say stop, we stop. No questions. No hurt feelings."

She lifted her arms over her head, silently urging me to undress her. Once her shirt joined mine on the floor, I wasted no time undoing her shorts and dragging them down her thighs. She placed her hand on my back and lifted one foot and then the other to help me.

My cock strained painfully against my zipper as I took in how her matching black bra and panties hugged every curve. Despite the pressure, I kept my jeans on as I kissed my way up her leg. I stopped to inhale her delicious scent before I continued my journey up her smooth skin until I was standing.

"You're so beautiful," I said just before I took her lips again. As we kissed, I unhooked her bra and tossed it. Her breasts fit perfectly in my cupped hands. I broke our kiss to lower my mouth to her rose-colored nipples, giving each equal attention, sucking and massaging until her legs shook.

I slid my hand into her panties and groaned when I found her soaked.

"There," she said, gripping my shoulder. "Touch me there."

I flicked my thumb across her clit once, twice, and she shattered with a strangled cry.

"That came out of nowhere," she said, panting. "I'm so sorry. That was too quick."

I grabbed her chin and tilted it until our eyes locked. "Never apologize for coming. I love that you're so responsive."

"Yeah, but I haven't even touched you."

"Any man who can't pull more than one orgasm from you doesn't know what he's doing."

Her eyes widened, and I knew without asking that she'd never had multiple orgasms, and so help me, I was going to show her exactly what her body was capable of with the right person.

"Lie on the bed, Angel," I said, guiding her backwards until her thighs hit the edge of my mattress. "We're just getting started."

She shoved down the comforter and stretched out on my bed, looking up at me with such a sweet expression my breath caught.

As I lowered my mouth between her thighs, she whispered my name and threaded her fingers through my hair. At the first taste of her, I lost what little control I had, devouring her like a man starved. The sounds she made with each swipe of my tongue made me painfully hard. I slid a finger into her tight heat and tested the angle until she tensed when I found the spot deep inside her that would heighten her pleasure.

When she came a second time, she writhed on the bed as I sucked her clit in my mouth, drawing out her orgasm until she dug her fingernails into my shoulders.

"Too much," she said.

I quickly sat back on my heels and stared down at her. Her cheeks were flushed, her chest heaving with labored breaths, and the dazed look in her eyes made me want to play with her all night before I found my release.

"I think we found the number of orgasms I needed before we rip off that Band-Aid."

I laughed, but then my stomach sank when I realized we couldn't. "That might have to wait. I don't have a condom."

"I do," she said, sitting up.

Why would she have condoms if she'd sworn off sex? I must have looked confused because she said, "Lauren had a feeling this might happen."

"Remind me to thank her tomorrow."

"Be right back," she said, smiling as she ran in all her naked glory from my room.

This was really happening. In a few minutes, I'd be inside the woman I'd wanted more than any other in life. This wasn't like the friends with benefits or random hookups I'd had before. I'd been infatuated with Cammie from the moment I saw her gorgeous face. Since then, I'd tucked away more adjectives to describe her: kind, brilliant, talented, and incredibly easy to love.

My dick didn't seem to care how significant sex with Cammie could be. I'd never been so turned on, and I hoped I could last long enough to make it enjoyable for her.

"Here," she said, returning to the room with a massive box of condoms. Well, at least we could go again if I made a fool of myself.

I stood and held my hands out to the side. "You're in charge, remember," I said, giving her a wink.

She blushed, seemingly shy despite the fact she'd just come all over my face. She set the condoms on the bed and reached for my belt, quickly undoing it with her graceful fingers. My breaths became shallow as she carefully unzipped my fly. She pulled both my jeans and boxers down with one quick tug, and my cock sprang free.

"That's going to hurt," she said, her eyes wide.

I know every guy likes to think he's got a massive one, but I'm realistic enough to accept that I'm only slightly above average. What kind of pencil dick assholes had she been with before? Even so, I couldn't help grinning at the shocked look on her face. "I promise it won't."

Though she still looked unsure, she nodded.

"You take me as slow as you want," I said, cupping her cheek gently. "Or not at all. You're in control here."

She reached for the condoms and tore one open before sliding it down my throbbing length. "I don't think I'm comfortable with you just looking up at me," she said, biting her lip.

"Then I'll sit up," I said, taking a seat on the edge of the mattress and sliding back far enough so she'd have room to place her knees on either side of me.

She looked so nervous walking toward me, I almost told her to stop, but once she'd straddled me, I couldn't bring myself to say it.

"You're incredible, Cammie," I said, tracing the lines of her face before placing a gentle kiss on her lips.

She grabbed my shoulders to steady herself, rocking against me and making me harder than I'd ever been in my entire life.

"Are you ready?" I asked, my voice strained. Fuck, she felt so good, and I wasn't even inside her yet.

She nodded and lifted on her knees, using one hand to guide me into her tight heat. We both groaned as she slid down my length, taking me all at once.

"Oh," she breathed, her hands shaking on my shoulders.

"Did that hurt?" I asked, the thought of causing her pain acting as a much-needed damper to the orgasm already building at the base of my spine.

She shook her head. "You feel so good," she said, raising up on her knees only to sink back down on me again. She threw her head back with a look of pure ecstasy and the words poured from my mouth before I could stop them.

"*Estoy enamorado de ti.*" I'm in love with you. Even stupefied by the most intense pleasure of my life, I'd at least had the common sense to say it in Spanish.

She tightened around me as if she understood anyway. Her eyes locked with mine and something so perfect passed between us, my eyes stung. We slowly rocked together, the pleasure building to an unbearable height. I fought against it as long as I could, but too soon my balls tightened and I groaned as my orgasm shot through me. She stilled and her walls convulsed, milking every drop of cum from my body with her own release. I wrapped my arms around her as we both fought to catch our breath.

"*Te amo cada día más.*" I said, rubbing my hands down her back.

"*Te amo cada día más,*" she repeated.

Though she pronounced it perfectly and with conviction, I had to remind my heart that she didn't know what it meant.

CHAPTER EIGHTEEN

Cammie

TE AMO CADA DÍA MÁS

Te amo cada día más

Te amo cada día más

If I repeated it enough times, I'd remember it well enough to Google later. The other phrase Wyatt murmured while he was deep inside me was too complicated to commit to memory. Not to mention, my brain wasn't focused on linguistics. But I thought I recognized a few of the last words he whispered to me, even repeating them out loud to hear them again.

"Are you OK?" Wyatt asked, as I carefully lifted my body from him. "Did I hurt you?"

He'd wrecked me in the best ways possible. "Not at all," I said, smiling at him, suddenly very aware of the fact we were completely naked with the overhead lights on. "I'm just going to clean up."

Rather than hunt around his carpet for wherever he'd thrown my clothes, I ran down the hallway naked, for the second time, and grabbed my phone from the kitchen table.

Más meant more. I'd seen *Te amo* on a Valentine's Day card in the pharmacy. I'd figured it meant "I love you" but that couldn't be right.

I hurried into the bathroom connected to my room and typed *Te amo cada día más* into my translation app. When it spat back "I love you more each day," I nearly dropped my phone in the toilet.

Maybe love was just a broad translation. I opened my browser and typed "Ways to say I love you in Spanish." Based on the results, there were several with subtle differences in the meaning and intensity. My stomach fluttered when I read Wyatt had specifically used the version meant for deep love, not friendship or mild affection.

And I'd said it back to him.

I didn't have to understand Spanish to hear the emotion in his voice, to know he was telling me something special. I might not have known exactly what I was saying, yet it'd felt right to repeat it back to him.

A gentle knock sounded on the bathroom door. "Everything all right?" Wyatt asked, the worry clear in his voice.

"Yeah, I'll be right out," I said, exiting out of everything on my phone. I heard him close the door to my bedroom on his way out, giving me another layer of privacy I hadn't bothered taking.

I cleaned myself up and changed as quickly as possible, but by the time I joined him in the kitchen, his face looked pale. He'd pulled on a pair of gym shorts but left his chest bare as he leaned against the counter facing my door, clearly waiting for me.

"How's your blood sugar?" I asked.

The question seemed to surprise him. His eyes widened before he walked to the table and grabbed his phone. "68," he said with a frown.

"You didn't finish your dinner," I said, pointing to the food we'd left on our plates and the nearly full casserole dish in the middle of the table. "And you took your insulin as if you were."

"Yeah," he said, reaching for his fork.

"Can I heat it up in the microwave for you, or do you need to eat right away?"

"I can wait sixty seconds not to eat congealed cheese," he said with a smile that untangled all the nerves that had crashed into me when I read the translation.

I reheated his food and then my own while he started eating again. When I joined him at the table, he did his best to keep the conversation going about anything and everything except what had just happened between us. He was trying to put me at ease, but it felt strange not to acknowledge that he'd just given me the most intense orgasms of my life, then declared he loved me.

The cats wandered in for their nightly cuddles, weaving between our legs under the table. Once they realized we weren't sharing our chicken, Desdemona let out a meow to get Medusa's attention before she led them to the sofa, which seemed to be their favorite place in the apartment.

"Main Street is busy tonight," Wyatt said as he pushed his empty plate away.

"Friday night," I said with a shrug.

"Must be hard to sleep with all the noise."

Peace Falls was far from wild and crazy. Even if someone had a little too much fun at Church, the window unit in my room drowned out most of the sound from the street. "It's not bad," I said.

He shook his head and let out a short laugh. "I was trying to ask if you wanted to sleep in my room tonight. It didn't come out as smooth as it sounded in my head."

I'm not sure how he did it, but Wyatt nailed adorable and sexy simultaneously. He was so open with his mistakes, self-deprecating in a charming way that brought out a playful side in me I didn't know I had. "You should have said something like 'My blood sugar might dip again. Want to help me keep an eye on it?'"

His eyes warmed, and he reached across the table and took my hand. "How about I'm not ready to say goodnight, but I'm fucking exhausted

and need to sleep if I have any chance of being half-functional tomorrow when I open Karma."

"Just sleep?" I asked, raising my eyebrow.

He rubbed his thumb across the back of my hand. "Like I said
before, you set the pace, Angel. Whenever you want more, just let me
know."

I looked at our joined hands. Only a few days ago, the thought of
letting another man touch me felt dangerous, wrong, yet being with
him felt like breathing. Reflexive, necessary.

There was so much about Wyatt I didn't know. I'd researched him
like I did everyone else in my life I needed to trust, somewhat, but
his digital footprint was faint. No social media. No criminal records.
I did, however, know his exact birthdate, and the fact he'd gotten his
driver's license in Northern Virginia. I'd slipped up when I chastised
him for not learning about Patsy Cline in his state history class, since
theoretically, I shouldn't have known he lived in Virginia when he got
his driver's license. It felt wrong now to know more about him than
he realized. "How old are you?" I asked, looking up at him.

"Twenty-two."

I smiled because he'd told the truth, not that his age was anything
he needed to lie about.

"I don't want to know," he said when I opened my mouth to speak.
"I figure you're older than me, and you're intimidating enough without the reminder that I'm dealing with a more experienced woman."

"Me, intimidating?" I squeezed his hand and giggled. "I'm only
two years older than you, and trust me, Wyatt. Tonight was my best
experience so far."

"So far?" he asked, raising an eyebrow. "Sounds like a challenge."

"Oh my word," I said, ignoring the clench in my core. "Let's clean
up dinner before we have to throw away the leftovers."

We worked together to get everything put away and were ready for bed and in Wyatt's room by nine. He flung back the covers and motioned for me to lie down first. I froze.

"Hey," he said, taking my hand. "You don't have to stay here with me if you'd rather sleep in your room."

"I just don't know what side to take."

His brow scrunched in confusion. "Whichever side you want."

"But what if I lay down on your side? The first time Bishop shoved me was to push me off 'his side' of the bed." I hadn't meant to say the second sentence out loud, though it felt good telling Wyatt why I was so hesitant to choose.

"Your ex's name is Bishop?" Wyatt asked before his mouth set in a tight line.

"No, it's Keith. But everyone calls him Bishop."

Wyatt nodded, as if that scrap of information told him everything he needed to know. "Just above a pawn. One of the weakest pieces on the board."

My eyes widened. Daddy and I sometimes played chess over video calls since he had access to a board, so I knew the basics of the game. I'd made the connection before. I doubt my ex ever had. "Yeah, but Bishop didn't know anything about chess. He was an altar boy when he was younger, and I guess the nickname stuck long after he stopped."

"Being decent," Wyatt said with a frown. "He sounds like an asshole. Sleep in the middle of the bed if you want, Angel. I'm just going to wrap myself around you wherever you are."

I'd always hated nicknames when I heard other couples use them, but for some reason, it didn't bother me when Wyatt called me Angel. I was far from angelic. Given how much I'd stolen from Bishop, the nickname should have grated my conscience. Even so, I found myself liking it a little more each time Wyatt used it. What's more, I liked who I was when I was with him.

I laid down on the left side of the bed, the superior side in my humble opinion. Wyatt settled in beside me before curving his body around mine and draping his arm over my waist.

"You weren't kidding," I said as my body warmed against his hot skin.

"Nope," he said, snuggling his face closer to my neck. "If you get too hot, just wake me up and tell me to roll over."

I waited for him to make a move. Part of me wanted him to lower his hand between my legs and ease the ache that started as soon as he held me, but a larger part wanted to rest in his arms. Within a few minutes, his breaths evened and the arm around my body grew heavy.

I wished I could fall asleep so easily, though then I wouldn't get to enjoy the simple peace of lying beside him. Of course, the more my body relaxed into his, the more my mind came alive.

Wyatt wasn't the first man to tell me he loved me. Bishop said it early in our relationship and kept on saying it through all the abuse. I believed he loved me. What's worse, I thought I felt the same. Maybe I did or maybe I just repeated what I knew Bishop wanted to hear. The thought made my stomach turn. I'd done the same thing with Wyatt, parroting back the words he said to me regardless of the meaning.

But Wyatt had meant them. I felt it every time his eyes locked with mine and with every touch. It's why Lauren warned me not to hurt him. She probably knew his feelings for me were stronger than a crush. Wyatt loved me, which meant what we'd shared tonight wasn't casual. At least not for him.

Or for me. The realization sent a shockwave of fear through my body. How had I gotten in so deep, so quickly? It had to be because we spent a lot of time together. We were so domestic, making meal plans and grocery runs. In a matter of weeks, we'd become an old married couple. Make that a sexually explosive married couple.

We were moving dangerously fast. There was only one way to keep myself from spending every night locked in Wyatt's arms: Stop living with him.

I had to move back to my apartment. If Bishop hadn't found me yet, chances were he wouldn't. He might not even know about the PO Box. Wyatt would understand that I needed space, even if I didn't want it. As if he could hear my racing thoughts, Wyatt's arm tightened around me. But rather than feeling trapped, it felt like an anchor holding me steady as I drifted off to sleep.

Chapter Nineteen

Wyatt

I WOKE THE NEXT morning before my alarm, which was pretty impressive given it was set for five-thirty. Cammie hadn't asked me to move over in the night, so my body was still molded to hers. She looked even more like an angel with her blonde hair spread across the pillow, her face relaxed in sleep. Morning wood didn't even begin to describe the situation in my shorts. I'd never felt so hard in my life, but instead of kissing Cammie awake, I eased out of the bed and tiptoed from the room.

I was scheduled to open Karma at six with Lauren, while Cammie would close later with one of the part-timers. I hated the idea of leaving her to work with someone else, but Cam was not a morning person. I checked my blood sugar and grabbed my overnight oats from the fridge, willing my dick to calm the fuck down so I could get dressed and downstairs.

I'd put my clothes in the hall bathroom last night, so I wouldn't disturb Cammie any more than I had to and did my best to get ready without waking her. She was still sleeping peacefully as I headed out, and for the first time in a while, I wished I didn't have two jobs. It'd been so long since I had a day off that the idea of spending the morning indulging in her felt like a fantasy.

The lights were already on in the backroom when I arrived downstairs, and I could hear Lauren moving around on the other side of the swinging door.

"Morning," I said, pushing through the door carefully, so I wouldn't bump into her. She was growing by the day, and I had nightmares of slamming the door into her pregnant belly.

"Hey Wy," she said and raised her eyebrows. "How did things go with Cammie last night? Everything good between you?"

Fucking incredible. I should have jerked off this morning because just the thought of last night gave me a semi. "Best night of my life," I answered honestly. Lauren could read me like a book, so bullshitting her wasn't an option.

Her eyes widened. "Holy shit, Wyatt," she said, slapping my shoulder like we were a pair of dude-bros in a locker room. "Did you sleep with her?"

I smiled, and kept my mouth closed.

"You know she tells me everything," Lauren said, crossing her arms over her chest.

"Then she'll tell you," I said, giving her a wink as I walked toward the espresso machine.

"I both love and hate that you're a gentleman," she grumbled, ripping open a bag of cup sleeves.

I laughed and checked the waterline to the machine. I swear the thing sometimes knotted itself just to piss us off. I was so focused on untangling it, I jumped when Lauren placed her hand on my arm.

"I know you care about her," she said softly. "And she's one of the sweetest people I know, but she's been hurt before. Don't be surprised if she freaks out and pulls back. She might even try to push you away."

"She told me a little bit about her ex," I said, my voice hardening.

"What has she told you?"

"Just that he hurt her physically. I'm sure in other ways too."

"That's all?" Lauren asked.

"Isn't that enough?"

Lauren started chewing on her bottom lip, which meant she knew something she wanted to tell me but wouldn't. I knew better than to ask her to spill it. Her eyes went glassy before she sucked in a breath and said, "She could break your heart if you're not careful. Don't go falling in love with her until she's ready."

I pulled Lauren in for a hug. "Too late."

She hugged me tighter and nodded against my chest.

"It'll be OK," I said, hoping to assure myself as well as Lauren.

By the time Cammie arrived, the late morning rush was in full swing. Lauren was reading to a group of kids in the stacks, so Cammie simply smiled at me and got to work helping with the orders. My shift ended at one, but I stayed behind the counter with her even after another worker arrived.

"Go eat lunch, Wyatt," Cammie said, narrowing her eyes at me. "We've got this handled."

"I don't mind staying," I said. "The espresso machine gets twitchy in the afternoons."

"The espresso machine is twitchy all the time," she said. "I promise I'll get you if we need help."

The nerves that had built all day refused to wait another moment to acknowledge that things had changed between us, at least for me. "Would you go out with me tonight after work?"

"On a date?" she asked, like the idea was unfathomable.

"Yes," I said with more confidence than I felt.

"I have plans," she said before her eyes widened. "That sounded like I was shutting you down, didn't it?"

I nodded, but some of the tension in my shoulders eased when she asked the question.

"I have plans to go to Church after work. Now that I think about it, I'd really like you to come along. I was going to be the seventh wheel with 'the couples.'"

She didn't have to explain who she meant by "the couples." Lauren was best friends with the Stevens sisters and Aiden was best friends with their partners, one of whom was Cammie's other boss Cal. Small town living was complicated in its simplicity.

I wasn't surprised Lauren hadn't invited me herself. Cammie was friendly with everyone in the group. I'd worked with the Stevens sisters briefly when Lauren was struggling with severe morning sickness, but my only interactions with Aiden's best friends had been serving them in the café.

"They won't mind?" I asked.

"Not at all." She frowned. "Um, just a heads-up, Cal is a little protective of me. So, if you hold my hand or anything, he might pull you aside for a chat."

I didn't give a shit if Cal sat me down under a spotlight and interrogated me if it meant holding hands with Cammie in public, letting everyone know that she and I were—whatever we were. "Noted. What time?"

"Right after we're done closing. Everyone else is getting there at six-thirty. I was planning to walk over if you wanted to go with me."

Like that was even a question. "I'll come down and help close, so you don't feel rushed."

"Sounds goods," she said and blushed. The smallest things seemed to embarrass her, and I loved watching her cheeks pink at random.

I glanced around, desperate to kiss her, but when I saw how packed the café was, I settled for leaning closer and whispering, "Last night was incredible, and I'd like to be with you again. The same rules apply though. It's up to you to start things and set the pace, OK?"

She nodded, her cheeks fully red now. Whether she was agreeing to what I'd said or more, I didn't know, and I couldn't wait to find out.

Even as I climbed the stairs to the apartments, I was itching to turn around and finish out her shift with her. Thankfully, Karma closed at six on Saturdays and didn't open until seven on Sunday mornings, so we had an entire evening ahead of us.

After taking a shower and eating some of the casserole Cammie made, I still had hours to kill and looked around the apartment for something to do. I didn't have free time often, so my to-do list should be endless. However, Cammie and I kept the apartment neat, and I'd already done the grocery shopping. I threw in a load of laundry and paced a bit. I'd already changed the cats' litter and the batteries in their trackers. They wouldn't need to be fed again until later. A normal person would pull up Netflix or read a book or, at the very least, doom scroll. I was too amped to sit still, and it wasn't just excitement that had me pacing the length of the apartment.

Like I always did when I needed to talk through something, I called Wade. He accepted my video request on the first ring, the tension clear on his face.

"Well?" he asked. "Did you kiss the shit out of her?"

The guy had clearly been waiting for an update, and I was more than happy to give it. "I left her in my bed this morning, and we're going out tonight."

"Finally!" Wade shouted before he let out a whoop and fist pumped so hard, the camera shook. "About time you got laid. What's it been?"

"Too long," I said, blowing out a breath and taking a seat on the sofa. "I, um, kind of did something stupid though."

"Bro, Papá gave us the sex talk in middle school. You know to wrap it up."

I laughed and shook my head. "That wasn't the stupid thing."

Wade frowned. "I kind of don't want to hear if you blew your load too soon or had trouble getting it up. We have the same DNA. I don't need that shit in my head the next time Megan and I are together."

"I told Cammie I loved her."

Wade was so still I thought the video froze until he leaned closer and whispered, "Are you insane?"

"I know. It just kind of slipped out. At least I said it in Spanish." Twice, in slightly different ways.

"*Te quiero?*"

"*Te amo.*"

"Fucking hell, Wyatt. I haven't even told Megan that and we've been together for months. Do you think she understood you?"

"Cammie doesn't speak Spanish, but she's a fast learner. When I teach her something, her pronunciation is perfect."

"So 50/50 she looked it up later."

"Yeah." I couldn't admit to Wade she'd said the entire phrase back with enough clarity to suggest it was closer to 75/25. She'd let me hold her all night, so maybe I'd gotten lucky, and she hadn't remembered it well enough to look it up. Or she had and spent the night in my bed anyway. I pushed that thought aside before I got my hopes up.

"Did you mean it?" Wade asked, lowering his voice again.

I nodded.

His eyes widened slightly, but he sounded sincere when he said, "Well, then it wasn't that stupid."

"We aren't even dating."

"Sounds like you are to me. You live together, you've banged, and you're going out later."

"With both my bosses," I said. "And two other couples."

Wade laughed. "Are you trying to convince me you're an idiot? Because if you want me to call you a dumbass, I can do that and call Megan back. Couldn't you think of something better than a group date?"

"You hung up on your girlfriend to talk to me?"

"I can never get you on the phone, so yeah. And stop deflecting. Why are you taking her on a group date?"

"She already had plans with them and invited me along. I'm just nervous I'm going to fuck this up," I said, gripping the back of my neck. "I really like her, Wade."

"No," he said in a tone he seldom used. "You love her." Wade was a joker, a charmer. Whenever he sounded serious, I knew he meant every word he said. "I might be the better half of our duo, but any woman who can't appreciate what a great person you are doesn't deserve you. Just relax," he added, his tone shifting back to normal. "You're awfully tense for a guy who just got his rocks off. You did get your rocks off, right? Or did only one of us pay attention to Papá's talk?"

"Fuck you," I said, trying not to laugh and failing. "Papá's talk was not that detailed."

"I know. I made you laugh though, didn't I?

"Thanks, man. Tell Megan I'm sorry for interrupting your call. And maybe next time, don't ditch her for me."

Wade shook his head. "She's chill. I'll still make it up to her when she comes over later. Have fun on your lame date. I can't wait until I get my license. I'm going to take Megan somewhere epic."

I'd been so distracted with Cammie, work, and my blood sugar problems, I hadn't even asked for an update on the van. "Have you been looking for wheels?"

Wade frowned. "Mamá wants to keep the van for herself and get me something with a chairlift on the driver's side. I kind of think it's a waste of money. I can use the ramp we have and just add modifications to the driver's seat. It's expensive enough to convert ours to something I can use, even if I transferred out of my chair. It'd be a hell of a lot easier if I didn't have to transfer, but then we'd need to find Mamá another car since she's not driving in a wheelchair."

"I think Mamá has the right idea. You should have whatever you need to make it easier for you. We'd have to get another car anyway, since you'll be driving everywhere once you get your license, and Mamá needs her own ride. Keeping the van would make it easier when you're a passenger."

Wade blew out a breath. "I'm being impatient. I know the cheapest solution isn't the best long term."

Wade had waited years to drive. He was the furthest thing from impatient.

"We'll get there," I said before saying goodbye.

As soon as the call ended, I sent my parents a thousand dollars electronically, which ate up all I'd saved in rent and half of my Karma paycheck. I didn't need to tell them what it was for. The entire family was scrimping for the same thing. I felt bad keeping more money than I needed for my other bills, but I wanted to take Cammie out as many times as she'd let me.

Assuming I hadn't royally fucked up and given her the ick. Even if it was true, telling a woman you loved her when you're only having sex to "rip off the Band-Aid" was bad. She must not have looked it up, which meant I needed to simmer down and wait for her to make the next move.

CHAPTER TWENTY

Cammie

WYATT WAITED FOR ME at the bottom of the apartment stairs. Whether he intended it or not, he'd created that girl-walking-down-the-stairs-all-dressed-up-for-a-date moment. I'd taken less than three minutes to throw on my favorite yellow sundress, slap on a couple coats of mascara, and take my hair down from the messy bun I'd worn to work at Karma. If I'd had more time to get ready, I would have put on some eyeshadow or lipstick. I'd always loved playing with makeup until Bishop complained about it so much, I'd stopped wearing it. Apart from my one open mic performance and Rowan and Cal's wedding, I'd been completely barefaced for years. A few weeks ago, I'd bought a new tube of mascara, though I hadn't gotten the courage to add anything else to my daily routine. Still, Wyatt's eyes widened as I walked down the stairs to him, making me feel like a '90s rom-com heroine.

"Wow," he said, taking my hand when I reached the bottom of the stairs. "You're always beautiful, but you're stunning right now."

My cheeks warmed, and I cast my eyes away from his. Compliments hadn't made me nervous until Bishop, and I hated how my body still reacted. "Do you have your insulin?" I asked, hoping to calm the butterflies in my stomach by switching the topic to something practical.

"In my pocket."

I looked up at Wyatt and frowned. "You have a needle in your pocket?"

"It's in a case," he said, his cheeks pinking.

I'd embarrassed him, which hadn't been my intention at all. "Sorry for asking," I blurted out, grabbing his other hand as well. "I know you don't like to make a big deal about it. I'm just nervous and you don't have a bag or anything, not that you'd carry a purse, but a backpack or something to store your insulin, so I asked." I sucked in a breath and added, "Sorry."

Wyatt frowned. "Are you nervous about going out with me or introducing me to your friends?"

"Both," I answered honestly, relieved when I realized I wasn't just a nervous mess because of Wyatt's compliment.

He rubbed his thumbs across the backs of my hands. "The only people I haven't worked with are Cal and Theo. And from what I can tell, Theo is chill. That just leaves Cal, and I'll do my best to assure him he has nothing to worry about."

I smiled. "No question, they'll like you. It's just they know how scared I am of guys, so seeing me with one will be a shock. I'm nervous about going out with you for the same reason. It's alarming how much I enjoy spending time with you."

He dropped my hands so he could wrap his arms around my waist and pull me close. "I've been waiting all day to kiss you."

Still he waited, giving me time to pull away. When I wrapped my arms around him, he lowered his lips to mine. The kiss started gentle enough, but soon it deepened, his tongue sliding over mine igniting a longing so intense I whimpered. Neither of us seemed eager to stop, yet eventually he broke the kiss, resting his forehead on mine while we both caught our breath.

He opened the door to the parking lot behind the building and motioned me forward. "After you."

The air practically vibrated with tension as I walked past him. I'd never felt so turned on by another person, practically reckless with need. If he hadn't stopped us, I would have let him take me on the staircase.

He grabbed my hand after he pulled the door shut and gave it a squeeze. "Thanks for inviting me."

"Thank me after you face the inquisition," I said as we walked toward Main Street. My stomach still jumped with nerves, and my palm felt a little sweaty in his.

"Hey," he said, stopping in the middle of the sidewalk. Someone walked around us with a huff, but my eyes stayed glued to Wyatt's. The rest of the world melted away, leaving just the two of us. It was the strangest feeling. Something about the intensity of his expression, focused so completely on me, blocked out everything else. "If you're uncomfortable, I'll go back to the apartment. There's still a ton of casserole left, and I can see you later tonight."

And he would. He wouldn't even be hurt or angry about it. Disappointed, maybe. My casserole wasn't that good and who wants to sit at home alone on a Saturday night when they'd planned to go out? But if he turned around and walked back, I felt confident he'd greet me with a genuine smile when I returned to the apartment. Which was why I really wanted to spend the evening with him and my friends. To share a meal with every person who'd made me feel welcomed in this tiny town. It just wouldn't be the same without Wyatt.

I shook my head and gave his arm a tug. "Come on. Poppy gets hangry, so we better walk faster."

And shorten the time I had to worry that Cal or any of my friends would snarl at Wyatt like a guard dog. It wasn't his fault I was such a mess. If I'd been anyone else, they wouldn't blink at a guy like Wyatt. He oozed kindness, just like Lauren, which put everyone at ease around him. I'd seen it a million times at the café. Heck, I'd experienced it myself. Unlike Lauren, who chose to be kind despite the terrible start she had in life, Wyatt just was. What's more, he was trusting and genuinely assumed the best in people. I might not know much about his childhood, yet I imagine it wasn't anything like mine or Laurens's. The fact he worked two jobs without complaint to help his family spoke volumes about the relationship he had with them.

"I got to experience Poppy's hangry firsthand," Wyatt said with a smirk. "To be fair, I get hangry too."

"Let's hope we get food into you both before that happens," I said, resting my head on his shoulder as we quickened our pace to the corner. The music from Church spilled into the warm night with the sounds of laughter and loud conversations. Clearly, the place was packed as usual.

Six pairs of shocked eyes stared at us as we approached the tables that had been shoved together to accommodate my group of friends.

"Pay up," Lauren said, holding out her palm to Aiden.

He let out a groan but had a huge smile on his face. "Win-win for me." He took out his wallet and put a fifty-dollar bill in her hand before standing and gripping Wyatt's shoulder.

"Theo, Cal, you've met Wyatt before."

Theo nodded and waved. His height and muscles were enough to make him imposing. The tattoos, piercings, and black clothing simply added to his screw-off vibe, which was completely at odds with his personality. He was a tiger with the soul of a kitten. Theo had his arm wrapped around Poppy, whose screw-off vibe was real for most of society, but who was a sweetheart once she decided to like you.

"Hey, Wy," Poppy said. "Congrats on thawing the ice queen."

"Poppy," Rowan yelled. "She didn't mean that, Cam."

"Yeah, she did," I said.

Poppy smiled, melting her RBF and her sister's irritation.

"Thanks, Poppy," Wyatt said, squeezing my hand, perhaps as an apology for basically agreeing with Poppy's assessment.

"And Cal there," Aiden said, pointing to him, "will not give you a hard time because everyone else at the table is thrilled you're here with Cammie, and he will be too once he acknowledges that the rest of us are excellent judges of character, and he has no reason to get his boxers in a twist."

My heart squeezed as I watched my boss glare at Aiden and then give Wyatt a begrudging nod to acknowledge his presence. Though they couldn't be more different, Cal watched over me like my father had before he went to jail. Even without knowing all the details of my last relationship, giving Wyatt enough grace to get to know him would be a challenge for Cal. I only hoped Wyatt wouldn't get too defensive.

"Have a seat," Cal said, pointing to the single empty chair beside him, the one intended for me. I started toward Cal, but Wyatt pulled the chair to the end of the table and stood behind it until I took the hint and sat. He asked the group next to ours for their empty chair and carried it over to the empty space beside Cal.

Aiden let out a sigh and sat down next to Lauren. "Behave," he said, pointing at Cal.

Wyatt sat and pushed his chair in before twisting to face Cal. "Nice to see you," he said, holding out his hand.

Cal shook it and gestured toward the pitcher in the middle of the table. "Want a beer?"

"Sure," Wyatt said, and Cal poured him some into a plastic cup.

"Here," Poppy said, shoving a half-full margarita across the table to me. "These go down too fast, and I have a feeling you're going to need it more than I do."

Wyatt took a sip of beer and frowned ever so slightly before he set the cup on the table.

"Not a fan of IPAs?" Cal asked, not missing a thing.

"Love them," Wyatt said. "I'm just not use to hanging out with people who can afford them by the pitcher. I was expecting Nattie Lite."

"I can get you one of those," Aiden said, already raising his hand to get the server's attention.

Everyone except Lauren and Wyatt gave him an odd look, and I couldn't help but do the same.

"Put your hand down, A," Theo said. "You're not making the new guy drink piss beer while you drink the good stuff. This isn't a frat initiation."

"IPAs have high carbs," Lauren said. Her eyes widened, and she started reading the specials menu with more focus than a tiny slip of paper about Taco Tuesdays and Wings Wednesdays could ever require. Smooth, Lauren.

"This is fine, thank you," Wyatt said.

Cal looked at Wyatt with genuine curiosity. "You a bodybuilder?" he asked.

"What do you think?" Aiden said. "The guy has less than ten percent body fat."

It wasn't exactly a lie. Wyatt had an incredibly lean and muscular body, and Aiden had posed the bodybuilder comment as a question, not a statement.

"That's impressive," Cal said, and the tightness in my shoulders eased with the admiration in his tone. "I can't get below twelve. I don't have that kind of discipline, and my wife is a fantastic baker." He placed a kiss on Rowan's red hair, and she smiled at him before turning her attention to Wyatt.

"Just before you two got here, we were talking about how much we love hearing Cammie sing. Did you catch the open mic she did last summer?"

"No, but she sang a couple songs for me the other night. She's incredible." He sipped his beer, oblivious to the shocked looks around the table.

"That's great," Lauren said, recovering first. "Maybe you can help us convince her to sing at the open mic here next week."

I shot Lauren a glare. What happened to working me *up* to a twenty-person wedding with my nearest and dearest? She mouthed sorry and went back to the specials list, not looking the least bit contrite.

"Oh, that's a great idea," Rowan said, clapping her hands.

"Simmer down, you two," Poppy said, glaring at her sister and Lauren, who continued her perusal of the specials. "We're not pressuring Cammie to do something that makes her puke."

And that's why she was a great friend.

"As much as I'd love to hear you again," Cal said, looking at me, "I agree with Poppy."

Wyatt frowned. "Performing makes you so nervous you throw up?"

"Why don't we plan a barbeque or something," I said. "I'll sing for y'all then? Just y'all."

I'd been considering it since I sang for Wyatt without hurling. If I could perform in front of a man I found attractive, singing for my friends should be easy. Right?

My offer seemed to appease everyone, and the table filled with chatter about when and where we'd be having said barbeque. The group finally decided on next Sunday at Cal and Rowan's house. Before Cal could resume questioning Wyatt, the waitress came by and dropped off several platters of appetizers, including a plate of the fried pickles I loved but no one else ate, and two full pizzas. By the amount of food on the table, I wasn't surprised when she ran off without taking anyone's dinner order. I doubted she'd be back except to refill drinks. It wasn't uncommon for Aiden to order a ton of food and put it on his tab before anyone arrived. There was more than enough to feed everyone an entire meal, though all of it was breaded or filled with carbs.

Wyatt studied the food and excused himself, saying he was going to wash his hands. I assumed he was taking his shot in the bathroom. How many times a day did he have to fib to manage his blood sugar? Though he'd likely wash his hands as well. Like the whole bodybuilding comment, it was still a half truth. Across the table, Lauren and Aiden whispered together, probably realizing there wasn't anything healthy for Wyatt, which, considering they didn't know he was coming, made sense.

When Wyatt returned to the table, Cal looked at the food and frowned. "Feel free to order a salad or something, Wyatt. No one here will judge you."

I wanted to hug Cal. He might not be smiling at Wyatt like everyone else, but he wanted him to feel comfortable in the group.

"It's OK to have a cheat day," Wyatt said. "Sometimes, you just need fried food and beer."

"Cheers to that," Aiden said, pulling off a slice of pizza.

"Cam, take your nasty pickles," Poppy said, grabbing the plate of deep-fried goodness and shoving them toward me.

"I love those," Wyatt said, eyeing the plate. I set it down between us and before long, we were all enjoying the food and conversation. Cal asked Wyatt questions and watched him with the shrewdness of an FBI agent, but he stopped short of drilling the poor guy.

About an hour later, though, Wyatt and Lauren both looked at their phone. They exchanged a glance across the table. Wyatt smiled at her and put his phone back in his pocket. She frowned at him but returned to her conversation with Rowan about the bridesmaid dresses for Poppy's wedding, which apparently were going to be white.

"Everything all right?" I whispered.

"My sugar is a little high. It'll come down now that I'm done eating."

The conversations continued around us, but I noticed Wyatt wasn't speaking as often as he had been, and his face looked flushed and tired.

Though he'd only had one beer, anyone who didn't know he had diabetes could easily assume he'd had too much to drink. He poured himself a glass of water from the center of the table and chugged the entire thing in one gulp. I put my hand on his leg, and he flashed me a smile that didn't reach his eyes.

That's it.

"Wyatt and I are opening tomorrow," I said, reaching for my purse. "So, we should head home. How much do we owe?"

"Wyatt, how's the closet coming on the Fitzwilliam project?" Aiden asked. He sounded casual enough, but his eyes bore into Wyatt, assessing.

When I first met Aiden, he terrified me. His eyes were the same ice blue as Bishop's and just as calculating. Over time, I learned Aiden watched others not to learn their weaknesses or ways to manipulate them, but for opportunities to help and support them. He'd still been the last man in the group I'd grown to trust.

"We don't want to hear about your work, Studman," Poppy huffed. "And I doubt that conversation would be incentive enough to keep two people at dinner who want to go home and bang."

Rowan buried her face in her hands, but Theo, Lauren, and even Cal, laughed.

"If Wyatt answers my question, I can call this a business meal and put the whole thing on my company card."

"So," Poppy said, turning to Wyatt. "How's that closet coming?"

"I should finish it up by Tuesday," he said.

"Fantastic," Poppy said. "So glad you could join us, Wyatt."

"You're not paying for all this, Aiden," Theo said, glaring at him.

"Absolutely not," Cal echoed.

Knowing these three, this conversation could last longer than I was willing to let Wyatt suffer. "Thanks so much, Aiden," I said, standing.

"No problem," he said without taking his eyes from Wyatt. "You two need a ride home?"

"Nah, we're walking," Wyatt said, pushing back from the table. "Thanks, Aiden, and thank you all for letting me crash your dinner."

I looped my arm in Wyatt's and started pulling him toward the door even as everyone said their goodbyes.

"How high was it?" I asked as we stepped from the crowded bar onto the equally crowded sidewalk.

"I'm fine, Cam," he said, taking my hand and giving it a kiss.

"You don't look fine," I said, surprising myself. I'd never talked back to Bishop, and I held my breath, waiting for his response.

Wyatt gave me a small smile. "I'll be fine once I get a little more insulin and some painkillers. My head is pounding."

I dropped his hand and fumbled in my purse until I pulled out a bottle of ibuprofen. "Here," I said, shaking out a few. "Can you swallow them without water?"

He nodded, an amused expression on his face.

"What?" I asked as he swallowed the tablets.

"You like taking care of people."

"So do you."

He nodded. "Yeah, I guess I'm just not used to people taking care of me."

"I'd take care of you more if you'd let me."

"Angel, I'll let you do anything you want to me."

Now my face was flushed. "Oh my stars, Wyatt," I breathed. "You seem like this sweet guy, but you're positively feral."

"I enjoy sex," he said with a shrug. "And I really enjoy watching you come."

"Well, I enjoy that too." I stared at the sidewalk in front of me as we kept walking. I was afraid I'd do something totally inappropriate if I looked at him, like making out in the middle of Main Street while his blood sugar started wrecking his kidneys. Because of course I'd read up on all the terrible things that happen with high blood sugar. "But I'm a little worried."

He nudged me until I looked up at him. "Talk to me. If something is bothering you, I want to know."

"I'm nervous that we're moving too fast. Sleeping together is a big step in any relationship, and we live together. It's like we went from roommates to live-in boyfriend and girlfriend in one night."

He nodded. "It doesn't have to be that way."

"Oh," I said, feeling embarrassed. Maybe Wyatt only wanted something casual, and I'd gone and assumed he wanted to be in a relationship with me. *Because he said I love you.*

"It shouldn't take much longer for the mold abatement."

I'd forgotten about the dang mold excuse. "Um, yeah. Any day now."

"So we won't be living together for long." He cleared his throat. "Though it's been really nice sharing dinner with you every night."

"It has."

"Like I said before, Cam. You set the pace. If you want to stop being physical until you can move back to your place, that's what we'll do. It's your call. I'm just happy to be with you, even if all I get to do is hold your hand."

As if to prove his point, he brought my hand up to his lips and kissed it.

"Thank you," I said.

He flashed me a grin that made my stomach dip. "And now that I've faced Cal's inquisition, can I thank you for bringing me along tonight?" he asked.

"You're welcome. Cal warmed up to you faster than I expected. I'm sorry if he still seemed a little cold."

"I know it's nothing personal. He cares about you. They all do." His face became serious. "They just want you to be happy, and I bet they saw the same thing I did when you sang in front of them. It's really too bad you have stage fright. You're an amazing singer."

"I don't have stage fright," I said, which brought him to a complete stop on the sidewalk.

"Then why would singing in front of people make you sick?"

I'd never told anyone the reason, not even Lauren, but I wanted to tell Wyatt. I wanted him to understand all the experiences that had cut me into the woman I was today.

"I'll tell you after you've had your insulin."

He seemed concerned but nodded. I didn't like how exhausted he looked or how his eyes were unfocused. We hurried the rest of the way to Karma.

I followed him silently up the stairs to the apartment and back to his bedroom. "Can you check the app and tell me my blood sugar?" he asked, kneeling in front of the fridge.

"Yeah, sure," I said, opening it. "350."

"Fuck," he breathed, pulling out a vial filled with liquid. "You can stay if you want, but if you're afraid of needles, you might want to step out."

"I'm good." I was better than good. He was letting me watch him as he filled a syringe and prepped his skin for an injection. I wondered if Lauren and Aiden had ever watched him before, or if I'd just become the only person in his life that he'd allowed to see him like this.

His phone vibrated in my hand as a text from "Your Better Half" scrolled across the top of the screen.

> *Forgot to ask when RU coming home?*

I stared at the text, trying to make sense of it when another came through.

Your Better Half

> *Your boys miss you. And OK, so do I.*

My heart lodged in my throat. He'd told me he sent money home to his family, and I'd just assumed he meant his parents. "Um, Wyatt," I said as he tapped an air bubble from the needle. "Your Better Half would like to know when you're coming home to see your boys."

Chapter Twenty-One

Wyatt

CAMMIE'S SHOCKED EXPRESSION WOULD have made me laugh if I didn't feel like shit. Fucking Wade. Taken out of context, and with the nickname he'd given himself, it's no wonder Cammie's eyes had doubled in size.

"You're married?" she asked after a beat of silence.

"That's my twin," I said, pushing the needle into my stomach and depressing the plunger. "He changed his contact in my phone, and I never changed it back. It's a joke between us because we're identical. The boys he's talking about are our friends from high school who'll be leaving to go back to their colleges soon."

"You have an identical twin?" she asked, looking only slightly less surprised than when she thought I was married.

Had I really never mentioned Wade before? I nodded and rubbed my eyes. Everything looked slightly blurry. Hopefully, the insulin would kick in soon. "Mind if I lie down?"

I hated to ask, but it was better than falling on my ass.

"Of course," she said, taking my hand and pulling me toward the bed.

I locked my arm around her waist and brought us down onto the mattress together. She let out a yelp, then giggled and nestled against me.

"You look like you don't feel great," she said, lifting her beautiful face to study mine. No doubt I looked like a piece of shit.

"I'll be good in a bit," I said, kissing her forehead. She smelled amazing, I wanted to bury my face in her hair and just lay together until my blood sugar went down. Despite how crappy I felt, my body reacted to having her in my arms. I willed my dick to simmer. I didn't need to be poking her with a hard-on after she'd told me she was nervous to sleep together while she stayed in the apartment.

"Can I ask you a question?" she said softly, placing her hand on my chest.

"Of course."

"What makes him your better half?" She flashed me a huge smile, and I swear my fucking heart skipped a beat. "Cause I'm having a hard time imagining you as the dud half."

"His name is Wade."

"What makes Wade better?"

"He's funnier," I said, taking her right hand and kissing the palm. She sucked in a breath, and I smiled against her skin. "Has way more game than I do," I said, placing another kiss on her hand. "And is by far the toughest person I know."

I sat up and grabbed my phone from the edge of the bed where Cammie had dropped it when I tackled her. I thumbed through my pictures until I found one of Wade and me before handing it to her. Watching her face, I said, "He also has cerebral palsy and has worked his ass off to crush every limit he's ever faced. He recently got medically approved for a learner's permit. It took him years of PT to build up enough strength and mobility in one hand to get that clearance."

"He sounds amazing," she said, smiling at me.

"He is. I'd video call him now so you could meet him except he's on a date with his girlfriend. And texting me," I said, shaking my head. Wade might have more game, but he sure as hell could use some lessons on how to treat a woman after he'd snared her interest.

"Maybe tomorrow afternoon. I'd like you to meet my dad too. We schedule a call every Sunday evening."

"I'd like that."

She studied me for a moment and frowned. "You said you hadn't told your family you're diabetic. Why?"

"Because it's not that big a deal. Not compared with what Wade deals with every day. And now that I've told you about my better half, I believe you owe me an explanation for why you don't like to perform."

She laid her head back on my chest and nodded. "I get a lot of attention when I sing."

"Because you're amazing."

"Thank you," she said, blowing out a breath. "But three years ago, I performed at a local bar where I lived, and this guy hit on me afterwards."

"Bishop?"

She shook her head. "I was already with Bishop. We started dating when I was eighteen, and I was with him for three years."

My stomach ached as a feeling of dread washed over me. "What happened?"

"Maybe we should wait to talk about this. You're not feeling well, and I can hear your heart racing."

My heart wasn't racing. It was trying to fly through my rib cage. "Please, Cammie," I whispered. "Just tell me."

"OK, but try not to get upset. This happened three years ago, and I'm fine now. Well, minus the throwing up after performing part."

I tightened my grip around her and waited.

"So this guy hit on me after I performed. I turned him down easily enough, but Bishop got jealous. He always did whenever guys talked to me. I guess he felt really threatened by this particular one because when we got home, he broke my hand, so I couldn't play."

I wanted to throw up. The thought of someone hurting Cammie made my stomach drop and the corners of my eyes sting.

"My hand healed, thankfully." She held up the hand I'd kissed earlier and moved her fingers up and down like a wave.

She almost sounded chipper. Like she'd broken her hand slipping on ice and was relieved it'd healed well. Maybe because a broken bone was easier to heal than the pain of being hurt by someone she cared about.

"This was three years ago?" I asked, forcing my voice to sound calm.

"Yeah."

"How long ago did you leave him?"

She tensed in my arms. "Two years."

She stayed with him a full year after he'd broken her hand. I didn't know why it'd taken her so long to leave him, though I knew judging her for staying wouldn't help her now. "Did he hurt you any other time?"

She nodded against my chest, and my stomach soured more than the pickles I'd eaten. "Have you been in contact with him since you left?" I was trying so hard to keep it together, my voice sounded robotic.

"I've done everything I can to prevent that from happening. Recently, he might have learned about my PO Box in Jericho, so he might know the general area where I am." She lifted her head and looked at me, her cheeks pinking. "It's why I moved into the apartment. There isn't any mold in mine. I panicked when I thought Bishop might find me and called Lauren. She didn't want me living alone, and I wasn't willing to put her or Rowan or Poppy at risk. Bishop isn't a big guy. If I thought for a minute that you were in danger, I'd have told you sooner."

"Thank you for telling me now," I said.

"Wyatt," she breathed, moving up my body to brush my cheeks. I hadn't even felt the tears spilling from my eyes. "I'm OK."

"You're incredible," I said, placing my hand on her cheek and rubbing my thumb across her delicate skin. It killed me that someone had hurt her, and she still carried the mental scars long after her body healed. "*Te—*" I started but stopped myself.

"I Googled it," she said in a small voice. *"Te amo cada día más."*

My entire body tensed in the silence that followed. I waited for her to jump from my arms, to tell me I was crazy for even thinking I was in love with her. She didn't move. Her eyes locked with mine, unsure, yet she stayed in my arms.

"And you're still here," I said, brushing my hand down her long, soft hair.

"I'm still here," she said with a small smile.

Thank fuck for that. The words could wait. I didn't need them. She was here, safe with me, and I'd do everything I could to keep it that way.

"How are you feeling now?" she asked, handing me my phone.

"Better." I opened the monitoring app and showed her that my sugar levels have fallen closer to the normal range.

"Good," she said, taking my phone and putting it on the nightstand by the bed. "Because I was thinking now would be a good time for me to make my move."

CHAPTER TWENTY-TWO

Cammie

"Wait," Wyatt said, as I placed my hand on his face.

"I'm sorry," I said, sitting back. "You probably feel terrible still. I have no clue how long it takes insulin to kick in."

His eyes softened, and he grabbed my hand. "Last night was the best sex I've ever had, Cam. There are so many ways I'd like to have you, and I'm more than ready to spend the rest of the night tackling a few."

"But?"

"But," he said, rubbing his thumb across my hand, "I don't want you living alone. Not after what you told me. As much as I'd like to explore every inch of your body, it's more important to keep you safe."

"Are you saying you'd rather be roommates than sleep with me?"

He let out a groan and dropped my hand. "If those are my two choices, yes."

Every man I'd ever been with had lied to me. Some, like my first boyfriend, to get me into bed. I'd been fed lines, cheated on, and gaslit before I even met Bishop. He might have been the first to physically hurt me, but he wasn't the first to cause me pain. "You honestly think it's a good idea to sleep together and live together so soon?"

"I know it feels like we jumped ahead, and maybe we have, but it's also been a long time coming. At least for me. I've wanted you since the moment I laid eyes on you, and getting to know you this past year only strengthened my belief that you're it for me, Cam. I don't want anyone to hurt you again, including me. So if you think we're moving too fast, we'll keep things PG because making sure you're safe is more important."

Wyatt was either the best manipulator I'd ever known, or he genuinely cared. Every instinct I had told me it was the latter. But if Bishop taught me anything, it's that my instincts were crap. My brain spun through all the ways Wyatt could be playing me. He could be telling me what I wanted to hear to gain my trust and lower my resistance, knowing it'd be the fastest way to get me to sleep with him again. Saying he loved me didn't mean he did. My stupid heart thudded rapidly in protest because he'd said it in a language that he knew I didn't understand. Sure, I'd looked it up easily enough, but the worry on his face when I'd told him I understood what he'd said felt genuine.

Because he was genuine.

With my mind finally on board, I crawled across the bed to Wyatt. His chest moved in rapid bursts, and he kept his hands balled at his sides. As I drew closer, the tension in his body grew, his erection pressing hard against the front of his pants.

I paused before our lips touched, breathing in the moment. I'd never felt so desired by anyone. The gentle kiss I pressed to his lips was all the permission he needed to wrap his arms around me and flip me to the mattress beneath him. It happened so fast. One moment I was kneeling down to kiss him, the next he was above me, his hands yanking down the thin straps of my sundress and rocking his hard length against me.

"Just so you know," he said softly as he peppered kisses down my throat. "Last night was pretty tame."

My eyes widened both at the sensation of him sucking the delicate skin at the top of my breast and his words. "You didn't enjoy it?"

He looked up at me, his pupils blown so large only a slight ring of the warm brown remained. "I meant what I said. Last night was the best sex I've ever had. But if you're comfortable with me taking the lead now, I want to make you come so hard and often you lose count. I want to edge myself until I think I'll die if you don't milk my cock with that sweet pussy." He sucked in a breath and closed his eyes. When he opened them again, he looked more controlled. "If you want to stop, we stop. If something is too much, tell me. You're still in control. Say it."

If I wasn't so turned on, I'd have pointed out that his entire statement suggested he wanted me completely boneless with pleasure to the point my brain stopped working. Instead, my panties soaked through at his tone and I whispered, "I'm in control."

And that's when he lost it.

He pulled my dress down my body, his eyes lighting when he saw I hadn't been wearing a bra. I arched off the mattress when he sucked one of my nipples between his teeth and bit down lightly.

"Oh," I said, pleasure shooting straight to my core with such intensity I arched off the bed.

He lifted my hand to my other breast before taking his head from my hardened peak. "Play with your tits, Cam," he said. He grabbed my other hand and placed it on my breast. "Lie as still as possible while I make you come on my tongue."

With that, he slid my ruined panties down my legs and gave my center a long, slow lick. He groaned like he'd just had the first taste of the best ice cream in his life. He kissed me everywhere but my clit, which throbbed to the point of pain.

"Are you ready for your first orgasm?" he asked, before dipping his tongue inside me, only to pull back a moment later.

"Yes," I cried, my legs shaking with my impending release. "Make me come, Wyatt."

He attacked my clit, flicking and sucking relentlessly until I shattered. He grabbed the box of condoms I'd left on the nightstand and quickly tore off his clothes. His thick cock jutted up to his stomach, where his abs contracted with each labored breath.

"I'm going to fuck you until I get close, then pull out and finish you with my mouth. I want you to come for me as many times as you can, Angel."

I nodded and he rolled the condom on before positioning himself at my entrance. "Touch your clit," he said. "Your breasts are mine this time."

I lowered my hand between my legs, and he thrust into me as my fingers connected with my slick nub. He stilled a moment before rolling his hips, stretching me in the most delicious way before he lowered his mouth to my breast and sucked my nipple between his teeth again.

"Oh shit," I said as my orgasm built. My fingers flew across my clit until I was clenching around Wyatt as he continued to take me with languid thrusts.

His pace quickened as I started to come down, building me right back up again, but before I could tip over, he pulled out and put his head between my legs, thrusting his tongue into me while I continued working my clit. One of his hands reached up and twisted my nipple while the other pressed down on the sensitive skin just below my belly in time with his tongue.

I didn't stand a chance.

I came, gripping his hair with my free hand to hold him in place while wave after wave of pleasure crashed through me. As my legs relaxed around his head, he moved up my body and slid deep inside me before lowering his mouth to mine.

I could taste myself on his tongue as it caressed mine. Before I registered what was happening, he pulled out again. "I want to fuck you from behind," he said, flipping me over and lifting my ass in the air. He moved my body with such ease and speed, I felt dizzy. I'd barely registered his withdrawal before he slammed into me again, so deep I whimpered.

"You OK?" he asked stilling.

"Don't stop," I said, grinding against him. He pressed forward, his body flush with mine as he lowered his hand to my clit. My orgasm built and built until he pulled out again.

"No," I said, looking over my shoulder at him. "I want to come around your cock. I want you to stop holding back."

When he slid back into me, he groaned. "I don't want this to end."

My body tightened to the point of snapping as his pace quickened. My legs shook beneath me, ready to collapse. "Lie forward," he said, his voice hoarse.

When I lowered myself further, he hit a spot inside me that made my vison narrow. "Wyatt," I said, surprised by the desperation in my voice. I felt like I was going to pass out I was breathing so hard, and my orgasm was building with an intensity that scared me.

"Give me one more," he commanded, tipping me over the edge.

I screamed into the pillow as my pussy gripped his cock. He swelled inside me and came with a roar.

"Fuck, Cam," he said, panting against my back. He pulled out gently and helped me from the bed.

When both our feet were firmly on the carpet, he wrapped me in a tight hug.

I rested my head on his chest, so his heart pounded against my ear. "Say it, please."

"*Te amo.*"

My eyes burned. "I've never felt this way before," I said as I tightened my arms around him. "And it terrifies me. Promise you'll be patient."

"Always," he said, placing a gentle kiss on the top of my head. "I'd do anything for you, Cammie."

I nodded against his chest before I lifted my eyes to his. "How long would you have kept going if I hadn't told you to let go?" I asked, hoping to lighten the mood.

"I was aiming for a couple more. I only got four orgasms out of you."

"I don't think six is possible," I said.

He smirked as if accepting the challenge, and I had a feeling we wouldn't be getting much sleep before we opened Karma in the morning.

Chapter Twenty-Three

Wyatt

"So, before we video call my dad, I need to tell you a couple things." Cammie shifted on the couch beside me, clearly nervous.

I nodded and took her hand. She gripped my fingers tightly, sat up straighter, and looked me in the eyes. "My father is serving a life sentence in South Carolina, so we'll be calling him in prison."

OK. Not what I was expecting her to say. I figured she was going to prepare me like she had for meeting Cal, and I'd assure her I could handle an overprotective father as well as I had her overprotective boss. I wanted to know what her dad had done to land a life sentence, but I wasn't sure that was something I should ask or she'd even answer.

"Your face has no filter," she said, trying not to laugh. "I'm sure you have questions. Let me give you the basics, then you can ask me anything you want. Just try to listen without judging, OK?"

"I can do that," I said, my stomach jumping with nerves. No matter how open-minded I tried to be, if she told me he'd done something violent, I wasn't sure my face could stay neutral. All bets were off if he'd hurt kids or animals.

"So, South Carolina has this thing called the three-strikes law," she said. "If someone is convicted three different times of certain offensives, they get a life sentence."

Meaning her dad was a repeat offender. I did my best not to react to the news.

"Before I was born, my dad went away twice for cooking and distributing meth," she continued.

On one hand, that was a lot less scary than a serial killer or rapist, but WTF. I couldn't imagine how different her childhood must have been from mine.

"You're judging," she said, frowning at me.

"I'm trying really hard not to," I said, blowing out a breath. "I'm sorry. This is just so outside anything I've experienced before."

She gave me a soft smile. "You had a great childhood, didn't you?"

"Yeah," I said, gripping my neck. "My parents always made sure Wade and I had everything we needed. I know they'd give us the world if they could, and they were always generous with their time."

Cammie nodded. "My parents were the same. After his second stint, Daddy got clean, met and married my mother, and they had me. He worked as a mechanic until my mom died, and for the first ten years of my life I had a childhood a lot like yours. We weren't rolling in money, but our home was filled with love." She smiled and showed me the photo on her lock screen. A woman, who looked like a carbon copy of Cammie with brown hair and slightly darker blue eyes, held her blonde mini-me on her lap while a man with blond hair wrapped them both in a hug. "These are my parents."

"You look just like your mom," I said.

Cammie nodded and her eyes turned sad. "For a long time after Mom passed, I think it hurt Daddy to look at me. He stopped spending as much time with me when he was home and started using again. Eventually, he lost his job, which was scary enough. Then he fell back into old habits and started cooking."

"With you in the house?" I asked, my voice rising. I know I'd promised not to judge without hearing all the facts, but anyone who'd put their kid in that kind of danger didn't deserve the consideration.

Cammie shook her head. "Even when he was at his lowest, he protected me fiercely. He'd have never put me in danger like that. We lived on an old farm in a rural area outside Charleston. He used one of the old outbuildings to cook and never let me anywhere near it."

Father of the year.

Cammie let out a sigh. "You're judging again."

"Kind of hard not to," I said. "I'm sure he was devastated when he lost your mom, but you lost her too. He owed it to both of you to keep it together. Who took care of you when he went to prison?"

She sat up straighter and her eyes hardened. "I love my father dearly, and if you're going to look at him like he's less than, I don't want you with me when I call him."

There was a fierceness in her eyes I'd never seen before, and I realized that whether or not he deserved it, Cammie's dad had her unconditional love and devotion. "I'm sorry," I said, giving her hand a squeeze. "Please go on."

"When I was twelve, he was arrested. I'm not naïve. I know he broke the law and what he did hurt people. He deserved to serve time. However, if we'd been in a state that didn't have the three-strike system, he'd have faced less than ten years for all the charges. Instead, the judge handed down a life sentence, even though there'd been over a decade between his second and third charges."

"Where did you go after he went to jail?" I asked again.

"Foster care," she said softly. "I won't sugarcoat it. The years I spent as a ward of the state were not ideal. Lauren and I bonded so quickly when I moved here because we'd both been foster kids and understood each other without having to go into the details of our pasts."

"I can't even imagine what that must have been like. For either of you." I rubbed my thumb across her hand, and she gave me a small smile.

"I kind of like that you can't. Your lack of baggage is refreshing. Even if I envy you a little."

"It just means I'm better able to help with yours. Whenever you're ready."

"Well, brace yourself. This is where my story gets scary. As hard as the system was, aging out of it was even harder."

If what she'd just told me was the easy part, I was afraid to hear the rest. But if she could live it, the least I could do was listen. "Go on," I said, wishing I could pull her into my lap and protect her from everything, even her memories.

"I was barely keeping a roof over my head working minimum wage jobs. That's when I met Bishop. His brother is serving time at the same prison as Daddy. We kept meeting during visitations. He was charming and offered me more stability than I'd had since my mom died."

In other words, he preyed on her when she was vulnerable.

Cammie blew out a breath. "What I'm about to tell you, I've never told anyone except my dad."

I felt sick after hearing all the things she'd survived, yet my heart beat a little faster knowing she'd chosen to share something with me she hadn't even told Lauren.

"I did something really bad," she said in a small voice.

"Whatever it was, I won't judge you." And fuck, I hoped I didn't. My track record in this conversation hadn't been the best. But this was Cammie. I couldn't imagine her doing something so terrible I wouldn't be able to look at her the same.

"I stole fifty thousand dollars from Bishop when I left him," she said in a rush.

My first thought was holy shit, that's a lot of money. My second thought was how did she do it? What came out of my mouth was, "Good."

Her eyes widened and a ghost of a smile tugged at her full lips. "Not the reaction I was expecting," she said.

"The asshole broke your hand because he was jealous. Even if you took every cent he had when you walked, it wouldn't be enough."

"Well, I have no idea how much more he had. I just took all the cash I could find."

Now it was my turn to gape at her. "Who keeps fifty grand in cash lying around?"

"People who don't earn it legally," she said. "Which is why I'm sure he never reported me to the police. I'd avoided any details about what he did for a living because I didn't want to know. I doubt there was a record of the money, so he couldn't claim it was stolen. Still, I've been saving every penny I could since I came to Peace Falls because I plan to pay him back."

"Paying him back would be breaking his hand." The sentence was in my mind and out of my mouth before I even registered the thought.

She shook her head. "I don't want revenge on Bishop. I'm telling you all this because I don't want to hide what I did from you. It's the reason Bishop is looking for me, and the last piece of my past I haven't put behind me. Well, not counting my father. I'll never leave him behind."

"So, do I get to meet him now?" I asked.

She glanced at the time on her phone and nodded. "Just one more thing. Daddy knows Bishop hit me, but I never told him anything specific. It wouldn't change what happened and it'd only upset him, so please don't tell him about my hand."

While she clicked around to connect the call, an endless stream of questions ran through my head. What had she done with the money she stole?

Could she really be certain Bishop only wanted money and not her? What had finally given her the courage to leave him? And finally, what did it mean that she'd told me about her hand and not her dad?

A second window appeared beside the image of us on Cammie's phone, and a man who looked to be in his forties or fifties popped into view.

"Millie," he said, smiling. When he noticed me, his grin fell, and he narrowed his eyes, which were the same crystal blue as Cammie's.

"Daddy," Cammie said, "I'd like you to meet Wyatt."

"Who the fuck are you?" he asked.

Cammie's mouth dropped opened. "Daddy!"

I glanced at Cammie, unsure how she wanted to define whatever it was we were and also a bit thrown by him calling her a different name.

"For fuck's sake, it's not a hard question," he said, getting pissed.

"I'm the guy who will do everything he can to make sure your daughter is happy and safe," I said. Unlike you, asshole.

His eyebrows raised slightly, and he dipped his chin in a quick nod. "Well then, it's nice to meet you. You can call me Gibs."

Cammie buried her face in her hand that wasn't holding the phone. "Sorry, Wy," she mumbled.

I smiled at Gibs so he'd know I was friendly, even if it was a little forced. "No apology needed."

"So," Cammie said, dropping her hand, "this is Wyatt and as you can tell, he's very easygoing."

"What do you do for a living, Wyatt?" Gibs asked.

I'd been grilled by dads before, which was apparently the same whether I was in a living room picking up a date or video calling a prison. "I have a full-time construction job, and I work part time at Karma. Cammie and I are on the same shifts."

"But he's going back to school to get a degree in architecture," Cammie added.

"Someday," I said. "I was diagnosed with type 1 diabetes last year, and it's been an adjustment, both physically and financially."

Cammie looked momentarily stunned before she smiled at me. I'd shocked myself a little. Maybe I'd told Gibs because Cammie had already shared so much about him, and it felt wrong to know the guy's criminal record before he'd learned my name. Or I just wanted to prove to him I had nothing to hide (at least from him). Either way, a guy in South Carolina now knew more about my health than my family.

Gibs nodded approvingly and said, "Sounds like you've got a good head on your shoulders and a strong work ethic. No doubt you'll get that degree."

He sounded so much like Cammie, I smiled. She must have gotten her optimism from him. It made me feel a little guilty for judging the guy. "Thank you, sir."

"You must be pretty important to Millie if she wanted to introduce you to me."

"I hope so," I said. "Cammie's the most incredible woman I've ever known. It took over a year for her to give me a chance, and I'm not wasting it."

He laughed and shook his head. "Oh shit, you sound like me when I met Millie's mom. But I guess you call her Cammie like everyone else there."

"Yeah," I said, pulling on my neck. "I hadn't realized it wasn't her name."

Cammie's father rubbed his chin. "Guess you don't know much about her."

I know some things you don't.

Cammie rolled her eyes at her dad. "My name is Camila, after my mom. She went by Cammie, and when I moved here, I started going by it too. I like hearing her name."

"Me too, sweetheart," Gibs said with a sad smile.

"And Wyatt knows about Bishop. He even knows about the money I stole."

Gibs's eyes hardened, making him look every inch a guy serving a life sentence. "Did you tell him why you took the money?"

Cammie shot me an apologetic look. "I guess I forgot to tell him that part."

Gibs shook his head. "My dear daughter didn't think the public defender was doing a good enough job on my appeal, so she went and took money from that asshole to hire a hotshot lawyer. Not that it did any good."

Cammie glared at him. This had obviously been a sore subject between them for a while. "Hey, they got further than anyone else. I'm confident we can get your sentence reduced if we get another appeal. We just ran out of money. I'm not backing down."

All the bits of information she'd given me slotted together like puzzle pieces. "Is that why you finally left Bishop?" I asked. "You wanted to help your dad, but you knew Bishop would hurt you if he found out about the money?"

She nodded.

"You leaving him was worth every penny of that money," Gibs said. "But I don't want you saving up for another appeal or to pay that jackass back. I'm here because of the things I did, and he owes you for the things he did. Wyatt, you know he's looking for her, right?"

"I do. I promise I'll do everything I can to keep her safe."

Gibs frowned. "You can't be with her all the time."

"He's staying with me in Lauren's apartment until I'm confident Bishop can't find me."

My stomach dropped to my feet. I expected Cammie's dad to go ballistic after hearing I was shacking up with his daughter. Instead, he let out a relieved breath.

"Good. I'll sleep better knowing you're looking after her, Wyatt."

In the span of a few minutes, I'd gone from "who the fuck are you?" to him approving of me living with his daughter. "Um, thanks."

Gibs smirked. "Yeah, kid. You're OK. Millie might have a terrible read on the guys she likes, but I don't."

Cammie practically melted into the sofa beside me. I wished I knew whether she'd been nervous about getting her dad's approval because she wanted him to like me or because she trusted his intuition better than her own.

"Has Todd bothered you again?" she asked. "That's Bishop's brother," she added to me.

Gibs shook his head. "I don't know whether to be happy about that or not. He could be leaving me alone because I beat the shit out of him or—"

"He already has what he needs," Cammie said in a small voice.

Gibs nodded.

"What if you told Todd I wanted to pay Bishop back? We could set up a bank transfer or something, and I'd never have to see him."

Hell no. I couldn't see a scenario where opening the lines of communications with Bishop would be positive for Cammie. I also didn't think she owed him a dime.

"No, Millie," Gibs said in a stern voice. "That's not up for discussion."

Cammie blew out a breath but didn't fight him.

I liked her dad more every minute I spent with him, though I figured it was time to give the two of them space to talk without me. "Sir, I assume you'd like some time with just your daughter. If you don't have any more questions for me, I'm going to give the two of you some privacy."

Gibs studied me for a moment. "You always this thoughtful or just when you're trying to get in someone's good graces?"

"Always," Cammie said, flashing me a smile that made me feel ten feet tall.

"Well, nice to meet you, Wyatt," Gibs said.

"You as well," I said before I waved goodbye and headed down the hallway to my room.

Cammie's soft voice moved into her room, where she shut the door. I'd have given anything to be a fly on that wall. And I realized it was more than wanting to hear what Cammie and her father said about me. With so many revelations in one evening, I couldn't help but wonder what else Cammie could be hiding.

CHAPTER TWENTY-FOUR

Cammie

WHEN I ARRIVED AT the PT office Monday morning, Cal and Skye were already inside. Both of them looked at the door when I opened it like they'd been waiting for me. Cal hadn't beaten me to the office since I moved in with Wyatt because I no longer had to wait in line at Karma for my morning caffeine fix. Lauren handed me a latte on my way out the door whether or not I asked for it. Skye ran over for some love before I even put my coffee down.

"Hey baby," I said, bending to give her a belly rub and placing my cinnamon toast latte on my desk.

"I owe you an apology," Cal said, shoving his hands in his scrub pockets. "At least Rowan says I do."

I laughed. Cal could be emotionally clueless sometimes, though in this case, his wife likely had a different take on his gruff behavior toward Wyatt Saturday night.

"You're fine," I said, giving Skye's belly a final pat before I straightened. "I know you're just looking out for me."

"Yeah," Cal said with a frown. "Aiden gave me a hard time too after y'all left, which is ironic since I've seen him do far worse to the guys who dated his sisters. Hell, I've seen him give his brothers-in-law a hard time more often than I can count."

"He likes Wyatt."

Cal nodded. "I'm guessing Aiden knows Wyatt has diabetes?"

I gaped at him.

"Come on, Cam. I've worked with a lot of diabetics. I know the guy didn't flat-out lie to me since I'm the one who came up with the body-builder question, and Aiden kept me on that track, but as the night went on, it became obvious."

"It did?"

Cal shrugged. "Maybe not to everyone. I noticed he got way more flushed than he should have after one beer and dinner. Also, I might have caught a glimpse of the blood sugar monitoring app on his phone when he checked it."

"It's not something he likes telling people."

"Yeah," Cal said, taking his hands from his pockets and scrubbing them down his face, "that's what worries me. Any guy who thinks he has to hide something like that must have a fragile ego, which means he'll expect you to fluff it, and he'll never treat you the way you deserve."

I put my hands on my hips and glared at him. "You've only spent one evening with Wyatt. How could you possibly conclude that? He's not required to shout out his personal health information to every person he meets."

"Obviously," Cal said. "But he could have avoided feeling like shit by the end of the night if he'd taken either of the opportunities we gave him to order more appropriately for his condition."

I couldn't argue with that. There were dozens of other drinks Wyatt could have chosen with lower carbs than an IPA, and Cal had told Wyatt no one would judge him if he ordered a salad. But that would have meant singling himself out. "He doesn't like to make a fuss."

"Doesn't like to make a fuss, or doesn't want to appear weak?"

I could count on one hand the number of times Cal had truly pissed me off, and every one of them was because he misread a person or situation. "Caleb Cardoso," I said, which was usually how I started a chewing out with him. "I've known more than my share of men who make others feel smaller, so they can feel bigger. Wyatt is not one of them. If anything, he's got guilt issues that keep him from complaining about his health or even drawing attention to it."

The wrinkle that always formed between Cal's eyes whenever he worried smoothed. Cal, Theo, and Aiden had each carried loads of survivor's guilt after the car crash that killed the fourth member of their friend group. "Did he lose someone?" he asked quietly.

I shook my head. "He's an identical twin, and his brother has cerebral palsy. Wyatt doesn't think his diabetes is anything to talk about compared with what his twin faces every day. He hasn't even told his family, including his brother. He's never told me straight out he feels guilty for being 'the healthy twin' but it fits. And yes, there could be some fear about people judging him as weak. It can be pretty debilitating, but he's been really open with me about it since I found out."

Cal blew out a breath. "Now I feel bad for the guy. I'm sorry. For how I treated him on Saturday and for being too quick to judge him. I just don't want you to get hurt. Things between the two of you seem to be progressing fast. And the fact you're living together makes it serious by default."

"Living together temporarily." The stab of disappointment surprised me. I'd been so proud to have a place of my own when I settled in Peace Falls. My tiny apartment was my sanctuary, and I never questioned if I was happy living alone. Yet the past few weeks living with Wyatt had been incredible. I hadn't felt this happy since my mom died. But eventually, enough time would pass that I'd feel comfortable Bishop hadn't found me, and I'd have to move back to my apartment. We'd only shared a bed a few nights, yet the thought of spending less time with Wyatt made me incredibility sad.

"Any idea when your mold problem will be fixed?" Cal asked.

I hated lying to him. I half considered spilling the entire story about Bishop. Instead, I just said, "You have nothing to worry about."

Which could very well be a lie too.

He frowned, which likely meant he had a hunch I was hiding something from him. "You've never told me about your life before Peace Falls, but whatever happened, I just don't want it to happen again."

Me either. Despite my track record of poor judgment with romantic partners, I couldn't even imagine Wyatt hurting me intentionally. "Wyatt is incredibly kind, Cal. You should be more worried I'll hurt him. I'm the one with baggage."

Cal shrugged. "Everyone has baggage."

"Not everyone is broken like I am. Or like you were."

He nodded. He'd come a long way in the last year, and I'd loved watching every forward step he'd made. It was downright inspiring. It also meant he could commiserate with me better than most.

"I'll admit, I'm a little scared," I said, softly. "Wyatt's a good man, and I could easily see myself falling in love with him. I might already have. I just don't know if my past is too much." Because it might not be the past.

He smiled at me for the first time since I walked through the door. "Well, like you told me, when you know, you know."

I may have told him that when he was about to blow things with the love of his life because I trusted Cal's instincts more than mine. When he said he was in love with Rowan, there was no reason not to believe him. But my definition of love was warped. I thought I was in love with Bishop and every guy I dated before him. I've been in love so many times, hurt so many times, it's hard to trust myself and my feelings for Wyatt.

"I don't care if he's the greatest man on earth," Cal said. "If he ever makes you uncomfortable, call me. Anytime."

My lip trembled unexpectantly. "Thank you," I said, my voice thick with emotion. "You have no idea how much that means to me. How much you mean to me."

Because when you got down to it, I loved Cal like a brother. He'd proven time and time again that he had my back. He was the first man since my dad who made me feel safe, and I'd never take him for granted.

"Shit, Cam," he said, pulling me into a hug. "Don't cry. We have a new patient in five minutes, and if her first impression is me making you cry, she's going to turn around and leave."

"OK," I said, sucking in a breath and giving him a hard squeeze before I stepped back.

Skye sprinted over for a snuggle and by the time the first patient arrived a few minutes later, I'd finished my lukewarm latte and gotten myself under control. Before I knew it, Thad arrived for his final therapy appointment. My spine stiffened as soon as he walked through the door. Cal called him back immediately, even though Thad had arrived ten minutes early. After putting him on the table farthest from me and setting him up with heat therapy, Cal finished with his patient, barely pausing to write chart notes between appointments.

I remained tense while he and Thad worked in the center of the room. Without looking up, I could feel Thad's eyes on me whenever he faced my desk. When Cal moved him to the treadmill by the window for his cardio, I let out a relieved breath.

Cal headed to my desk with Skye as soon as he'd programmed Thad's workout. "I need to chart," he said. "Will you be OK out here?"

"Yes, go get your work done," I said.

Cal glanced over his shoulder at Thad. "Skye, stay," he said and went into his office, leaving the door open.

The amount of effort Cal made to make sure I was comfortable at work was embarrassing. I was mad at Bishop for making me so afraid and mad at myself for allowing him to affect my life still. I stabbed at my keyboard as I cleared out my inbox, and soon enough, my focus shifted to the mountain of tasks required to run the practice smoothly.

"So," Thad said, so close I jumped. "This is my last session."

I looked up from my computer and found him leaning on my desk. "Congratulations," I said, sounding more annoyed than celebratory. Cal was on the phone in his office, and Skye had fallen asleep at my feet. I could get their attention easily enough, but I felt more pissed than paralyzed.

"Maybe I can have your number now that I'm not a patient."

As if that was the sole reason I hadn't accepted his advances. "I'm not interested," I said, shocking myself with how firm I sounded.

Skye's ear twitched, but she kept her head on her paws.

"Come on. Don't be like that. I've seen the way you watch me."

Like a lamb watches a lion.

"You're making me uncomfortable," I said. "If you're done with your session, you need to leave."

His eyes widened, and he took a step back, holding up his hands. "Sorry, didn't mean to upset you."

I almost said it. The words were on the tip of my tongue. *That's OK.* Don't make him mad. Smooth over the awkwardness. Instead, my silence made him shift on his feet.

"I'll just go then," he said, shuffling toward the door.

The moment it closed behind him, Cal started slow clapping from the doorway to his office. Skye bolted awake before rolling over on her back for tummy rubs.

"That was awesome," Cal said, crossing the room to my desk. "I take back everything I said about Wyatt. I've been trying to get you to stand up for yourself for years. A couple weeks with him, and you're a complete badass."

"I wouldn't call me a badass," I said, feeling my cheeks heat.

He smiled. "Call it whatever you want, and I hope you won't take this as condescending, but I'm proud of you, Cam."

I smiled at him because the truth was, I was proud of myself too.

CHAPTER TWENTY-FIVE

Wyatt

DR. HUANG LOOKED AT his laptop and frowned. I knew I'd been having issues regulating my blood sugar since I started working for Aiden full time, and seeing the concern on my endocrinologist's face confirmed it.

"Your numbers are all over the place, Wyatt," he said, looking up from the screen.

"I know," I said with a sigh. "Ever since I started doing manual labor, I'm having a hard time figuring out how many calories I need not to crash. So, I've been trying to take less insulin, but that's making me run high."

"Well, that explains why your ketones are elevated," he said. "Have you been testing for them at home?"

I nodded. "I've been watching to make sure they didn't get dangerously high. My blood sugar went so low once I completely lost it. There's an entire chunk of time gone from my memory. I don't want that to ever happen again, so I've been running high on purpose. It might make me feel crappy, but at least I'm not passing out."

Dr. Huang shook his head. "You might feel the low blood sugar swings more in the moment than the highs, but you're damaging your body either way. Every time you have sustained high blood sugar you risk damaging your liver, your heart, you name it. And that's not even the worst of it. Even if you're testing your ketones, diabetic ketoacidosis can happen quickly, and it can be fatal."

I gripped the crinkly paper on the exam table as his word sank in. "It's just really hard with the type of work I do."

Dr. Huang shook his head. "That's not an excuse, Wyatt. Don't let the choices you make today ruin your chances of living a full life later. I've had patients go blind, lose limbs, and go into kidney failure. I've also had patients manage their condition so well, they're healthier than most of their non-diabetic peers. You're fortunate to live in a time where we have tools like insulin pumps. I strongly recommend you get one."

"I just can't swing one yet."

"Make it a priority. In the meantime, get a better handle on your blood sugar before you do serious damage to yourself."

I thanked him as he stood to leave. He stopped in the doorway of the exam room, his hand on the frame. "I lost a patient very much like you several years ago," he said in a low voice. "He was young and strong, but he didn't manage his blood sugar well. He gave me excuses until he slipped into a coma and died. So forgive me for being harsh. I promise it's for your own good. I want to see you in a week and then twice a month until we get your levels under control."

"Yes, sir," I said as his words settled like lead in my stomach. Of course, I'd read a ton about the risks of uncontrolled blood sugar, but hearing my doctor had experienced someone my age dying from it was sobering. It still didn't give me a clue what I should do about it.

By the time I arrived at Karma, I felt drained. Cammie took one look at me and abandoned the customer at the counter who was trying to buy a stack of new releases.

"What's wrong?" she asked, taking my hand.

My phone buzzed in my pocket because, of course, my blood sugar had tanked from the stress of the doctor's visit. I reached into the cooler and grabbed a juice. "I'm good, Angel. You can finish helping the customer."

She yanked Lauren's stool over to the register and glared at me until I took a seat beside her. After she'd finished with the customer, she placed her hand gently on my arm.

"You look worried," Cammie said.

"I'm fine," I said, holding up my phone where I'd been watching my blood sugar rise at a snail's pace.

"Your hair is dry. You didn't come from a job site."

"You don't miss a thing," I said, winking at her. "I had an appointment with my endocrinologist."

"I'm guessing it didn't go well," she said. Other than Lauren, and occasionally Aiden, I wasn't used to people worrying about me. I was conflicted by the concern on her face. It bothered me that I'd upset her, but I felt an undeniable warmth in my chest because it showed she cared about me.

I wrapped my arm around her waist and pulled her closer. Despite waking up beside her, it felt like we'd been separated for weeks. "I missed you today."

"I missed you too," she said with a frown. "And I'd really like to know what's wrong."

I rubbed my forehead. "I'm not managing my blood sugar well."

"No shit."

I stared at her. Cammie rarely cursed. Some of the expressions she used instead were downright hilarious. "Ms. Gibson," I said, laying my palm on my chest as though she'd shocked me.

Her eyes turned sad. "You've terrified me too many times lately to tiptoe around it."

"Fair." She started running her fingers through my hair, her touch soothing. I wanted to carry her upstairs and forget about ketones and comas. Though more than her body, I wanted Cammie's heart. Ignoring my problems and keeping her in the dark was no way to get it. "The doctor wants me to get an insulin pump. The problem is they're crazy expensive, and I want to help Wade get the van he needs."

"Wants," she said, tipping my chin up to meet her eyes.

I shook my head. "It's more than a want. Having a van he can drive himself would make him so much more independent."

"Which is something he wants. Controlling your blood sugar is something you need, Wyatt."

"I just have to be more careful and react faster when my levels change. People managed diabetes for generations without a pump. So can I."

"Maybe you should ask Wade what he thinks," she said, raising her eyebrow.

"You know I can't do that. I'd have to tell him everything. He's dealing with enough. He doesn't need to worry about me."

"Well, that doesn't seem very fair to Wade," she said, narrowing her eyes.

"Exactly. It's not fair that he has to deal with so many obstacles."

"And you don't," she said, softly. "I've never met Wade, so maybe I'm completely off base here, but would he take your money if he knew you needed a pump?"

I shook my head. "Which is why I haven't told him or my parents. After I help buy the van, I'll start saving for the pump."

"Which will delay when you can go back to college and potentially damage your body. How much is a pump?"

"Anywhere from five to ten grand, plus another three to six thousand every year in supplies."

"Oh," she said. "Wow, that's really expensive. And I'm guessing the van is as well."

I nodded.

"I could loan you the money," she said, worrying her lip.

"You're saving that money for a reason. Besides, Lauren and Aiden already offered, and I said no. I don't like owing anyone."

"I'm not just anyone. Am I?"

The doubt in her eyes broke me. I stood and took her face in my hands. My heart thudded in my chest. I'd told her I loved her several times, but never in English. The words were the same to me no matter what language I used, and while Cammie may have looked up the translation, I hoped hearing them in her native tongue would erase any lingering doubts she had. "You, Camila Gibson, are the woman I'm head over heels in love with," I said, running my thumb over her cheek. "But I'm not borrowing money from you or anyone. I'll just be more careful, OK?"

Her eyes filled with tears, and she nodded. She gripped the front of my shirt, her shoulders tense.

She wasn't ready to say it, yet she'd clung to me instead of running. "I love you," I said, kissing her forehead. I pulled her into a hug, burying my face in her neck.

"Hey, *Novato!*"

When I lifted my head from Cammie's shoulder, I found my foreman Sam weaving through the bistro tables toward the counter.

"Can't call me that here," I said, reaching across the counter to give him a fist bump. "I'm a seasoned barista. Sam, this is Cammie. Cammie, this is my foreman, Sam."

"Now, I see why you kept working here." Sam smiled at her.

Cammie blushed but straightened as though the word "work" had reminded her where we were. "Can I get you something?"

"Maybe in a minute," he said, his eyes pinging around the café.

He looked on edge, which was never an adjective I'd use to describe Sam. Sure, he got tense whenever we ran behind, but he looked downright jittery.

"What's going on?" I asked.

He cleared his throat and pulled his phone from his pocket. "I'm meeting a blind date."

I looked around the café. The only person sitting alone was a guy old enough to be my *abuelito*. "Doesn't look like they're here yet."

Just then, Maddie, the woman who'd shoved juice down my throat, pushed through the café door.

"Fuck," Sam muttered, staring.

"Hey," Maddie said to me as she headed for the counter. "How have you been feeling?"

Sam shot me a look full of questions I ignored. "Good to see you again," I said.

Cammie walked around the counter and pulled Maddie into a hug. The young woman's eyes widened, suggesting they weren't on a hugging basis, but softened when Cammie whispered something in her ear.

"Maddie, this is my friend, Sam," I said when they broke apart. "He's here to meet a blind date. You wouldn't be meeting someone too?"

I figured there was a 50/50 chance they were at Karma to meet each other, whether they knew it or not. Judging by their shocked expressions, I'd say my assumption wasn't off base. They stared at each other, neither blinking for so long, I worried for their eyeballs. Cammie walked back around the counter, and together we watched whatever silent exchange was happening between them.

"Why did you use a fake picture?" Sam asked, finally snapping out of it.

"Dude," I said, shaking my head. Maddie was one of those conventionally attractive women most men would fall over themselves to date. She probably looked better in real life than whatever picture Sam had seen.

"I'm in med school," she said with a shrug. "I didn't want to put my picture online."

"So you just catfish people?"

"I use a picture of my cousin, with her permission. We look similar. Besides, you have a beard in your photo."

Sam gripped his bare chin. "Yeah, I do, don't I?"

I looked between them, trying to understand the issue when something clicked. "You're Aiden's little sister," I said to Maddie.

"Technically, no," she said. "We grew up next door to each other."

"And he treats you like a sister," Sam said, blowing out a breath. "I'm sorry, but this isn't going to work."

Maddie put her hands on her hips. "Because of Aiden?"

"Yes," Sam said. "I'd like to keep my job."

"Unbelievable," she said before spinning on her heels and storming out of the café.

"Aiden's a great boss," Sam said as the door shut behind his almost-date, "but damn, I wish he wasn't mine right now."

"Pretty sure he's more bark than bite," I said, thinking back to the conversation I'd had with Aiden the night Maddie saved my ass. I was certain he'd come upstairs to fire me. Instead, he kept me company while I ate dinner and offered to buy me a pump, which I declined. I finally asked if I still had a job. He said of course, and we spent the rest of the time shooting the shit about football.

"I agree," Cammie said.

Sam shook his head. "Not when it comes to his family. I've seen him throw down too many times to believe that."

"Aiden?" I asked.

Sam shrugged. "He's calmed down a lot since he got with Lauren, but the man has a temper."

"What kind of temper?" I asked. It's not that I didn't know some men hit their partners. Hearing Cammie's stories and watching her continue to struggle to move past the pain Bishop inflicted on her, had me wary that a guy with a short fuse, even one I liked and respected, was in a relationship with Lauren.

Sam threw his head back and laughed. "Shit, Wy, you look just like him when he gets all protective. Not the kind of temper you have to worry about for Lauren. He'd rather cut off his arm than hurt a woman."

"He's right," Cammie said. "Aiden's one of the good ones."

"Wyatt's one of the good ones too," Sam said, winking at her.

Cammie wrapped her arm around my waist. "I know."

Sam shot me a shit-eating grin. The guys were going to rib me relentlessly tomorrow, and I kind of looked forward to it. "Well, if you'll excuse me," Sam said. "I'm going home to widen my online dating profile to North Carolina since all the single women in this town are off-limits."

"I guess there are some drawbacks to living in a place like Peace Falls," I said, watching him walk down the sidewalk.

"Maybe," Cammie said, squeezing my waist, "but I wouldn't want to live anywhere else. Do you think you'll ever move back to Northern Virginia?" she asked in a small voice.

I smiled down at her. Even if she didn't love me yet, or couldn't say it, she was thinking about the possibility of us long term. "I'd rather convince Wade to move here. Our parents will follow wherever he goes."

"When was the last time you saw them?" she asked. "In person, I mean."

"Easter," I said. "I've been avoiding going back."

"Because you're hiding your diagnosis," she said, more as a statement than a question.

I nodded.

"I haven't seen my dad in person in over two years," Cammie said, her eyes shining. "If I don't settle things with Bishop, I might never visit my dad again. It's too much of a risk."

I felt like an asshole. Though she didn't come out and say it, the implication was there. She'd visit her dad in a heartbeat if she could, and I'd avoided my family simply because I didn't want to tell them I had diabetes. "I'd go with you to visit him in person."

She smirked at me. "I'd go with you to tell your family you're not perfect."

"Oh, they know that already," I said. "And I appreciate the offer. But I'm not ready yet. Maybe after we get Wade's van."

"Are there any assistance programs you might qualify for? Or Wade?"

I'd been so caught up in my new relationship with Cammie, I'd completely forgotten about Doña Valentina and the form I'd helped her complete.

"Maybe," I said. "I know programs like that exist for some medications. A lot of them are needs-based though, and I doubt I'd qualify while working two jobs. Wade only works part time and makes minimum wage, so my parents have been looking into options for him."

Cammie's eyes brightened. "Let me research it. If there's a program out there for either of you, I'll find it. We recommend several to Cal's patients for rehab and mobility equipment. Just give me whatever details you have about the vehicle Wade wants."

"Needs."

"Fine. Needs. I'm assuming any insulin pump is better than none."

"That's my assumption."

"Great. I'll look into it and see what I can find." She flashed me a broad smile that instantly brightened my mood.

"You're incredible, Cammie," I said.

Her smile softened. "I just might be addicted to the way you look at me."

She didn't have to explain what she saw. I felt like a cartoon character walking around with little red hearts instead of eyes. "Well, that's convenient, because I'm absolutely addicted to you."

Chapter Twenty-Six

Cammie

By the time our Sunday shift rolled around, Wyatt couldn't keep his hands off me. Each time he passed me, he'd kiss my neck or wrap his arms around my waist. I'd have worried customers might complain to Lauren that we were being unprofessional, but the Karma regulars seemed thrilled to see us together.

"You're going to get us in trouble," I said, pulling his hand from my waist for the hundredth time.

"Who with?" he asked.

I rolled my eyes. "Just because Lauren is our friend, doesn't mean we can goof around at work. This is her livelihood."

"We don't mind," a woman in a mom group shouted from the café. "You two are adorable."

"See," Wyatt said, smiling at them. "We're adorable." He planted a kiss on me that had the mom group whistling like a bachelorette party at a strip club.

"Oh my stars, Wyatt," I said after he pulled away. My cheeks were on fire, yet I couldn't remember ever feeling so happy or light. "Would you please shelve the book delivery before you do something indecent in front of the customers?"

The group of ladies actually booed when Wyatt walked out from behind the counter toward a dolly full of boxes that needed unpacking in the stacks. They went back to their conversation, and I focused on restocking the paper goods as we neared closing time.

I didn't even look up when Bishop walked in. I was balancing two stacks of disposable cups, trying not to drop any, when the bell over the front door rang. By the time I turned to face the counter, he was leaning against it, mere feet from where I stood.

"Long time no see, Millie," he said.

Somehow, he'd chosen the day I felt the happiest, when my guard was completely down, to saunter back into my life. I closed my eyes and opened them, hoping the man at the counter would morph into anyone other than the person who'd broken me to pieces.

"You're looking good," he said, raking his eye down me in a way that made my skin crawl. "Better than I remember."

He looked the same. Same dark blond hair tousled to look effortless but carefully gelled in place. Same cold blue eyes boring into me as though he was reading my every thought and calculating what response he'd use to gain the most control. He had a few new tattoos on his forearm, and a couple more pounds around his middle, but otherwise, he hadn't changed.

I could only hope his personality had grown more than his midsection.

He narrowed his eyes at me. "Aren't you going to say hello?"

It'd been over two years, yet the fear crashed into me as if every bruise he'd given me was still purple. I gripped the counter to conceal the shaking in my hands. My mouth went so dry I wanted to cough. More than that, I wanted to speak. I needed to speak.

"Didn't think I'd find you, huh?" he said, leaning over the counter and bringing his face closer to mine. "Thought you were smart enough to hide from me using a PO Box." He shook his head and tsked like I'd disappointed him. "You're a dumb bitch, Millie. You always were, always will be."

I glanced behind him at the busy café. He wouldn't do anything to me here, with so many people watching. I was safe. For now.

"I don't need you to talk," Bishop said, leaning so close I could feel his hot breath on my face. "Never did. I just want my money." The familiar scent of cigarettes and Mountain Dew brought back every memory of the times he'd pinned me against the nearest hard surface and yelled in my face. At least he'd kept his voice hushed now.

I opened my mouth to speak but choked on the words in my throat.

Bishop held up his hand. "Spare the bullshit excuses. Nobody steals from me. So, I'm going to use that pretty face of yours and that tight little body however I see fit until you've worked off what you owe me. And if you don't come with me, Todd will take out your dad."

"I have the money," I said, the words ripping from my throat like they'd been buried in glue. "I can write you a check."

Bishop threw his head back and laughed. "A check? Fuck, Millie. I forgot how funny you were. Not that you ever meant to be, but shit, a check?"

"Fine, a money order."

He narrowed his eyes at me. "You don't got that kind of money. And even if you did, I want cash, same as you took from me."

"I can do that after my bank opens tomorrow."

He studied me for a moment and nodded. "My number hasn't changed. Text me when and where."

He turned to leave, but I knew I had to tell him the truth. Things would only be worse for me and my dad if I shorted Bishop. "I can't get it all by tomorrow. I can get you forty-five in cash and send a grand a month until I've paid off the final five."

He turned back to face me and shook his head. "You're fifteen short. Interest. And I want all of it tomorrow."

My stomach dropped. Not only did I not have all the money I'd taken, but the interest Bishop also expected added an extra twenty percent. No doubt he'd intended to use it against me, even if I had every cent I'd taken from him. "I can't come up with that by tomorrow. If you give me more time, I promise I'll pay you back."

The slow smile on Bishop's face turned my blood to ice. He reached across the counter and gripped my wrist, pressing so hard I knew he'd leave a mark. "I have a better idea. You'll come back to South Carolina with me and work off the rest. Should only take you six months or so. I'll even take you to see your old man and let you stay at my place for free as long as you suck—"

Before Bishop could finish his sentence, he was ripped back and tossed on the floor. Wyatt stood over him with his hands fisted at his sides. The warmth in his usually kind eyes had been replaced with a steely stare as he glared down at Bishop with undiluted hate. The entire café fell quiet as everyone watched the spectacle unfolding.

"Who the fuck are you?" Bishop asked, jumping to his feet.

"The guy who's going to kick your ass if you don't walk out of here right now," Wyatt shouted.

Instead of heading for the door, Bishop took a step toward Wyatt, severing his last thread of self-control. He pulled his arm back and punched Bishop square in the jaw. What my ex lacked in size, he more than made up for in experience. He quickly recovered from the hit and pulled Wyatt to the floor. They threw punch after punch, rolling into the bistro tables and sending customers scrambling out of the way.

"Stop," I yelled, running around the counter and right into the scuffle.

"I wouldn't do that," one of women in the mom group said as I yanked on Wyatt's shirt.

Someone's foot caught my leg, and I tumbled onto Wyatt, who let Bishop land a punch to his face because he was using both arms to protect me.

"I've called the police," the woman who had tried to stop me shouted.

Bishop used the nearest table to pull himself to standing before spitting a mouthful of blood onto the floor. He pointed at me and said, "Tomorrow. Bring it all or else."

"Or else what, *cretino*?" Wyatt said, helping me to stand. This time when I tugged on his sleeve, Wyatt wrapped his arm around my waist and pulled me close. I could feel his heart thudding in his chest as he sucked in huge gulps of air.

Bishop looked between Wyatt and me, his expression cold. "You know what to do," he said, pointing at me before walking through the silent café and out the door.

Several of the women rushed us and forced Wyatt and me into chairs side-by-side.

"I'll grab some ice for his face," one woman said.

"Do you want me to call a doctor?" another woman asked.

When the lady returned with the ice, Wyatt pressed it to his face and turned toward me. He opened his mouth to speak as a member of the Peace Falls Police Department pulled up in front of the café with his lights flashing and siren blaring.

Wyatt stood as the police officer entered Karma, but I shoved him back into his seat. The last thing we needed was the officer to think Wyatt was a threat. Without sparing the cop a glance, I took Wyatt's hand in mine and held it.

The women in the mom group surrounded the cop and started speaking at once.

"I've never seen that man before."

"I got a picture."

"Seemed to be threatening her."

"That young man stepped in to help and got hurt."

At the word hurt, the police officer gently pushed through the women and came closer. When he took off his hat, I recognized Officer Stafford, who came into Karma at least a couple times a week.

"Cammie, Wyatt," he said, kneeling down to look us in the eyes. "Y'all OK?"

Wyatt nodded. Officer Stafford didn't look convinced. He reached for his radio, but stopped when Wyatt said, "I'm fine, Levi."

I'd never called the man anything but Officer Stafford. Apparently, he and Wyatt were on friendlier terms, which made sense since I'd always been a little terrified of him, both because he was a cop and ridiculously good looking.

"Can you tell me what happened?" Officer Stafford asked.

Wyatt looked at me, and I realized if I didn't want the entire Peace Falls Police Department looking for Bishop, I had to tell the officer something. Unfortunately, the truth wasn't an option if I wanted to keep my dad safe.

"My ex-boyfriend came in here. Wyatt asked him to leave and when he wouldn't, they fought." I shrugged like a coffee house brawl was no big deal. "Everything is fine."

Officer Stafford nodded, like he heard people minimize violence every day, which he probably did. "Any idea why he came to see you?"

"Come on, Levi," Wyatt said. "Isn't that obvious."

Officer Stafford remained quiet.

"What would you do if some guy was trying to get back with the woman you love and didn't leave after you told him to?" Wyatt said.

Officer Stafford cracked a hint of a smile at that and nodded. "Do you want to press charges?" he asked Wyatt.

"Can I do that if I hit him first?" Wyatt asked.

"Hypothetically," I added, shooting Wyatt a warning glare.

"I wouldn't advise it," Officer Stafford said. "He'd likely press charges against you."

"Then I think we're good," Wyatt said.

Officer Stafford narrowed his eyes. "You don't look good."

"Damn, Levi, way to kick a guy when he's down," Wyatt said, flashing a smile.

Officer Stafford remained stoic. "How's your head feel?"

"Like someone punched me in the face. Go ahead and check me for a concussion if it'd make you feel better."

Officer Stafford shone a flashlight in Wyatt's eyes and started asking him questions, and with each correct answer, my heart rate slowed.

"Thank you for your help, everyone," I said, smiling at the group of ladies once Officer Stafford put away his flashlight. "I hate to do this, but I think we should close a bit early today."

"That's twice we've had to close Karma because of me," Wyatt said, rubbing his forehead.

"Don't you worry about it," a lady said. "It's only fifteen minutes early. Do you want us to stay and help you clean up?"

My eyes burned. I could tell by the earnest looks on their faces they meant it. "We're fine. Thank you again."

Officer Stafford stayed long enough to make sure everyone was out of the building. He pulled two cards from his pocket and handed one to each of us. "If you have any trouble in the future, call me." He glared at Wyatt. "And try not to be a hero, Romeo. It only makes more paperwork for me."

As soon as I locked the front door behind the officer, I ran back to Wyatt and wrapped my arms around him. "Are you OK?"

He held on to me tightly. "I should be asking you that. I'm assuming that guy was Bishop?"

Before I could answer, Lauren pushed through the swinging door from the back and stormed around the counter with Aiden at her heels.

"Oh shit," she said, seeing Wyatt's swollen face. "Where is the fucker?"

She started off toward the stacks, but I jumped in front of her. "He's gone. For now."

"You break your hand?" Aiden asked.

For the first time, I looked down and saw the raw skin on Wyatt's knuckles. I sucked in a breath as my stomach twisted. "That doesn't look good."

"Brandi Fitzwilliams texted me because a friend texted her and said Wyatt got into a fight with some guy who came in here and messed with you," Lauren said to me. "She even sent along a picture. Was it Bishop?"

"Who's Bishop?" Aiden asked.

The tears I'd been holding back burst through, and I buried my face in my hands. "A few weeks with me, and Wyatt looks like a boxer."

Wyatt wrapped his arms around me and kissed the top of my head. "Shh. It's OK, Angel. Look at me." He pulled my hands from my face and tilted my chin until our eyes locked. "I would do anything to keep you safe."

"What the fuck is happening?" Aiden yelled.

Lauren, Wyatt, and I exchanged glances, which only pissed off Aiden more.

"OK, that's it," he said. "The three of you are getting in my truck and we're going to Cal's."

"I'm not sure they're in the mood for a cookout, My Love," Lauren said, taking a step closer to me.

"Tough shit. Clearly, something big is happening. I'm saving you having to repeat everything to the rest of the group. Clean yourself up and grab your insulin, Wyatt."

"Please," I said, looking at Lauren. "Keep everyone else out of it."

Lauren shook her head. "I told you, if I ever thought you were in danger, I couldn't keep this secret. Either you're telling them, or I am. Cal will probably take it better hearing everything straight from you. It's time, Cam."

Wyatt swallowed hard, his eyes locked on me. He didn't say a word before he turned and headed upstairs to the apartment, but there was no mistaking the pain in his eyes.

"If you run," Lauren said so softly Aiden, who was flipping chairs onto the tables, couldn't hear, "promise you'll give Wy the chance to go with you."

"I'm not running," I said, and she pulled me into as tight of a hug as she could with her baby bump.

"I want to believe that," Lauren said.

I stepped back and looked her straight in the eyes. "Running isn't an option."

She nodded, her shoulders relaxing. Unfortunately, it might be the only truth I'd be telling her about my plans for tomorrow.

Chapter Twenty-Seven

Wyatt

Cal burned the hamburgers. He'd taken one look at my face when I walked into his backyard and abandoned the grill. When he noticed the red marks on Cammie's arm, I thought I'd have to get into my second fight of the day.

"A little help, Theo," Aiden yelled as he wrapped his arms around Cal's waist and held him back.

"Cal, stop," Cammie said, holding out her hand. "Wyatt protected me from the guy who grabbed my arm."

Cal instantly stopped lunging toward me. Even so, Theo Makis stepped between us. "Why don't we all sit down?" he said in a calm voice.

After everyone had found a place at the patio table, Cammie blew out a breath and told them a summary of what she'd shared with me about Bishop and her dad. By the time she'd finished, the burgers were burned to a crisp. After he'd turned off the grill, Cal sat the charred meat pucks in the center of the table, which everyone ignored, and jumped back into the conversation.

"I still don't understand why you won't call the police," Cal said, which was the only piece of information I didn't already know and had been dying to ask. "The guy never reported the money stolen, and I doubt he'd ever admit it existed. What he's doing to you is harassment."

"Bishop said if I don't pay him back, he'll have my dad killed," she said.

"There was nothing stopping him from doing that before," Theo said softly. I didn't know Theo well, but I'd heard enough whispers in the café to learn he'd served time in prison himself.

Cammie shook her head. "Bishop's brother just got moved to the same unit as my dad."

"That might make it easier," Theo said, "but he wasn't safe before the brother moved to the block, and he won't be safe even if you pay Bishop. You know this."

Cammie nodded, her eyes filling with tears. "I'd never forgive myself if something happened, and I could have maybe prevented it. Plus, I've felt guilty about the money since I took it. I just want to pay him back."

"How much do you need?" Aiden asked.

"I saved forty-five. He says I owe him another ten with interest, so fifteen total."

"That's bullshit," Poppy huffed.

"I get paying back what you took," Rowan added, "but you don't owe the asshole interest."

Cammie shook her head. "If it gets him out of my life, it's worth it."

Aiden nodded. "OK. You've got it."

Cammie gaped at him. The rest of the group seemed unsurprised by Aiden's offer.

"You barely know me," Cammie said. "I wouldn't even speak to you for over a year."

He shrugged.

"I can't let you do that," Cammie said.

"Then let me," Cal said. "Consider it an early year-end bonus."

"Cal—" Cammie started.

Cal shook his head. "Let me do this, Cam. I've got a line of credit for the practice I can use."

"I can get the cash without paying interest on it," Aiden said, glaring at him.

I seriously doubted she'd accept that much money from Aiden. Cammie might let Cal help her if he didn't have to take out a loan himself, but she'd never put him into debt, no matter how much she needed the money. "You can take it from my pay," I said to Aiden.

"No," Aiden said, rubbing his forehead. "You need a damn pump."

Poppy, Rowan, and Theo exchanged confused looks while Cal stared me down as if daring me to explain. "I have diabetes," I said. "I need an insulin pump."

I'd more than doubled the number of people who knew about it now. Cal gave me a chin dip of approval I didn't quite understand. I returned it anyway since I was doing the best I could to get on his good side.

"Well, then I'm with Aiden," Theo said. "You can't give Cammie that much. I can throw in a few grand."

"I can cover her," Lauren said.

"Oh, for fuck's sake," Poppy said, throwing up her arms. "Theo, Lauren, Aiden, and Cal, you'll give her three grand each because, let's face it, the four of you have it to give. Wish I had that much lying around. With the bakery just getting off the ground, Rowan and I together can only kick in two thousand." She paused and waited for her sister to nod. "Wyatt, can you handle the last thousand?"

"Wyatt doesn't need to cover anything," Aiden said.

"Oh come on, Studman," Poppy said. "He just got into a fistfight for her. Do you honestly think he's going to sit on his hands while everyone else gives her money?"

"Fine," Aiden said, before he pointed at me. "I'm covering it now and taking it out of your pay two hundred at a time after you get your pump."

I nodded since it might be the only way anyone would let me help.

Cammie's eyes shone and her voice wobbled as she said, "I can't thank y'all enough. I'm paying each of you back as soon as I can."

Cal cleared his throat and pulled out his phone. "I'm ordering pizza. I know a place that can make cauliflower crust. What do you want on your pie, Wyatt?"

"Do we all have to eat cauliflower crust?" Poppy asked, wrinkling her nose.

"Yeah, I'm with Hell Cat on that," Aiden said.

"I'll get everyone's usual," Cal said. "I just don't know Wyatt's yet."

My head hurt. Not just from the last hit Bishop landed on my chin, but from trying to process everything that had happened in the last hour and a half. "Whatever is fine," I heard myself saying.

"Trust me, Wyatt," Poppy said. "You don't want to risk it. The man puts pineapple on his pizza."

"Pepperoni, supreme, or meat lovers?" Cal asked, ignoring his sister-in-law. "I assume you need protein."

How they could go from Cammie's gut-wrenching confession to pizza toppings blew my mind. "Supreme," I said, rubbing my forehead. Now that the adrenaline had mostly left my body, my face throbbed.

I stayed sitting while everyone else left the table to help Cal get rid of the burned food and clean the grill. After a minute, Rowan came over with a bottle of ibuprofen and a glass of water.

"Cammie asked me to bring you these," she said, taking a seat beside me. "If you need to lie down while we wait for the pizza, there's a guestroom upstairs."

"I'm fine," I said for what felt like the millionth time.

"You know it's OK not to be," Rowan said, putting her hand on my shoulder.

"I'm good. We should focus on Cammie," I said, pointing to where she was now standing in the yard, surrounded by her friends. Poppy was shouting something about superglue and feathers, which Lauren seemed very excited about.

"And yet, Cammie is focused on you," Rowan said with a smile.

I'd worked with Rowan quite a bit while Lauren was suffering through the worst of her morning sickness. She had a sweetness that always put me at ease. Watching the dynamic of this little group, I'd quickly learned that despite the varied personalities, each person softened around her and put down their walls. I'd almost told her about my diabetes twice when we were sharing shifts.

"What if he doesn't leave her alone after he has the money?" I asked, voicing the worry that had twisted my stomach from the moment I saw Bishop with his hand around Cammie's wrist. "We can't be with her all the time. What if he attacks her? Hearing some of the specifics of what he did to her damn near wrecked me. What if she runs because he knows where to find her?"

Rowan nodded. "Those are all realistic worries. But look at them," she said, pointing to the group where the conversation had moved on to restraining orders and self-defense classes. "She's not alone, and neither are you." Rowan bumped my shoulder gently and motioned to the pill bottle in my hand. "Take care of yourself first, so you can take care of others, Wyatt. The sooner you learn that the better."

CHAPTER TWENTY-EIGHT

Cammie

I LEFT THE COOKOUT with eleven-thousand dollars in a reusable shopping bag and strict orders from Cal not to leave Karma until he escorted me to my bank in the morning. One by one, my friends had made trips to ATMs and brought back cash. Lauren ended up covering Wyatt's portion because Aiden's bank capped his daily ATM withdrawals at $3K. She, on the other hand, had cash hidden around Karma.

Wyatt and Aiden looked stunned as Lauren pulled stacks of fifty-dollar bills from various hidey holes throughout the building.

"Why do you have cash in the heating ducts?" Aiden asked.

Lauren shrugged, and my heart cracked. Like me, she hadn't always had everything she needed growing up. The difference between us was that the last half of my childhood was uncertain, while the first half of hers sucked. Despite all my hangups, Lauren's scars came from older and deeper cuts.

"Thank you," I said, wrapping her in a hug. "I know what this money means to you, and I promise to pay you back as soon as I can."

"He's meeting you in the café tomorrow afternoon, right?" Lauren asked, repeating the lie I'd told everyone at the picnic.

"Yeah," I said, fighting to keep my voice neutral. If anyone could tell I was lying, it'd be Lauren. "I figured it was safer that way, though he made a point of telling me not to bring Wyatt."

"Like I give a shit what he thinks," Wyatt said. The bruises on his face were already deepening. By tomorrow morning, half his face would be black and blue.

"Let's not piss off the asshole and give him a reason to take it out on Cammie," Aiden said, fixing Wyatt with a glare. "Cal, Theo, and I will be in the café in case he tries anything. We'll keep Cammie safe, and you'll stay up here and keep my pregnant girlfriend from going Scarface on this guy."

Wyatt looked pissed but nodded. Something everyone agreed on: Lauren needed to be kept far away from Bishop. While she lived to do good in the world, she was a fighter to the core. She'd had to be.

"Just one punch to the nuts," Lauren said. "That's all I want."

"No," Wyatt, Aiden, and I said together.

"Come on, Princess," Aiden said, holding out his hand to her. "Let's get you home so you can work out all that aggression on me."

"You're going to let me punch you in the nuts?" she said, raising a sculpted eyebrow at him.

"I had something else in mind, but if that's what it takes to keep you and the baby safe tomorrow, sure." He winked at Lauren, and she rolled her eyes.

"Try to get some sleep, y'all," she said.

"You're taking sick time," Aiden said, pointing at Wyatt. "I want to make sure your hand is OK before you come back on site. Sleep in for one damn day of your life and get an x-ray if the swelling doesn't go down."

"I will," Wyatt said. "Thanks."

I locked the apartment door behind them and let out a sigh. I felt wrung out. Seeing Bishop and telling my friends the worst pieces of my past had left me emotionally drained.

"Let's get ready for bed," Wyatt said, rubbing my back.

He looked as exhausted as I felt. I placed his right hand in my palm and ran my fingers across his swollen knuckles. Cal had examined Wyatt after he'd disinfected and bandaged all the cuts. When he suggested Wyatt get an x-ray if his hand hadn't improved by the morning, I'd had to hold back tears. "What if you broke a bone? Will you be able to work?"

"Hey," Wyatt said, tipping up my chin with his other hand. "If Cal thought something was broken, don't you think he'd have made me go to urgent care or the ER? I can move my fingers fine. He's just being cautious."

"I'm sorry," I said as tears leaked down my cheeks.

"For what? You did nothing wrong." He stared down at me with so much tenderness, I'd have cried if I wasn't already. "I look worse than I feel. Right now, all I need is to hold you."

Neither of us spoke as we got ready for bed. When I walked into his room, Wyatt pulled back the covers and gathered me in his arms.

"Seeing his hand around your wrist—" He shook his head. "I've never been so angry in my life. The thought of you being near him tomorrow makes me sick."

"He just wants the money," I said, tracing my fingers down the hard muscles of his chest where another bruise was forming. "As soon as he has it, he'll be out of our lives." I hoped. Bishop wasn't a forgiving person. Even an extra ten grand might not be enough for him to walk away. Whether he ever cared for me or not, he thought he owned me. It had to have been a blow to his ego when I left. I only hoped enough time had passed that he'd be willing to let it go, to let me go.

"I want to be with you tomorrow," Wyatt said quietly.

"I know you do. And knowing that is all I need. You being there could only make things worse." Any of my friends being there could set off Bishop, which was why I'd lied to everyone.

I'd never forgive myself if anything happened to any of them. They might keep me safe while I gave Bishop the money, but by doing so, they'd expose themselves as someone I cared about. Someone Bishop could use against me like he had my father, and like he could with Wyatt, now that he knew about him. Going alone was the best way to minimize the damage Bishop could do if he decided the money wasn't enough. I also had to do everything I could not to bring my ex's wrath down on my father. As much as I loved and appreciated my friends, I couldn't trust any of them to keep a level head around the man who'd hit me.

"I just wish there was something I could do," Wyatt said.

"You already have. The way you've treated me has changed everything. I'm finally strong enough to face him and close this chapter of my life. Before you, I worried about the power Bishop had over me. Not just what he could do to my dad, but to me. When we were together, he broke my self-esteem down to the point I felt grateful to have him, even when he hurt me. You showed me what it's like to be loved with kindness. Lauren, Cal, and the others started my healing, but these past weeks with you have taught me so much."

Wyatt tightened his grip on me. "I don't know how I'm going to let you out of this bed tomorrow to face him."

"Because this is something I have to do for me," I said, running my hand down the contours of his stomach. "If you're up for it, I'd really like to be with you tonight instead of thinking about tomorrow." And talking meant lying, so I needed to avoid it as much as possible.

Wyatt's eyes closed when I wrapped my hand around his hardening cock. "Fuck, that feels good."

I loved touching him, feeling the strength of his body and the effect I had on him. He made me feel powerful in a way I'd never experienced before, like I could bring this incredibly strong man to his knees with only my fingers. I'd been dying to see how he'd react to my mouth, and I wanted to get both our minds off Bishop.

I gathered my hair and pushed it aside before I lowered my head. His eyes snapped open as I gently licked his swollen crown. He let out a hiss and my core clinched. I slid my tongue down his length, pulling a groan from deep in his chest. His abs flexed as he fought to keep still. Wyatt wasn't the type to shove a woman's head down, which made me eager to give him the best blow job of his life. I sucked him into my mouth, hollowing my cheeks as I lowered my head, taking him so far back my eyes watered. Heat pooled between my thighs as I saw the look of pleasure on his face. I'd never gotten so turned on pleasing a partner before.

"Cammie," he said, placing a gentle hand on my hair. I pulled back, curling my tongue along his length before taking as much of him again as I could. I wrapped my hand around the base of his cock and moved it up and down in tandem with my mouth. His legs started shaking with the effort to hold still, and I realized I didn't want him to be careful with me. I wanted him to lose control. When I started humming, he thrust up into my mouth with a groan. I matched his rhythm, bobbing up and down with his frantic pace. "Fuck, I'm going to come if you don't stop."

Instead of answering him, I hummed again and cupped his balls with my free hand, tugging gently. He closed his eyes and exploded in my mouth with a roar. I swallowed every drop he gave me as my arousal dripped down my thighs.

I sat back on my heels and smiled at him. Before I could even catch my breath, Wyatt flipped me onto my back and lowered his head to my throbbing center. "You're so wet," he said, running his callused fingers up my thighs. He locked eyes with me as he flattened his tongue and licked my sensitive flesh. I let out a strangled cry as he pulled my clit between his teeth and flicked his tongue back and forth.

Within moments, I came, my vision dimming as white-hot pleasure washed through my body. Wyatt rose to his knees and gripped his already hardening cock. "I need to feel you," he said, sliding his tip against my wet folds.

I arched against his silky length. My orgasm had barely receded, yet the sweet ache in my core started to build again. "Wyatt," I breathed as his tip brushed against my entrance. "Please."

He sank into me an inch, the feeling of him bare so exquisite my eyes rolled back in my head.

"I can grab a condom," he said, even as he sank deeper.

"I want to feel you," I said, between pants. He stared deep into my eyes as he entered me inch by inch. We both stilled when he'd buried himself to the hilt.

"I love you," he said, brushing his hand down my face.

I wrapped my legs around him and pulled him closer, digging my heels into his firm butt while he rolled his hips. He made love to me slowly at first, our eyes locked as we moved together. As I tightened around him, his thrusts became less measured, wilder. He braced an arm against the headboard and pistoned his hips so forcefully the bed smacked against the wall.

"Don't stop," I begged as the pleasure continued to build.

"Cam, I'm—"

"It's OK," I said before I lost all words. He crashed into me again and again until my body felt electrified. I shouted his name as the most intense orgasm of my life ripped through me, and he swelled, finding his own release deep inside me.

He collapsed onto his back before pulling me on top of him. We were both breathless, clinging to each other as though we feared we'd float apart. He rubbed my back as his heartbeat slowed and his breaths evened. "I'm sorry," he said, kissing my shoulder. "I should have pulled out. I'll go to the pharmacy tomorrow for a morning-after pill."

I rubbed my hand across his chest. "No need. I have an IUD. And I'm clean. I've been tested since I moved to Peace Falls."

"I had a complete workup done when the doctors were trying to figure out why I was so sick last year."

"Guess we didn't need Lauren's jumbo box of condoms then," I said, lifting my head from his chest.

"Guess not," he said. His eyes grew serious as he took my face in his hands. "I didn't think it was possible for sex to be any better than what we've had before."

"Me either," I said. "That was—"

When I couldn't find the right word, Wyatt leaned forward and placed a gentle kiss on my mouth. "Special. *Te amo.*"

He was so damn patient with me. He was already flipping back the covers to go clean up because he'd grown accustomed to my silence after he told me he loved me. What I felt for Wyatt was stronger than any emotion I'd had with Bishop or anyone else. He didn't demand the words I told the others to keep the peace, but he sure as hell deserved them. "*Te amo* too," I said.

Wyatt froze. His eyes were wide when he turned back to face me. "Can you say that again in English?"

"I love you too."

"*Te amo también,*" he said with a face-splitting grin.

"*Te amo también,*" I repeated.

He pulled me into a hug that started out innocent enough, but before long, we were lost in each other again. By the time he fell asleep, he'd given me so many orgasms they bled together, and I honestly lost count. I lay still, willing my eyes to stay open, as his body relaxed and his breaths evened.

Once I was certain he wouldn't wake, I carefully left his arms and headed to the kitchen.

I had so much more to lose now than when I left Bishop. Friends who were like family and a man who held my whole heart and loved me more than I ever thought possible. I knew the moment Bishop walked out of the café that the only way to keep everyone safe was to meet him alone. I just hoped they'd forgive me for deceiving them one last time.

When I first came to Peace Falls, I lied easily and often to keep my past hidden. As time passed and my relationships deepened, I only lied by omission. My fingers shook as I typed out the text to a number I'd never entered in my new phone's contacts, but had memorized along with every insult that dropped from Bishop's mouth.

> I'll have all your money after my bank opens to-morrow. Meet me at ten at Centennial Park by the fountain.

Despite the late hour, Bishop replied immediately.

> Don't be late and come alone.

> I understand.

My eyes stung as I carried a chair from the table where I'd shared so many meals with Wyatt into my room. I placed it by the closet, climbed onto the seat, and lifted my suitcase from the top shelf.

CHAPTER TWENTY-NINE

Wyatt

THE MOMENT I STRETCHED my hand across the cold sheets beside me, I knew she was gone. Cammie was not a morning person. Not once had she ever gotten up before me. I jumped out of bed anyway and went through each room of the apartment, hoping to find her making breakfast or taking a shower. The cats lifted their heads from their paws when I ran past the sofa to the door leading downstairs. Instead of sprinting through Karma like a madman, I went straight to the parking lot in my bare feet.

Cammie's car was gone. My stomach dropped as the reality of the situation sank in: She'd left. Whether Peace Falls or just me, she'd lied to Cal when she promised to go with him to the bank this morning. She'd lied to all of us. I checked the time on my phone, hoping like an idiot that maybe it was after ten and they'd maybe taken her car instead of Cal's, but it was just before eight. The banks weren't open.

I took my phone from my pocket to call Cammie and found a text message she'd sent me around four.

Check on Desdemona for me.

That was it. No, I'm sorry I told you I loved you and bailed. Or even a remote clue of where she'd gone. Just check on the cat. Which made me kind of worried for Desdemona. If Cammie had taken the time to text me about her before she ran, there must be something wrong.

A blood sugar alert flashed across my screen as I tried to call Cammie. Her voicemail picked up on the first ring. I let it play through, but when the message ended, I struggled to find the words that might convince her to come back to me.

Instead, I hung up and retreated to the apartment at a much slower pace. What if she'd lied about loving me too? I quickly pushed the thought aside. We could have gone to bed like usual after I told her I loved her. Instead, she'd shocked me by saying it back. The only question was if it was also her way of saying goodbye. I was so lost in my head, I didn't realize I'd cut my foot until I turned around to shut the apartment door.

"Shit," I said, hopping to the couch.

Desdemona let out a startled yawl and shot off into Cammie's bedroom with Medusa close behind, which wasn't anything out of the ordinary. The cats seemed fine. I was not. I lifted my foot and found a gash across the heel. It didn't look deep enough for stitches, though I had to take care of it before I did anything else, or I'd get blood all over Lauren's carpet. I hobbled to the kitchen and grabbed a paper towel to catch the blood on my way to the half bathroom. The face that greeted me in the mirror was so swollen and bruised it startled me. I hoped Bishop looked worse. Other than his final cheap shot, we'd been going blow for blow. By the time I'd washed and bandaged my foot, I could tell my sugar was dropping.

I was about to look for the cats when a second alert flashed across my screen, so I grabbed a jar of peanut butter and a spoon, and dropped onto the couch. As soon as they heard me open the peanut butter jar, Desdemona and Medusa returned to the living room to investigate. Medusa sniffed the bandage on my foot while Desdemona pawed at my hand holding the jar. They both seemed fine to me, making Cammie's message even more confusing.

I'd just swallowed a spoonful of peanut butter when my phone rang. My heart sank when Lauren's name appeared on the screen instead of Cammie's.

"I know it's low," I said instead of hello. "We've got bigger problems. Cammie's gone."

Lauren blew out a breath. "Are you sure?"

The knot in my stomach tightened as a thread of hope I hadn't considered snapped. "So she's not with you?"

"She's not, Wy," Lauren said softly. "You're sure she's gone?"

"She's not at Karma. Didn't you notice her car was missing when you opened today?"

"I'm still at home. I have a doctor's appointment later, so I wasn't scheduled to open. You need to eat more."

"I know," I said, jabbing my spoon into the peanut butter jar. "Hold on a sec." I shoveled in another spoonful. "Do you have any idea where she might have gone?" I asked as best I could with half my mouth stuck together with goo. I should have grabbed something else to eat, though the peanut butter had drawn out the cats like I intended.

Lauren sniffed, and when she spoke again, her voice wavered. "She promised me she'd give you a chance to leave with her."

"Yeah, well, she promised she'd wait for Cal to go anywhere. We can probably forget any promises she made."

"Did she take her things?"

I hadn't even thought to check her room to see if she'd packed up. My foot ached as I walked across the living room to Cammie's and flicked on the light. The book she'd been reading was still on the nightstand beside a framed copy of the photo she'd shown me of her and her parents. I turned on the bathroom light and let out a relieved breath.

"She didn't take anything from the bathroom," I said. "She left her toothbrush and everything."

"Check the closet," Lauren said in an even tone, clearly not sharing my excitement and making me consider whether I'd pause to grab an old toothbrush and a half-empty bottle of shampoo if I was running. The photo on the nightstand was also the lock screen on her phone, so even that was replaceable.

I opened the closet door and frowned. "Her clothes are here, but her suitcase is missing."

"Are you sure?"

"I put it on the top shelf myself after she unpacked. It's gone."

"Damn it, Cammie," Lauren hissed. "She's about to do something incredibly reckless."

"That doesn't sound like her," I said, walking back to the living room. "She's one of the most careful people I know."

My foot throbbed, so pacing wasn't an option to ease my nervous energy. I collapsed on the couch, pulling the peanut butter jar away from the cats. They both started cleaning sticky globs from their whiskers.

"People do stupid things to protect the ones they love," Lauren said.

"It sounds like you have an idea of what she's doing." I leaned back on the couch and stared into the jar, which now had pieces of cat fur stuck inside. That pretty much summed up the morning I was having after the best night of my life. I set the jar between my feet, hoping to keep the cats away until I could throw it out.

"How would you deliver sixty-thousand dollars in cash, Wyatt?"

The peanut butter in my stomach threatened to make a reappearance as I put my head in my hand. "She's meeting him on her own." Desdemona walked across my lap and rubbed her face against mine.

"That would be my guess," Lauren said.

"She still has to go to the bank to take out the rest of the cash. You know what bank she uses because you direct deposit her paycheck, right?" I asked. "We could catch up with her there."

"It's not a bad idea. The problem is there's about twelve branches of that bank within an hour of town and even more out of state," Lauren said. "I told her to open an account there, so she'd have access to the most ATMs. She could go to any of the branches. And Cammie's bright. I'd say the only branch you could eliminate would be the one in Peace Falls."

"Fuck. Maybe I should call Levi," I said, rubbing my forehead. My head was pounding at the same tempo as the ache in my heel. "Get the police to check each branch."

"Officer Stafford? Absolutely not, Wyatt. If she wanted the police involved, she'd have filed a report yesterday. She knows Bishop better than we do. Whatever she's doing, she must think it's for the best."

Desdemona rolled onto her back and meowed. I lifted my head from my palm and reached down to scratch under her chin. My hand stopped short when I saw her collar. "She wouldn't," I said as I opened the app on my phone.

"Wouldn't what?" Lauren asked.

The app showed Medusa's tracker was online and right beside me, but Desdemona's wasn't showing up at all.

"What's going on?" Lauren asked again.

"Cammie sent me a text while I was asleep, telling me to check on Desdemona. The cat's fine, but her tracker is gone and offline. Even if it fell out of her collar, it should show where it is in the building. Cammie must have taken it with her." Check on Desdemona *for me*.

"Wouldn't it show up wherever she is now?" Lauren asked.

"Not if she wasn't in range of a cell tower or she took out the battery."

"I'd bet she took the battery out," Lauren said, blowing out a breath. "She and I share locations with our phones. I checked as soon as you said she was gone, and she's not coming up. She must have her phone off too because she doesn't want anyone to interfere with whatever plan she has. At least she could use the tracker if Bishop takes her phone and tries to force her to leave with him."

"That explains why it went straight to voicemail when I called her. I'm going to keep my eyes glued to the cat tracker app. You should reinstall it too. I'd hate for the tracker to come online briefly and miss it."

"I never deleted the app," she said, a little sheepishly.

"Keep an eye on it. I need to call Cal before he shows up here thinking he's driving Cammie to the bank."

As soon as I hung up with Lauren, I dialed Rowan's number, since Cal and I had never exchanged ours. When I got him on the phone and told him Cammie was gone, he didn't even wait for me to elaborate. He just said he'd be over as soon as he could. By the time he arrived at the apartment with Rowan, I was halfway through cleaning the peanut butter the cats had smeared across the sofa while I stared at my phone, doing my best not to blink. They took one look at me and ordered me to sit down.

"How long have you been staring at that app?" Cal asked as he examined my right hand. I could tell by the tension in his shoulders and face that he was barely holding his shit together.

"About an hour," I said, not looking away from the screen.

"OK," Rowan said. "You can either give me the phone while you make yourself breakfast or tell me what you want me to make you."

"It'd be good to give your eyes a break," Cal said. "Maybe put some ice on your hand while you're eating."

"I promise, Wyatt," Rowan said. "One or both of us will watch the app."

I nodded and handed her the phone. "Lauren has it too," I said, before limping to the kitchen.

"What happened to your foot?" Cal asked, following me.

"Cut it on something in the parking lot when I ran outside to see if she'd taken her car."

Cal shook his head. "I'd have done the same, but shit, Wyatt, you've got to take better care of yourself. You know, diabetics have a higher risk of infection from wounds, right?"

I nodded as I pulled the oatmeal from the cabinet. "It kills me to say this, but I can't be the one to go after Cammie if that tracker comes online. I'm sure Bishop doesn't want me there, and I got so worked up the last time I saw him, there's no telling what my blood sugar would do if we were face-to-face again. Add in the busted hand and sliced foot, and I'm basically worthless."

"I don't know," Cal said, leaning against the counter. "Being honest with yourself and putting her first might make you the only person I know worthy of being with Cammie."

"I consider that high praise coming from you," I said.

"You should," he said with a smile, just as Rowan gasped and ran toward us.

"The tracker's back online," she said, holding up my phone. "And it's in Centennial Park."

Chapter Thirty

Cammie

Bishop was late. As the minutes ticked past ten, my nerves built. I wanted to get this over with, and it needed to happen before Wyatt used the air tag to find me. I couldn't exactly pull the tracker from my shoe and turn it off in case Bishop was somewhere I couldn't see.

Before I left Karma, I'd sent my dad a quick email warning him about Bishop's threat, stopped sharing my location with Lauren, and shut off my phone. Then, I'd driven to a branch of my bank outside of town and waited in the car until it opened. It had taken some convincing, but eventually, the branch manager allowed me to cash out my account in fifties and hundred-dollar bills rather than drafting a cashier's check. If my time with Bishop had taught me anything, it was all the reasons he didn't have a standard checking account.

I'd had to turn my phone back on briefly to show the branch manager a listing for one of the refitted vans I'd been researching for Wade, and the email exchange with the current owner where we'd discussed the price. The listing was real, though if she'd looked close enough, she'd have seen that the seller's email address was missing a letter.

When I put the rest of the money into the suitcase with the eleven thousand from my friends, I almost laughed. I could have fit everything in the reusable shopping bag Rowan gave me with room to spare. The money I stole from Bishop had been in smaller bills. The stacks of cash the banks gave me and my friends were tiny in comparison. Even if the suitcase was overkill, it felt right to return the money to Bishop in the same bag I'd used to take it.

I knew what I was doing was dangerous, which was why I'd grabbed Desdemona's tracker. If Bishop forced me to go with him, he'd toss my cell, but hopefully I could keep the air tag hidden in my shoe.

I'd pulled up to Centennial Park with a suitcase of cash fifteen minutes before ten, then waited until the last minute to turn on my phone, share my location, and pop the battery in the tracker. Other than one missed call from Wyatt, I didn't have a single call, voicemail, or text.

The lack of texts or voicemails put me on edge, even more than I was already. My heart pounded as I considered reasons for the silence. What if Wyatt hadn't understood my message? What if he hadn't told anyone? If he hadn't called me, I would have considered that he was still asleep, though Wyatt never seemed to need an alarm to wake when he opened Karma on the weekends.

My unease grew the longer I waited. When I first dragged my battered suitcase to the fountain at the center of the park, there were only a few moms and toddlers at the playground equipment. As the minutes passed, more and more people entered the park.

First, Dr. Evers walked to a nearby park bench and took out a crossword puzzle book, which was odd since he was usually working at this time. My blood pressure spiked when Poppy strutted in and plopped down beside him on the bench. She ignored me completely and focused on filling in the puzzle with Dr. Evers. The chances of Poppy being out of bed before noon were too slim for it to be a coincidence. When I turned around and looked behind me, Cal and his brother-in-law Chris were tossing a football back and forth. Theo entered the park on my left with his boss from the tattoo parlor just as Aiden entered from my right with Sam.

Everyone ignored me as more and more familiar faces filled the park. Rowan and her mother walked right by without saying a word and headed straight for a nearby rose bush with a pair of scary-looking pruning shears.

By the time Bishop finally sauntered into the park twenty minutes after ten, dozens of my friends and acquaintances were scattered around me, including Officer Levi, who'd joined Cal and Chris. Thankfully, he wasn't in uniform, but seeing a cop so close by made my palms sweat. I wasn't doing anything illegal, other than maybe lying to my bank to take out my own money, though I had stolen the cash I was trying to pay back. Money I'm certain hadn't been clean. At least Wyatt and Lauren weren't in sight.

Bishop walked toward me with a smirk on his face and his hands in his pockets. He looked terrible. Bruises colored his jaw, and his nose and left eye looked swollen. Wyatt clearly hadn't held back during the fight.

Bishop didn't seem to notice when everyone in the park fell silent for a moment before catching themselves and returning to whatever ruse they'd selected.

"Still dressing for attention," he said, slowly scanning my body. "You look like you're asking for a dirty fuck."

I can't believe I ever found this man's personality attractive enough to start a relationship with him. The fact he'd controlled every aspect of my life for so long felt inconceivable now. I'd even considered putting on baggy, dark clothing before deciding against it. It was bad enough he'd haunted me for years and wanted ten thousand more than I owed him. I was going to wear whatever the hell I wanted when I handed him the money. My dress was bright red and hugged every curve of my body. I'd even dug around and found a tube of Lauren's lipstick to match. The outfit screamed "look at me" which was exactly what I wanted if Bishop tried anything.

"Good morning, Bishop," I said in an easy tone. He could say whatever he wanted as long as he left me and the people I loved alone after I paid him. "It's all here." I patted the handle on the roller bag and took a step back, hoping he'd just grab it and go. It's not like he could unzip the thing and count stacks of cash in the middle of the park.

He raised his eyebrows at me. "Impressive. What are you into these days that you could pull that?"

I shook my head. "I just borrowed from friends."

He huffed out a laugh. "How many friends you got?" he asked, adding air quotes like I'd whored myself out multiple times last night for the fifteen grand I needed.

Over his shoulder, I saw Poppy narrow her eyes. Dr. Evers put his hand lightly on her knee, and she looked down at the puzzle book between them, balling her hands into fists on her lap. I should have moved further away from Poppy, but putting distance between us only brought me closer to someone else who'd likely react the same.

"More than I deserve," I said, feeling my throat tighten. I was humbled by the number of people who had shown up for me, even if their presence was making me a nervous wreck.

"That's for damn sure," Bishop said, shaking his head. "When I first drove in, I wondered why you'd stopped in this piece of shit place instead of heading to New York like you always said you wanted. I guess they took to you easy here." He looked around the park and let out a huff. "Must be boring as hell though."

"If by boring you mean peaceful, then yeah," I said, surprised at the irritation in my voice.

Bishop narrowed his eyes at me. "Watch it."

I lowered my head on instinct. As I stared down at my neon yellow sneakers, something in me snapped. I lifted my chin and looked straight into his cold blue eyes. "Here," I said, pushing the suitcase toward him. "We're good now."

"Are we though?" he said in a low voice. "I think you still owe me."

"What else do you want, Bishop? An apology? If you think you deserve one from me more than I do from you? Fine. I'm sorry I took your money. I thought I was just trying to help my dad, but looking back on it now, that was just the excuse I needed to finally leave you."

The look on Bishop's face made my stomach turn. "I thought you loved your old man more than that. You want to hurt him?"

"Never," I said, shaking my head. "But I can't let you hurt me anymore either. I'm happy to pay you back what I took, even the interest. I've felt guilty about taking it since I left, but it ends here."

"It ends when I say it ends," he said, taking a step closer.

He'd spoken so low no one could have heard him, yet with that tiny step toward me, every voice in the park hushed. This time, the crowd's attention stayed glued on us. Bishop's eyes widened as they bounced from one person to the next.

"What the fuck is this, Millie?" he whispered.

"All the reasons you're going to take that suitcase and leave me and my dad alone."

When we were together, Bishop had done an incredible job isolating me from anyone who could have convinced me to leave him. It would have killed my dad if he'd known what was happening and couldn't help, so I'd hidden the abuse from him until after I came to Peace Falls.

Bishop's eyes widened. Seeing me surrounded by so many people who were clearly there to protect me left him speechless. He grabbed the suitcase and yanked it toward where he'd parked his car on Main Street. After he tossed the bag in the trunk, he glanced over his shoulder at me before climbing into the driver's seat and speeding off.

Everyone started talking at once. Poppy reached me first, practically knocking me over with a hug.

"Your self-control is impressive," she said, stepping back. "I don't know how you kept yourself from punching him in the throat."

"You good?" Cal asked, running over with Chris. Instead of following them, Officer Stafford walked out of the park.

"Yeah," I said, watching the cop climb into a car and drive off, thankfully not in the direction that Bishop had taken. "Whose idea was it to invite Officer Stafford?"

"His," Cal said, pointing behind me.

I turned and watched Wyatt and Lauren cross the street from The Doctors on Main. He favored one foot as he walked, which I hadn't noticed yesterday.

"I don't know whether to hug you or smack you," Lauren said. "I was scared out of my mind."

Wyatt kept back while Lauren hugged me. Despite the warmth of her embrace, for the first time this morning, I was terrified. I'd lied to him. I'd *left* him. What if I'd broken us beyond repair?

Lauren stepped back and glanced between Wyatt and me. "Why don't we give y'all a minute," she said, practically shoving me toward him.

The bruises on his handsome face had deepened overnight, though he seemed better off than Bishop. "I'm sorry," I said, before bursting into tears. "I didn't want any of you getting hurt because of me."

Without saying a word, he wrapped his strong arms around me and pulled me close. "I'm so proud of you for standing up to him," he said.

I was so relieved he wasn't mad, my knees almost gave out. I cried so hard I couldn't draw a full breath. Pressing my face to his chest, I let go of all the stress and worry. Wyatt rubbed his hands down my back and held me until I'd cried myself out.

By the time I got myself under control and stepped back, much of the park had emptied and my closest friends stood around us in a circle like they'd been protecting me from the well-meaning people who'd dropped everything in the middle of the day to help me. I'd be writing thank-you letters for a month, but my found family needed to hear it now.

Cal walked to Wyatt and gave him a fist bump before squeezing me so hard my boobs ached. "I hope you know one of us will be glued to you for the foreseeable future. I don't trust that guy as far as I could throw him."

"That's further than he deserves," Theo said with a smile.

"I took a picture of the asshole for the town's social pages," Poppy said, messing with her phone. "If he steps foot in Peace Falls, we'll know."

"Thank you," I said. "You have no idea how much y'all mean to me. I can't thank you enough for what you've done and for letting me be a part of your lives."

Aiden gave me a quick hug, and when he stepped back his eyes looked a little misty.

"He's turning into such a softie," Cal said with a smirk. "Well done, Lauren."

"Pretty sure Logan has more to do with it than me," she said, rubbing her belly.

The group started talking about the baby and his namesake. And not for the first time, I felt a twinge of sadness that I'd never get to meet Logan Hendricks.

I turned to Wyatt, who seemed lost in thought, staring off at the fountain where I'd stood with Bishop. "If the people he left behind are any testament," I said, "Logan must have been pretty remarkable."

He nodded. "I have a feeling you're right."

His voice was quieter than usual, and I took a moment to study him. "You're mad at me, aren't you?"

He blew out a breath and nodded. "And myself."

"What for?"

"For not managing my blood sugar as well as I should. For letting it affect how I act. What if I hit you?"

"I've considered that," I said. After he snapped at me before collapsing, I knew it was a possibility. "It's a risk I'm willing to take to be with you."

He shook his head. "It's not a risk I'm willing to take."

The pain in my chest was so cutting, I put my hand to it. "What are you saying?"

His eyes widened, and he rush forward. "Angel, no," he said, cradling my face. "You're not getting rid of me. I just meant I've decided I need to make my health a priority. No more hiding it. I'm going to tell my family and everyone on the crew, so they can help me until I get a pump, which I'm doing as soon as I can."

"That's wonderful," I said, my voice still wobbly. "That still doesn't explain why you're mad at me."

"I think you know why," he said, rubbing his thumbs under my eyes to catch the tears I hadn't realized were falling again.

"I lied to you and left."

He nodded.

"I thought it was the best way to keep everyone safe," I said.

"Everyone but you." The pain in his eyes made me wish I could go back in time and never leave his side. "You have my entire heart, Cammie. You carry it with you wherever you go. If something had happened to you," he pressed his lips in a line and shook his head like he couldn't even bear to say the words out loud. "I'm mad because you didn't consider what losing you would do to me, to all of us." He pointed to the others, who had started listening in at some point. "We're the people you would have left behind, which by your own logic, makes you remarkable."

They all looked back at me with so much love, I worried I'd start ugly crying again.

"You two are staying together today, right?" Cal asked, looking between Wyatt and me.

My eyes widened. "I forgot to cancel today's patients."

"I canceled everyone last night," Cal said. "I knew neither of us would be able to focus."

"I'm not taking my eyes off her," Wyatt said. "Or my hands," he whispered as Cal and Rowan walked away with the others.

Chapter Thirty-One

Wyatt

"I don't understand," Mamá said. "Why wouldn't you tell us?"

Even through the tiny phone screen, the pain on her face was obvious. It made my chest ache that I wasn't there in person to give her a hug after upsetting her. I'd at least waited for the bruises on my face to fade, so I didn't have to explain those as well. "I figured I could handle it on my own."

"We're your family," she said, her eyes going glassy.

"I didn't want to worry you," I said. I shouldn't have told them over a video call. I could still have Cammie wrapped in my arms instead of dropping a truth bomb on my entire family from a distance.

Mamá was upset, Papá was pissed, and I was at a loss for what to do. I looked to Wade for backup like I always did whenever I aggravated my parents, but he was staring at his hands, refusing to make eye contact.

"Wade," I said, trying to get his attention, so he could help me calm down our parents.

Wade just shook his head and kept his eyes on his hands. Fuck, that was a first. Wade and I got into disagreements like any normal siblings, but we'd always been a united front with our parents anytime one of us was in trouble.

"So, can we assume you're telling us now because you aren't handling it well?" Papá asked, narrowing his eyes. My old man was as astute as they came. He knew I wasn't telling them about being diabetic on a fucking video call because I suddenly woke up and decided they should know after keeping it a secret for over a year. His observation seemed to surprise Wade and Mom, who were both so optimistic their minds never went to the worst-case scenario.

"What's wrong?" Mamá asked, her eyes widening. "Do you need me to come down there? I can be there before midnight if I leave now."

"That's why I didn't tell you," I said, pointing to the screen.

"Answer the question, son," Papá growled. "Why tell us now?"

I blew out a breath. "I haven't been doing a great job managing my blood sugar. It's lead to some unfortunate outcomes. The doctor thinks I should get an insulin pump, and they're really expensive. I'm telling you because I won't be able to send home money while I save up for one."

"Unfortunate outcomes," Mamá shouted. "What does that mean?"

"How expensive?" Papá asked. Neither he nor I wanted Mamá to know in detail how my body was falling apart. She'd be in Peace Falls by eleven and never leave.

Cammie and I had researched all the options, so at least I had a concrete number to work toward. "Six grand, plus four more every year for supplies."

My parents exchanged a look, both of them no doubt tallying the money they had.

"Order it," Wade said, speaking for the first time. "Now."

"I don't have the money yet."

"Yes, you do," he said in an angry tone. "Order it."

"He's right, son," Papá said. "If you need it, you need it. We'll send you the money."

I shook my head. "You're saving that for Wade's van."

"Seriously, Wyatt?" Wade snapped. "You've got to be fucking kidding me."

"Hey, don't talk like that in front of your mother," Papá said.

Mamá waved her hand. "It's fine. I agree with what he said. Well, the sentiment, not the language."

"Give us a minute, please," Wade said. "I'll talk some sense into him."

My parents shuffled out of the room behind Wade's wheelchair while my twin shot me a death glare. My palms started to sweat. "Wade—"

He held up his hand to stop me. "Do you have any idea how much you just hurt all of us?"

I shook my head. "Mamá's upset because she's worried. Papá's pissed I kept something from him."

"Of course he is," Wade snapped. "Pissed and fucking hurt, like Mamá and I are, that you didn't come to us the moment you found out."

"You all have enough to worry about," I said.

"So should I not have told you about wanting a van because you had enough to worry about on your own?"

"That's different," I said.

"Why? Because it's for me and not you?"

I didn't answer him.

Wade rolled his eyes. "I might be the better half, but that doesn't make me more important than you. Honestly, Wyatt. I'm more than pissed. I'm insulted."

"Insulted?"

"Yes, insulted. Look, I get that I have to work harder to do some things, and fine, I'm probably never going to win a hula hoop contest, but the fact you wouldn't come to me for help when you needed it—that's fucking insulting. Like you think I'm incapable of helping you just because I'm in this chair."

"What? No," I said, my stomach dropping. "I called you just the other week to get advice about Cammie."

"You did, didn't you?" Wade said, cracking a smile. "Be honest though, you didn't want to tell me about your diabetes because you've always felt guilty that I'm the one with CP, and you were born fine. You figured what's a life-threatening auto-immune disease to Wade's problems?"

"Well, maybe," I said, blowing out a breath. "Now I kind of feel like an asshole."

"You should. My body's not perfect, but I've always done everything I could to live the life I want. And you've always supported me. So yes, I'm fucking insulted that you didn't think I'd be willing and *able* to support you."

That one word felt like a dagger to the heart. People were always underestimating Wade. They saw his chair and thought of all the things he couldn't do instead of all the incredible ways he'd adapted and thrived. "Fuck, Wade. You're right. I'm sorry."

"I expect you to grovel for my forgiveness for at least the next month," he said with a hint of a smile. "Or you could introduce me to Cammie."

"You don't think now would be a weird time? She does want to meet all of you, and she's right in the other room."

Wade's eyes brightened. "No. Now's perfect. Let me get Mamá and Papá. They'll calm down faster if she's with you." He wheeled off camera without another word. I left my phone on my bed and walked down the hallway to the kitchen, where Cammie was stirring something on the stove.

"Would you like to meet my family?" I asked, feeling excited and terrified at the same time. I'd never introduced someone to my parents before. Wade had met a few of the women I'd dated, but none of those had been serious enough to meet Mamá and Papá.

"Of course," she said, beaming at me. "Right now?"

"If you don't mind."

She switched off the burner. "Do I look OK?" she asked, tucking a piece of hair behind her ear that had fallen from her messy bun.

"Gorgeous," I said, holding out my hand to her.

By the time we got back to my room, my parents and Wade were crowded together, far closer to the screen than they'd been earlier.

"Hi, I'm Cammie," she said with a small wave.

"How'd you pull her?" Wade asked in Spanish, looking a little dazed.

Mamá glared at him before she turned her attention to Cammie. "It's so nice to meet you," she said in English. "I'm Wyatt's mom, Nina, and this is his dad, Paul."

"Did you know my son needed an insulin pump?" Papá asked, skipping right past the small talk.

"Yes, and he's being stubborn about accepting help," she said, giving my hand a quick squeeze.

"He's going to call the doctor tomorrow and order one," Mamá said with a firm nod.

Cammie's eyes widened and she smiled. "Oh my stars, that's wonderful!"

"Seriously, how?" Wade asked in English.

"You must be Wyatt's better half," Cammie said, flashing a smile directly at my twin that made the fucker blush.

He recovered quickly enough and turned on his famous charm. "Did Wyatt tell you why I'm the better half?" Within minutes, he had everyone doubled over laughing and a huge weight lifted from my chest.

"You need to bring Cammie home so we can meet her properly," Mamá said to me. "I want to hear all about her family."

"Do your parents live in Peace Falls?" Papá asked.

Cammie tensed beside me, and I kicked myself again for being so judgmental when she told me about her father. Given how I reacted, she was probably terrified of how my parents would take the news.

"Cammie's mom passed away when she was ten," I said. "Her dad lives in South Carolina where she's from."

"He's not perfect," Cammie added. "But he's a wonderful dad."

The email Cammie's father sent her in reply to the one she'd sent warning him about Bishop's threats had made my balls shrivel. The video chat they had later that day reinforced for me just how much he loved her. She ended the call with strict orders to never let Bishop near her again and to let her father handle his own problems.

Papá nodded like he was reading all the subtext, though I doubt even he would suspect Cammie's dad was serving a life sentence. "No one is," he said. "I hope you'll come up for a visit soon."

"It was lovely to meet you," Mamá said.

"Call us after you order the pump, so we know how much to transfer to your account," Wade said, suddenly taking over our dad's uber-practical role in the family.

"Yes," Papá said, looking a little startled, like he'd almost forgotten the first half of our conversation.

After we'd said goodbye and I'd ended the call, Cammie turned to me and asked, "What did your brother say in Spanish?"

I undid her messy bun and ran my fingers through her golden strands before wrapping it around my hand and tugging her gently toward me. "He wanted to know how I pulled you."

"Oh, that's easy," she said, straddling me. "Patience." She rolled her hips, making me instantly hard. "And a shockingly voracious sexual appetite."

CHAPTER THIRTY-TWO

Cammie

THE MORNING OF POPPY'S surprise bachelorette party felt like the first real day of fall. There was a chill in the October air to match the leaves changing at the top of the mountains. Most of the trees in town were still green, but the ones lining the Skyline Drive would be brilliant hues of yellow, orange, and red. I couldn't have asked for a better day, weatherwise.

I'd scoured the internet and stores for the pinkest, frilliest decorations I could find. The penis-shaped sandwiches and desserts Rowan made were tucked in a cooler. Our outfits were perfect. I'd never worn so much eyeliner in my life. We were decked out head-to-toe in black, combat boots and all. Rowan had even bought a black wig. It was longer than Poppy's pixie cut, but I couldn't wait to see them standing side-by-side.

There was only one problem.

"The limousine isn't coming," Lauren said, glaring at her phone. "Pink or otherwise. Some issue with the engine that sounded like a bad excuse. I told them any color would do. Apparently, Jericho's homecoming is tonight, and they're booked solid."

"Probably double booked," Rowan said with a sigh. "We'll just take two cars to the picnic spot."

There'd be six of us total with Poppy, her mother, and Theo's, who was the only person outside our little group who knew the wedding was taking place next weekend. She'd flown in from Greece earlier in the week to "meet Poppy's family," which had been a reasonable enough excuse for Rose. Somehow, we'd done the impossible and planned the wedding without Poppy's mother finding out, and I'd managed to sing in front of my friends twice without getting sick.

Lauren frowned. "We'd all fit in Aiden's truck."

"No," Rowan and I shouted in unison. The plan had been for the guys to "kidnap" Theo the same time we grabbed Poppy and take him to his surprise bachelor's party. They were rock climbing somewhere deep in the mountains, and Aiden's truck was all packed and ready to go.

"I have an idea," I said, grabbing my phone to text Wyatt.

When the van pulled up in front of the farmhouse twenty minutes later, I couldn't stop the smile on my face. It had taken a lot of research, and even more paperwork, but Wade's parents and I had found him enough help that he'd been able to finance the van with a low interest rate. Two weeks ago, he'd passed his driver's exam and earned his full license.

"Your ride has arrived," Wade said, leaning out the driver's side window.

Wyatt hopped out of the passenger side and ran up to help with the cooler.

"This was so nice of you two," Rowan said, grabbing an arm full of decorations. "I'm going to start decorating the inside of the van."

"Happy to do it," Wyatt called after her as she headed for the van. He wrapped his arms around me and kissed me like he hadn't seen me in days, despite the fact I'd just left him and Wade after breakfast. "This is a nice surprise," he said, smiling at me. "I thought I wouldn't get to see you until tonight."

"You sure you and Wade don't mind? We're wrecking whatever plans you had."

"Going to lunch at Church and driving around town to show him all the houses I've worked on are hardly plans. We'll hang out in the front, and you can pretend we're not there."

Aiden walked outside with his arm around Lauren, who at seven months pregnant had been tasked with absolutely nothing for the party or wedding prep, though she'd jumped in and taken charge more than once.

"How long has your brother had his license again?" Aiden asked, frowning at the van. "Those mountain roads are twisty."

"The better question is how hard he worked to get it," Wyatt said. "I promise there's no one more careful, and if he gets too nervous or doesn't want to drive, he's taught me how to work the hand controls."

Aiden nodded.

"I hope he knows we'll be stopping every thirty minutes for me to pee," Lauren said, laying her hands on her black lace maternity dress, which may or may not have been an Elvira costume in another life.

"We'll stop whenever you need," I said. Aiden kept his arm around Lauren as they crept to the van. The woman ran around Karma with the energy of a toddler, yet she let Aiden baby her.

"He's going to scare the daylights out of your brother," I said, as Aiden approached the driver's window and leaned in to talk to Wade.

"Doubt it," Wyatt said. "If Wade could talk our mother into letting him drive down here alone from Northern Virginia, he'll convince Aiden to relax. I already explained to Wade about the car accident, so he knows not to take Aiden's concern personally."

"I'm a little surprised Lauren lets Aiden treat her like glass. That woman is tough as nails."

"And he knows it," Wyatt said. "Allowing him to take care of her is an act of love on her part."

My chest warmed because I knew he wasn't just talking about Lauren and Aiden. After Bishop left, Wyatt asked me to install his blood sugar monitoring app on my phone. He even brought me along to the doctor's appointment where he learned how to use and maintain his insulin pump. Having diabetes didn't define him, but he'd accepted that it was part of who he was and had learned to ask for help when he needed it. As a result, he hadn't had any scary lows or highs in a while.

"Let's get over there just in case," Wyatt said as the conversation between Wade and Aiden dragged on. He lifted the cooler and made a beeline for the van.

Aiden laughed as we approached, and I shook my head. "Your brother should go into sales or something. He'd make a killing with his charm and persuasion skills."

"Wade definitely got my share of those," Wyatt said with a smile.

He probably meant it, which was both adorable and a little sad. "You're charming too," I said, feeling the need to defend him from himself. "And you persuaded me to date you. That's a monumental achievement given I'd sworn off men for eternity."

"I did, didn't I." He shoved the cooler into the back and pressed a quick kiss to my lips. "Now, go have fun. Pretend we're not here."

It didn't work out that way. The fun part happened. The pretending they weren't there part didn't last long.

After we picked up Rose and Theo's mom, Aiden grabbed Poppy from her studio, literally, and buckled her into the van.

"Have fun, Hell Cat," he said, before cutting through the backyard to Cal's house, where my boss and Chris were distracting Theo with some Christmas present project for Rose.

"What the fuck?" Poppy said, looking around the inside of the van, which could have passed for the bedroom of a princess-obsessed five-year-old about to throw a tea party for her stuffed animals.

"Surprise," we all shouted.

Her eyes bounced around the van, taking in our outfits, and she put her face in her hands and cried.

Wade shot me a worried look in the rearview mirror. I just shrugged and told him, "She's fine."

Poppy looked up to see who I was talking to and her mouth fell open. "Holy shit, you two really are identical."

"Not any more than you and Rowan," Wyatt said, laughing. Poppy turned to take a second look at her sister and laughed so hard she snorted.

"You must be Wade," Poppy said, unbuckling herself so she could lean between the passenger seat and Wade's wheelchair. Thankfully, we hadn't pulled away from the curb yet, or I'd have told her to stop distracting him. I owed Aiden that much. "I'm not sure how you got roped into this, but I apologize in advance for whatever weird thing they have planned."

"Don't worry about it," he said. "Just pretend we're not here."

"Sit down, Poppy," Lauren said. "We're saving the blood ritual for *after* we get back."

"She's joking," I said. I hoped. Lauren was into some pretty woo woo stuff, though I'd never seen her do anything dark. Yet.

"You'd better have brought your guitar," Poppy said to me as Wade drove us out of town. "There's three new people for you to practice in front of before—"

"Open mic," Rowan yelled.

"Oh, how nice," Theo's mom said. Somehow, in the rush to get things together, I still hadn't learned the poor woman's name. Apparently, I was the only woman in the group she hadn't met already, and Wade and Wyatt were trying to blend into the background.

"I'm sorry, I didn't introduce myself. I'm Cammie."

"Kamilia, but please call me Milia."

Well, that'd be easy to remember. "What a coincidence. My name is Camilla. I actually went by Millie as a kid because my mom went by

Cammie. After she passed, I missed hearing it, so I started going by it when I moved here."

"What a beautiful way to honor her," Milia said. She gave me a sweet smile that told me where Theo had gotten his soft side.

It took me a moment to notice that all the other women had leaned forward to listen. Lauren had seen my driver's license when she hired me at Karma, but I'd never told her the rest about my name. It made my heart ache when I realized how eager my friends were to learn more about me. Wyatt had even turned in his seat to smile at me because he knew how little I shared with everyone. Only Wade, who was focused on driving, and Milia, who didn't know me, seemed unaffected by the tidbit of info I'd shared.

I cleared my throat and reached for my guitar. Now that everyone knew the darkest pieces of my past, I needed to share with them the lightest. "She's the one who taught me to play and sing," I said, strumming the strings lightly. "But never this song," I said, smiling at Poppy.

I launched into an unplugged version of Balance and Composure's *Tiny Raindrop*. The emo song was unlike any of the classic love ballads I'd played for them before. I'd heard Poppy listening to it several times and had a feeling it resonated with how she felt at the start of her relationship with Theo. As I sang about the hope of a flawed person giving into the lover they were pushing away to protect, everyone watched me with slightly shocked expressions.

"Sing it again," Poppy said in a quiet voice when I finished.

After I'd played the song a second time, everyone erupted in applause.

"That was incredible," Wade said, sounding slightly dumbfounded. "Seriously, how Wyatt? I've seen your game."

Wyatt twisted in his seat and smiled at me.

"I'd tell you, but I don't think Lauren or you really want to hear," I said, trying not laugh.

"Please no," Lauren said holding up her hands. "My stomach is still weak and the curvy roads aren't helping."

Without saying a word to each other, Wade pulled over and Wyatt jumped out of the front seat before helping Lauren switch places with him. After that, we gave up any pretense of pretending the twins weren't part of the party, which never would have worked for me anyway. I certainly couldn't have ignored Wyatt when he was only a few feet away, let alone when he was sitting beside me.

Wyatt drew my attention like a magnet whenever he was near. I'd always been hyperaware of the men I dated before. With them, I was trying to anticipate anything that would anger them. Wyatt pulled my attention with his warmth. I wanted to be near him any moment I could because he made me feel cherished, safe.

We sat for hours at the scenic overlook, admiring the mountain views and celebrating Poppy in a way she not only seemed to tolerate but enjoy. As everyone laughed and ate, I took a moment to appreciate how much my life had changed since I came to Peace Falls. I'd built a family here, one that became stronger with each person I let in. I'd also built myself into a person I was proud to be. When I left Bishop, I couldn't have imagined how full my life would become, or all the love I would find. By the time Wade dropped off everyone at Sullivan Street, my face hurt from smiling.

"That was way more fun than driving around looking at houses," Wade said as he pulled into the parking lot at Karma. "No offense, bro."

"Agreed. You sure you don't want to go out to dinner?" Wyatt asked.

Wade shook his head. "The number of dick sandwiches and cookies I ate is shocking. I'm stuffed. Driving is also a lot more tiring than I thought it'd be. I'm going straight to the hotel and crashing."

"Thanks again for chauffeuring everyone," Wyatt said, giving his brother's shoulder a squeeze. "We'll see you at Karma for breakfast in the morning. Take your time."

Lauren was filling in for us, so we could spend Sunday with Wade before he drove back, but we were opening the cafe and working until he joined us.

"I was thinking," I said as Wyatt unlocked the back door to the building. "We should really find a place with an elevator, so Wade doesn't have to stay in a hotel when he comes to visit."

Wyatt paused with the keys in his hands and turned to face me. We'd never discussed our living arrangement. I still rented my tiny studio apartment, though I hadn't slept in it since I moved into Lauren's room. In a couple months, she'd need the space for the baby to nap in while she worked. Wyatt and I hadn't talked about what would happen then. At first, I'd worried he'd take me moving out as a sign I was pulling away. Now, I couldn't imagine living somewhere without him.

"Let's go inside and talk," he said, his tone suddenly serious.

A wave of uncertainty crashed through me. Had I completely misread where we were in our relationship? Maybe he didn't want to keep living together. He'd probably been wondering why I hadn't moved out yet. By the time we walked up the stairs, my stomach was in knots.

As soon as he flicked on the apartment light and saw my face, he rushed to gather me in his arms. "Angel, no. Whatever you're thinking, stop."

"I guess sometimes it just feels too good to be true," I said, letting the weight of his arms erase all my panic.

He guided me over to the couch and held my hands in both of his as we sat turned toward each other. "First, things first, I am deeply in love with you, Camilia Gibson. I'm not going anywhere unless you tell me to."

"That's never going to happen," I said, squeezing his hands.

"OK, good, because what I'm about to tell you might not be exactly what you want."

"I want you, Wyatt. As long as we're together, we can work through anything else."

He leaned forward like he was about to kiss me, but I put my hand on his chest. "Don't even think of kissing me until you say whatever it is you need to say. We both know where that will lead, and I really want to hear what's going on."

He smirked and sat back, still keeping a tight grip on my hands. "Lauren fired me."

"Oh," I said, feeling too shocked to say anything else. As far as I knew, we were still opening the café together in the morning.

"Let me back up," he said. "You know I've been working two jobs to save up for college, and I never seem to get anywhere."

I nodded. Wyatt had kept up his frantic work schedule along with mine. We both felt like we had debts to pay, though no one we owed now seemed eager to collect.

"Lauren and Aiden sat me down earlier this week. Aiden's business is getting big enough to support an in-house architect. Right now he pays out the nose to independent contractors and—"

"He wants to hire you instead."

I nodded. "Clearly, that wouldn't be until after I graduate, and at first, he'd probably pay someone to double check any plans I drew up, but that's the idea. He had a whole spreadsheet of savings over five years. Then he'd calculated what my salary would be using the market rate for an entry-level architect."

He paused and laughed. We both knew Aiden paid his crew well above the market rate.

"Even padding that number twenty percent," he said, "it would still save him money. He asked how much it would cost for me to graduate, and we spent a couple minutes calculating everything. Turns out, it's not as much as I thought, especially when I compare it to what I'd be making once I had my degree. Aiden started saying some bullshit about a tuition reimbursement program, but I shot that down fast. If he did it for me, he'd feel like he had to offer it to everyone and that could get expensive fast."

"He and Lauren both want to save the world one person at a time."

He nodded. "Once they have Logan, I'm hoping they'll use their money to hire people and cut back on their hours. Besides, I can swing the tuition payments with a loan, though I want to take out as little as possible. I told my parents I wouldn't be sending money again until I graduate, and they told me I'd done enough already. Wade will be graduating soon and working full time, so they don't really need my help like they did before. Aiden said I could still work on the crew part time. Since it's the best money I'd make per hour, I'd need to schedule as many classes as I could at night to maximize when I could work with him. Not to mention, all the coursework will take up a significant portion of my time."

"So, Lauren 'fired' you," I said.

"Her exact words were 'I won't let working for me hurt you, and you're too loyal to quit.'"

That sounded about right.

"Since I won't be working full time, I need to keep my living expense low. Like, zero rent low."

"I can cover rent," I said. "We'd probably need a bigger place than where I am now, but I can handle the difference."

Wyatt shook his head. "Not if you want to save up for your dad's appeal. Which you could do faster if you also didn't have to pay rent. If you moved in, officially. I plan to pay Lauren back however I can. Fired or not, I'm going to work in the café here and there and upkeep the building."

"I'd still be taking advantage of her generosity," I said, pulling my lip between my teeth. He freed it gently with his fingers and placed his palm on my cheek.

"I figured you'd say that, so Lauren came up with a solution. We'll turn my room into a nursery for the baby since it's quieter on the back side of the building, and Logan won't need a room with a bathroom for naps. Lauren will move out whatever you don't need to make space for your furniture, and you'll pay her half of what you're paying now."

"That's too low," I said, frowning.

"What other renters would allow her to keep her baby in the second bedroom? Or would she trust enough to leave her baby with?"

I shook my head. "She told you to say that, didn't she?"

"Yeah, I told her you'd want to pay whatever you're paying now. She was firm you shouldn't and added that Desdemona and Medusa relied on us."

Both cats were stretched on the floor by the heating vent, looking every inch the pampered kitties they were.

"Good thing she has no idea what I actually pay," I said with a smirk.

Wyatt held up his hands. "Don't tell me. I want plausible deniability."

"So, we're living together, officially," I said.

Wyatt smiled and nodded.

"Why would you think it wasn't what I wanted?"

"Well," he said, gripping the back of his neck. "It means I won't be sharing shifts with you at Karma, so we won't see each other as much. I plan to study downstairs while you're working whenever I can. That way, I'll also be there in case Doña Valentina or anyone else needs me to translate. I agree this apartment isn't ideal for when Wade visits, but a hotel night here and there is a lot less than rent somewhere else. Plus," he said, leaning forward and pressing my back onto the sofa, "it will give us privacy that I intend to take full advantage of."

By the time he finished with me, I couldn't have agreed more.

EPILOGUE

Wyatt

THE ENTIRE YARD FELL silent as Cammie strummed the intro to *Can't Help Falling in Love with You.* I'd never tire of seeing the joy on her face when she performed.

Her hair was curled and her smoky eyeshadow made her eyes impossibly large. She was stunning in a different way, and I loved how she looked, whether she was in full glam or waking up in my arms with bedhead. When she finished the song, everyone applauded so loud I thought for sure Logan would wake up, but little man stayed conked out on my shoulder.

"That was amazing," Aiden said as Cammie climbed down from the stage.

"You could be a pro," Lauren said, pulling her into a hug. "How do you feel?"

"Great," Cammie said, coming to stand beside me.

"It's not like we're the first reception she sang at without puking," Aiden said.

"A backyard get together with twenty people is not the same as this," Poppy said, waving her hand at the crowd who had gathered near the temporary stage I'd helped Aiden set up in his backyard. "Being the center of attention here sounds like the tenth circle of hell to me."

"Does that mean you don't want us to sing *Happy Birthday* to you later?" Aiden asked.

Poppy's eyes widened in horror. "Don't you dare. I swear, Studman, I will go home right now."

"I promise," Lauren said, placing a gentle hand on Poppy's arm. "You will remain firmly in the social shadows at all times unless you should choose otherwise."

Poppy narrowed her eyes at Aiden. "Swear on Logan."

"I'm not swearing on my son," he said, holding out his arms to me as if even the suggestion made him long to hold his child. Logan stayed asleep while I transferred him to Aiden. As soon as my arms were free, I wrapped them around Cammie, and she snuggled against me.

Poppy closed her eyes and sighed. "When's it happening, so I can brace myself?"

"When's what happening?" Lauren asked.

"You want it before we cut the wedding cake or after?" Aiden asked.

"Get it over with," Poppy said, rubbing her forehead.

Aiden lifted his chin at Rowan and Cal, who ran off toward the house.

"What's going on?" Theo asked, rushing over when he saw Poppy's distress.

"I'm holding a baby," Aiden told him. Which wouldn't make a bit of sense without context. Theo glared at him and wrapped his body around Poppy like a shield. The scowl left his face when Cal and Rowan started across the yard with a large sheet cake topped with a single sparkler candle.

I sang along with the rest of the crowd, though I kept my voice low since I'm practically tone deaf. Poppy blew out the candle before hiding her face against Theo's chest.

"I decorated it myself," Rowan said proudly.

"I hate you all," Poppy mumbled into Theo's tux.

"Did you really have to do that, Aiden?" Cammie said, stepping from my arms and glaring at him. "She's shaking. You need to apologize."

He held up his palm to her. "High five, Cam. You're right. Thanks for handing me my ass."

Poppy lifted her face from Theo's chest, threw her head back, and laughed.

"Were you in on it this time?" Cammie asked Poppy.

"No, that scared the shit out of me. Aiden went rogue."

"Well, that wasn't really my intention, Hell Cat," he said, pulling her into a side hug with his free arm. "I'm sorry. I just didn't want to ignore your birthday."

"Feel free to ignore it every year from now on," she said, giving him a playful elbow jab to the stomach.

Cammie had been working on being more assertive. It was easier when she was speaking up for someone she cared about. Unfortunately, she still struggled at times when guys came on too strong. Aiden had taken to ribbing her any chance he could to draw out increasingly sassy responses. He often brought in other members of the group until it became something of an inside joke.

"At what point are you going to realize she can handle herself?" Poppy asked.

"Oh, we're way past that. I'm just having fun now," Aiden said.

If I didn't know him better, I'd think he was a complete asshole. Though as strange as it seemed, he had helped Cammie stand strong in conflicts. If Bishop ever showed his face again in Peace Falls, she'd be well conditioned to tell him off.

She certainly wasn't getting that from me. Whenever we disagreed on something, we talked it out in a way that never made either of us angry. I'm sure we'd have our first big fight at some point. Maybe.

Rose came over and gave Cammie a quick kiss on the cheek before doing the same to me. Since Poppy's bachelorette party, she'd decided we fell into the brood of people she mothered. "Your song was absolutely beautiful," she said to Cammie. "There's a couple here who want to talk to you about singing at their wedding."

"Go talk to them," Lauren said, squeezing Cammie's arm.

"When do I have time to become a wedding singer?" she asked.

Lauren took a step back, gripped Cammie's hands, and said, "You're fired."

Cammie was still reeling on the ride home. "I can't believe Lauren fired me at her own wedding reception."

"I have to confess, I'm not mad," I said, glancing at her as I turned onto Main Street. "Between our day jobs, my schoolwork, and your shifts at Karma, I don't see you nearly enough. Based on what that one couple offered you, you could earn as much in one night as you earned working a week at Karma."

"I could, couldn't I?" she said with a smile.

"Just don't book anything for the weekend we're going to South Carolina."

She shook her head. "I wouldn't miss that for the world."

In a couple of months, Cammie and I were taking a trip to visit her father in person. Cal asked if he and Rowan could join us, and the concern on his face left zero doubt they'd be joining, officially or otherwise.

I didn't like the idea of Cammie returning to the place where she'd met Bishop and where his brother still lived in the same unit as her father. But I wasn't about to let Bishop hurt Cammie ever again, and that included keeping her from seeing her dad.

I also had a very important question to ask him, face to face, and was relying on Cal to distract Cammie while I did. The longer I knew Gibs, the more I respected him. I didn't need his approval to ask Cammie to marry me, yet I knew it would make him feel more a part of her life if I did. My grandmother's ring had been taunting me for weeks to propose. I'd asked Lauren to put the little box in one of her hidey holes to help me resist the temptation. Until then, I'd just have to work out my nervous energy the best way I knew.

As soon as the apartment door closed behind us, I leaned down and kissed the spot below Cammie's ear that drove her wild. She let out a sigh and turned to face me, placing her arms around my neck.

"Do you have any idea how sexy you make me feel when you watch me sing?" she asked. "I was so turned on, I was sure everyone noticed. My panties were drenched by the end of the song."

"How are they now?" I asked.

"Gone," she breathed with a smirk. "I threw them out because they were so soaked."

"Show me," I said as my cock went rock hard and pressed painfully against my zipper.

She looked up at me with a playful smile before pulling the thin straps from her shoulders and letting her dress pool on the ground.

I let out a groan at the sight before me. She stood naked except for her high heels and a strapless corset that made her tits look amazing. I brushed my hand slowly up her thigh. She was panting even before I dipped my fingers inside her.

"Wyatt," she breathed as her legs shook.

"Do you want to come on my hand, my face, or my cock first?"

Her walls tightened around my fingers. The question had pushed her so near the edge, she was about to fall over.

"Stop," she said, placing her hand on mine. A gorgeous blush spread across her cheeks. "I want to ride you."

She whimpered as I pulled my hand from her, and we practically ran into our bedroom.

I started to unbutton my shirt, but she placed her hand on mine to stop me a second time. "Let me," she said, running her hands over my chest.

She stared into my eyes as she quickly undid every button and slid the shirt from my shoulders. She lifted my undershirt over my head and tossed it on the floor.

"May I?" she asked, running her hand across my stomach. "I want to be rough."

I nodded, too turned on to speak, let alone think straight enough to remove my pump on my own. She placed it gently on the nightstand before reaching for my belt buckle. By the time she undressed me, pre-cum leaked from my crown, which she licked off before taking me deep in her mouth.

"Holy shit," I said as pleasure shot through my body. "You better stop if you want me to last at all."

She smirked and released me with a pop before shoving me down on the bed and straddling my body. Her mouth fell open as she took my length at once. She tightened around me without moving, and all the air left my lungs in a hiss.

"You feel so good," I said, looking up at her. She leaned forward and started rocking her hips. The corset trussed up her gorgeous breasts, so they bounced whenever she moved. I pulled down one of the cups and drew her hard nipple into my mouth.

She sat up suddenly, digging her nails into my chest as she moved faster and faster. "Wyatt," she shouted as she threw her head back and came, her pussy tightening in waves that made my eyes rolls back in my head. Somehow, I managed not to fall over with her, and as the last pulse of her orgasm stopped, I flipped her onto her back and started fucking her with everything I had.

"Oh," she moaned, "I'm—"

She tightened around me again and let out a cry that almost sent me over the edge.

"That's it," I gritted out. "One more time, and I'll fill you."

"Together," she said before she moaned, lost in pleasure as I fucked her so hard the bed gave an ominous creak.

I slammed into her again and again. She gripped the sheets, holding herself back. My entire body went rigid as my balls tighten. "Come for me, now."

We found our release together, the sounds we made feral. I held her in my arms as we came back down, wishing I hadn't told Lauren to hide the ring, but thankful she had before I did something stupid like propose post-sex.

Still, I felt the words on my tongue, so I took her face in my hands and said, "*Te quieres casar conmigo.*" I kissed her forehead, hoping it would be enough until I could ask her in June.

When I pulled back, she smiled at me and said, "I thought you'd never ask."

More from Hannah

Can't get enough of Cammie and Wyatt? Sign up for my newsletter for a bonus epilogue featuring a very special wedding. Visit https://dl.bookfunnel.com/8kiehb58mx

If you enjoyed *For You Always*, you'll love the rest of the *Peace Falls Series*:

Book 1: *For You I'd Break* Available Now

Book 2: *For You I'd Mend* Available Now

Book 3: *For You I'd Bloom* Available Now

Red Blossoms Christmas: A Peace Falls Christmas Novella (Available in eBook October 6, 2025)

LETTER TO READERS

Dear Reader,

I was two books into the *Peace Falls Series* before I realized what kind of romances I wrote. I didn't even know the subgenre existed. I'd been typing along, thinking I was writing small town romances with spice. Which, they are. It wasn't until I did a reverse search on how readers found my books that I discovered I wrote "angsty" or "emotional" romance. I mean, isn't all romance emotional?

I shouldn't have been surprised. As a nonfiction writer, I alternated between humor pieces and the kind that make you ugly cry, but my literary fiction had always been dark. And not the good kind of dark with morally gray heroes and a touch (or a lot) of taboo spice. Dark like soul-crushing, no-one-is-coming-back-from-this-with-their-mental-health-intact dark.

In real life, I'm an optimist who adores florals and tries to be as kind as possible. I've always presented to others as a perky good girl. Then they'd read my fiction and be utterly baffled how someone who lives like I do has a mind that could come up with the things I wrote. Long story short, I enjoyed shocking people, and I hated being put in a box.

For better or worse, romance has *very* specific boxes that align with readers' expectations. I once downloaded a hockey romance and was confused when all the male POVs started piling up. My first thought was: "Is someone going to die?" No, my friends. No one died, and I learned I'd stumbled into the why choose genre (with a side of hockey).

All of this to say, that when I started writing romance, I knew I had to meet certain expectations. And apparently, the box I put myself into was still a little dark at times. Because that's life. And more than anything, I want my characters and their stories to feel real. So, thank you, for letting me break your heart a little before the well-deserved HEA.

There are more stories to come from Peace Falls as well as a new series set on a barrier island in South Carolina. I debated attempting a rom com, and I still might, eventually. However, when it comes down to it, I am who I am, so whether the story is set in the mountains or at the beach, brace for all the feels. To hear about my upcoming releases, visit https://hannahjordanauthor.com and sign up for my newsletter.

Thanks for reading! I would love if you'd leave an honest review.

Hannah

f   facebook.com/hannahjordanbooks/

   instagram.com/hannahjordanbooks/

Acknowledgements

To my friends and family who welcome me back every time I disappear into the world of Peace Falls, thanks for making my reality more beautiful than I could ever put into words. To James Carpenter and Gerri Mahn for hyping me up when I need it and mercilessly tearing my writing apart the rest of the time. None of this would have been possible without our little critique group and the many hours you've given to this series and to me. To Melyssa, thank you for your invaluable feedback and continued support. A special thanks to Kaytalin McCarry for your beautiful cover designs. As a writer, I'm always worried I'll get something terribly wrong. Fortunately, this introvert was adopted decades ago by two extroverts who know a lot of people with a lot of knowledge and experience. To Tess and Talleri, thank you for your insights on cerebral palsy. To Raina, many thanks for your help with Spanish (and for being the kind of reader every author hopes for). My first year as an indie romance author has been a rollercoaster of emotions, but hearing the positive feedback from readers has kept me going. Thank you for taking the time to read my books and give reviews. I can't wait to share with you all the stories to come.

ABOUT THE AUTHOR

HANNAH JORDAN GREW UP in the Blue Ridge Mountains of Virginia but moved to South Jersey after falling in love with her complete opposite. Though she's got all the advanced degrees of a "serious" fiction writer, she only smiles when she's writing romance. She lives with her husband and two daughters in a picturesque town outside Philadelphia where she enjoys reading in all genres, especially the spicy ones, and confusing people with her half-Southern, half-Northern accent.